IN TOO DEEP
Copyright © 2019 Ron Ramsay Hagg

International Standard Book Number  ISBN-978-0-578-51741-4
Ron Ramsay  Hagg
ronhagg@hotmail.com

# IN TOO DEEP

By Ron Ramsay Hagg

We learn the vulnerabilities – the self-denial – the guilt
– and how three people meet – struggle - want that sense of balance
– of being whole.

Ted Lewis is a bug trapped in amber.
Buried in Ted's past is a shame that cannot be spoken
– his violent act that keeps him trapped in himself.

Amy Nelson, recently retired, has kept a secret about that
terrible day twenty-six years ago.

Alice Humphrey moved to Humboldt from San Diego,
but wasn't able to break from her past that held her down wrapped in
sadness and depression.

Also about Ron Ramsay Hagg

Novels:
*Jesus of Kneeland*
*Dreams of a New Day*
*To Keep From Drowning*

These novels are available on
Amazon.com
or
ronhagg@hotmail.com

*Escape In Time*
Full-length feature film:
Based on Ron's novel: *Escape In Time*
Ron produced it.
It can be viewed on Netflix – DVD only
And on YouTube.

More information is available at:
www.haggmedia.com

*To all of us who struggle with our pasts.*

# TED

A thousand Celtic warriors pound their spears - waving their axes - on my roof. Gods long forgotten make themselves known raising watery weapons on this cabin. Bitter cold wet winds whip the world. Even the trees work to keep their balance. I am no tree. And the warriors pound on my roof - past a day - beyond a week - never ending - sun refuses to come out. How long can they dance in the gusts of wind in the dim light of the storm? Water invades the once dry earth forming miniature lakes surrounding me like a moat. And here I exist and try to find answers. I sit in the glow of the fire that can't keep out the gloom. Nowhere to turn - cannot hide - cannot go anywhere without the hard rain.

How long will it be - rain crashing into the earth in a cold fury leaving no prisoners. I withdraw within myself, not really knowing who I am, with nowhere to go - in my cabin - protected from the hard - cold - very cold rain. Celtic spears from the ancients continue their rant on the roof - non-stop.

I know I've got to get up – go out, the cupboard is bare. If I don't show up for my job, as lousy as it is, it too will be gone. Then what will I do. At least I've got wood in the cabin. Come on – get up – can't stay here forever. My old bones creek and rebel against movement, but up on my feet – slowly moving. I want coffee – that will do it.

Wood stove is still warm from last night's fire.

Gathering a few pieces of wood I put them in the stove. This is how I cook - on my wood stove. This cabin is one room and a small bathroom, which seems to have been an after thought. No one has ever bothered to put sheet rock or some other cover on the interior walls. The wood seen on the inside is the same wood seen from the outside. No insulation.

I've taken two wood fruit boxes and nailed them on the wall for shelving. The queen bed, couch, and kitchen table take up a good portion of my life in this cabin under redwood trees. I have no neighbors that I can see from my place. Isolated and very quiet.

Slowly make my way to the sink – dirty dishes – it's a mess. Water in the pot. Back to the stove, I get out my coffee, and put it in the coffee filter. This will do it. Looking around waiting – my life. Seventy years old and this is what it is. You'd think I would be in a much better place in life - not having to work - pushing brooms, tidying up. I have a hard time doing this in my own cabin, but no one pays me to clean up here. Water boiling – coffee will be ready soon. Back on my old couch – coffee in my hand - I sit. That first sip – yes. I open up the wood stove door to look at the fire. People have been looking at fires for thousands of years – almost hypnotic and the coffee slowly goes into me fusing me with alertness, but mostly warmth. Clock says I need to go or I'll be late. Pants cold when I put them on. Hate to take off my shirt – guess I won't, just put the hoodie on over it. Look around. Need to shut the stove door and dampen it down. My God, it's wet out - just one giant puddle. I practically have to wade through water to get to my old VW. Who drives these antiques anyway? Mine didn't even come with a gas gauge. Hope it starts, but at least it's parked on a small hill. Damn it's cold. I knew a guy who lived in Germany. He'd actually start a small fire under his VW to warm it up - pretty drastic measure. Don't think I'll ever do that. In the driver's seat. Shit the keys are still in the cabin. Leave the car and muddle through the water to retrieve the keys. Back towards the car – shit, my right foot steps into some kind of hole. It's all wet - neat way to start my workday. I should just go back inside. Standing, now getting even wetter I re-enter the VW and put the key in. There's this wonderful sound of the car wanting to start, but not. Getting out again I push it, jump back in, put it in 2nd gear, and pop the clutch. It catches. The engine not exactly purring - is running. Down from Fickle Hill I drive on my way to a new day - same as yesterday - same as tomorrow.

Shit, a tree's fallen across the road – for sure going to be late now. No need to get out of the car; I'll just have to wait until it's cleared. Sitting and looking out, there are no other cars. Wet road – leaves and needles in contrast to the dark pavement. If I didn't have to get to work I could enjoy the serenity this provides. Oh my gosh, there appears to be some room on the hillside of the road. Getting out to look, there's enough space for me to drive around the fallen tree. I knock on my gearshift knob – it's wood. Carefully I drive off the road to get around my obstacle. Sliding a little, this old car makes it around the tree. VW's are good at this sort of thing, the driveline is under the engine, giving it weight, and that helps with the traction. Good. I wonder if I'm going to be late and if I am will they believe me about the tree. Fuck it – whether they believe me or not, I'm on my way. I've been working for almost a year as a janitor at the "Welcome Gym". Very strange name – guess they're trying to drum up business. It's been two days since I showered – feeling a little grungy as I walk in the door at the gym. I could shower at my cabin, but the water pressure's very weak - just dribbles of water. So, instead I take my showers at the gym. And the best aspect about this job is I can use the pool, which I do almost daily.

No one notices me as I saunter in. I'm only five minutes late – I'll be OK. At 8 am there are only a few people "getting into shape". The whirl of the treadmill machines, the clinking of weights is the backdrop for my job. I don't use this part of the gym – only the pool. But I do like to watch people working out. Today, an old woman is lifting what looks like 3 lb. weights over her head. Her yoga pants cover her long legs. A blue bandana wrapped around her forehead to stop the sweat, but there's no sweat, but she's ready if it comes. Maybe later in her workout she'll need it. It's kind of cool seeing her, graceful in her movements. I mostly sit on my butt, except to swim. I'm nuts about swimming. It's one of the ways I define myself.

Enough of this - got to start working. Walking around, I empty all the wastebaskets, and pick up the occasional paper off the floor. Next, I get the polish, rag, and shine the various pieces of equipment, even though they really don't need the polishing. In the reception area I take my cleaning rag, feather duster, wipe and dust all of the areas people see - the reception counter, the desk. This is called surface cleaning - hitting the spots everyone can easily see. This keeps me occupied. It's important to always look busy. Getting my trusty broom I sweep. I could use a vacuum cleaner, but this is so much quieter. The grime behind and under is rarely cleaned. Hate when I have to clean the out of the way – unseen grime.

# TED

I've doodled around all day – looking busy. It's close to quitting time. My routine – go swimming at the end of my workday. Boy, another lifetime ago I was a beach lifeguard for the State of California in San Diego. This didn't work out so well. San Diego didn't work out – had to flee. Why this comes up today I don't know. Don't want to think about San Diego – cannot think about it – wish the memories would just go away. Back to the here and now. There's only one other person in the pool when I enter the water. My gosh, it's the same woman I saw in the morning lifting weights. Her old self cruises across the pool. She's a good swimmer. Good for her – being active. I wonder what her life has been like – is like now. I spit in my goggles, rub them with my fingers, rinse them out, and put them on. Entering the water I push off the wall and glide. This first length of my workout I take a deep breath and swim under water using only the dolphin kick – hands in front until I reach the other side.

It's hard to describe the freedom I feel in the water. Gravity takes a back seat as I pull myself across the pool. Sometimes I don't know what life would be like for me if I couldn't swim. In the summer I go to the Mad or the Trinity rivers to swim – see to the bottom clear – every inch of me caressed by the cleansing water – cleansing my soul – what there is of it to be cleansed. Trees grace the hills alongside the rivers and if I'm lucky – an eagle or osprey will look down at me. One time a turkey vulture followed me on the Trinity River – probably hoping I'd die – his meal. The warm air is brushed by cool breezes coming up from the ocean. Other than the ocean, rivers are the best. One thing I like so much about swimming in rivers is when I swim downstream - moving fast - spinning in the water - eyes open - sun distorted. A freedom that's beyond.

The ocean up here is too damn cold; so, I don't go in, but I love watching the waves. I can watch waves for hours on end. Sometimes Brown Pelicans fly just above the waves in single file only occasionally moving their wings as air is thrust upward by the waves. One time there was huge surf - at least 20-foot face waves. These waves weren't closeouts - they had great shape. People couldn't surf them - there were huge rocks. Anyway, the seagulls were hanging around these waves. Then one seagull flew in front of a wave catching the air driven by this gigantic mass of water. The seagulls were surfing the wind currents caused by the great upheaval of the ocean. After one seagull did this, another from the line up took off, and surfed the wave and so it went.

Fortunately the Mad and Trinity rivers are warmer than the ocean, though they're never actually warm. The pool? Not as good as the ocean or rivers, but it's what I have now. I have to wait until summer to swim in the rivers.

Today I'll swim my usual 64 lengths of the pool – half freestyle and half backstroke. The old woman gets out of the pool and I'm the only one in it. She dries off with a white towel - again I wonder about her life as she walks to the women's dressing room.

Swimming is a solitary activity. My mind often wanders while swimming either that or I hear songs in remembrance. I guess swimming mirrors my life – a solitary existence. My last length in the pool I do spinners - swimming as fast as I can – not as great as the rivers, but nonetheless I enjoy the feeling. I remember in first grade I spun around so much on the playground, I got dizzy, and fell on the asphalt. Haven't changed much in the following 64 years.

Time to go, my workday is over, and I finished my swim. I got paid two days ago, so I have money for beer and groceries. I could shop at Safeway, but I shop at a locally owned market: Wildberries. This store is often crowded – mostly with students from Humboldt State University. Lots of chatter – people meeting up with friends - walking the aisles. I like all of this activity as I also walk the aisles looking. I grab some beer, splurge on some fresh trout, get a few other items, leave the store, and get into my VW for the trip home. I've not paid attention and the car struggles and sputters – it's out of gas. No worries though, since this car wasn't built with a gas gauge it has a lever on the floor near the gas pedal. When the car runs out of gas – sputter-sputter, I simply nudge this lever down, a new line is then opened to the carburetor, and I have another gallon of gas. This is what I do. It's only about 4 miles up Fickle Hill to my cabin. I'll be fine. I reach down on the floor and grab a little stuffed octopus and put it on my dash to remind me to get gas tomorrow. Amazing to think the car was made without a gas gauge. Now cars have GPS, cameras for backing up, phones that are hooked up. Times have changed so much in my little life. I haven't really kept up with the changes. Don't want to keep up.

Miraculously the rain has let up. This is good because I can bring more wood in from the shed without getting soaked. Best to be prepared. And prepared I am. I have lots of wood in the shed next to my cabin.

# TED

Standard time is a bummer, gets dark way too early. It's dark when I get home now. Entering my cabin, I turn on the light, and put the beer in the fridge. The other food I put on the makeshift counter. It's actually a very cool counter I made from a very old virgin redwood plank 3 feet by 6 feet. It's more than an inch thick. It's a treasure I found under an old Victorian house in Eureka. Crawling under that house – musty – rat shit - got very dirty grabbing it, but it was worth it. The oil I rubbed into it makes it the pearl of my cabin. I don't like to cook – usually have a sandwich and avocado, but even before I do this I'll get out a frosted glass from the freezer and a beer. There's this game I play. I want the beer to come just over the top of the glass, but no spillage. Maybe I'm practicing for a bartender's job. On my couch I turn on the lamp that sits on a tree stump. Recently eBay was selling one just like my end table for $199. When I was making my chopping block, I made two of them, and brought this one into the cabin for an end table. Maybe that's what I should do, make a bunch of these and sell them on eBay. Yeah right. I try not to drink too much, but since it's dark so early, this is hard to do, but I'm pretty disciplined and usually only have two beers. The beer tastes so good going down.

After this beer, I reach for my small pipe and fill it with herb. The smoke fills me. I find it hard to believe anyone could live without some alcohol and or herb - I know I don't want to. Some of my best ideas come at this time. I used to wake up in the morning and think to myself - what was that idea I came up with last night? This was to no avail. I now write down my thoughts so I can work on them later.

I like to make up stories about people I see out and about. I get my pen and make a brief outline about the old woman at the gym. In it, she is a good person trapped in a life she didn't really choose. A life that came at her strong – reacting - trying to be the best she could. She lived a life almost as a monk – hidden away. Then age jumped out at her and before she knew it she was old and at the Welcome Gym. Shit, she was probably some socialite buzzing around in her social world.

Putting down the pen. What's the use of this. I write and write and no one sees what I've written. Maybe what I write isn't any good. Well, at least people don't tell me my writing stinks.

Looking at the clock – it's only 7. Wish it were later so I can go to sleep. I just can't go to bed at 7. Getting another beer I return to my place on the couch. Time for some music. The one aspect of technology I really like is YouTube. I've created a play list of songs I've "liked". Music takes me to places beyond my cabin - beyond my life. Funny, when I was young and living with my parents, that's what I did at night – listen to top 40 AM radio. I wanted to be a disc jockey.

*Lazarus* by David Bowie is on. It's very eerie - he's talking from heaven. It turns out this album was released two days before he died of cancer. I have to respect him. No one in the public knew he was dying. This was his personal business. This song, *Lazarus*, was his legacy. What will my legacy be? Not so good – in fact, damn disgusting, and that's putting it mildly. I'm now trying to accomplish something with my writing, but at my age almost certainly a wasted effort.

# TED

These fall days continue – me in my routine. I try to write everyday. There is no clear story, just vignettes and short, short stories. I decide to swim. Driving down Fickle Hill I am, once again, shown how beautiful it is here. Dark. Redwoods - tall - drape and cover this steep drive. Damn, there's the tree. A few years ago a bicyclist was going fast when his brakes failed. Instead of dropping the bike – this bicyclist tried to stay on the road. Unfortunately for him he flew off the road and smashed into this tree. Since it's so steep he hit the tree about 30 feet from its base. He died. I try to imagine the horror of flying through the air just before slamming into the tree. I don't ride bikes.

Without incident, I arrive at the gym and since it's the weekend I was slow getting out the door. The clock says 11. Getting into my trunks I wander slowly into the pool area. There she is again. She's really a good swimmer. The one thing I like about swimming is when done correctly it's very graceful...and she is graceful.

It takes me a moment to enter the pool. I sit at its side - then drop in. I think if I had another life before this I would have been an ocean mammal. Wish it were a dolphin or whale, but probably a seal. I know fear and seals aren't at the top of the food chain, like dolphins and whales. Think I'll ask God if she can exchange my life now for a dolphin. Gosh, I'd do this in an instant. I begin my workout in earnest. Pushing myself hard. I once swam 10 miles in a pool without stopping and another time, 5 miles in the ocean. If the ocean is warm - with its salt water, I feel I can swim forever. Back and forth. Looking over, the woman, long legs, is moving fast in the water... smooth and graceful.

She gets out of the pool and dries off with her white towel. She turns, sees me, and smiles. I think of the vignette I wrote about her, doubt it's anywhere near the truths she known. She saunters off. I continue my swim.

# TED

Done with my workout. Glad I came into town. On my days off I usually stay home and do very little all day. The wind is out and brisk air rushes at me. I forgot to bring my jacket, but I have my scarf – it's blue and gray with small white lines. It's my Scots Clan's Tartan. I'm glad I have it. It helps keep me warm - this isn't easy to do - cold winds from my past do not bring me comfort. When will I learn to bring warm clothes with me when I come to town? It's often warmer up Fickle Hill than down on the coast.

Arcata isn't a big town - I'm at the market in the matter of minutes. I've made a list of what I need. Now just to find the list. That's what happened the last time I went grocery shopping - I forgot my list. Seriously, without the list I'm lost in the store. I shop the best I can without it.

Wildberries is a former Safeway. It's on the top of a hill. Previous to this Safeway a very large Victorian house resided here. My god, the view they had. Then Safeway came into this residential neighborhood and demolished the grand old house. In today's economy this Safeway was too small – they have to be very large now, so, Safeway abandoned it, demolished more old houses for its new and improved store. This store on the hill laid vacant for a few years until a local guy bought it and turned it into the market it is today. I wonder what life was like before the corporate world took over. In this instance, beauty surely took a back seat.

Leaving the store, for some reason I turn, and look back inside. There she is. I'm I going to see her everyday? Let me explain. I am interested in meeting her, but I know I won't. I don't meet anyone, what's the use. The reason. My memories won't leave me – stay inside all wrapped up. This is who I am.

What to do. I drive to the Arcata Marsh. This place gives me peace of mind – such as I can have. This used to be where the town dump was - at the edge of Humboldt Bay. I remember going there. Trash in piles right next to the bay – seagulls flying in masse overhead searching for food. The town decided to turn the dump into marshes where used water from the town is filtered in the various ponds and finally into clear healthy water. What a difference. I park the car and get out to walk.

I wonder if I'll run into the old woman. I hope not. Hands in my pockets, again I vow to always have warm clothes in the car. I walk briskly in the cold wind. A dog looks at me. I continue my walk. Stopping to look out at the bay, the dog follows me. He's a fair sized dog – maybe 50 pounds – thick in his chest. Looks like a nice dog. I continue walking. Brown pelicans and seagulls fly about. A white elegant egret stands in the water - still as can be - looking down – waiting for a frog or such to come near. There – it gets a frog. Head back and down it goes. I'm getting cold and decide to leave. A car parks near mine. Is it that woman again? Why is this old woman in my thoughts so much? It's not her. A young couple, all bundled up, gets out of the car.

The dog. Does he have a home? I begin my way home, but I don't go that way. Instead, I go back to the Marsh. Maybe I'll see the dog. In the parking lot, there he is - dark fur – all alone – looking about. He appears to be well fed; maybe he's just wandered off. The young couple comes back to their car. The dog goes over to them. They ignore him, get in their car, and drive away. The dog - still there in the parking lot. Stopping my car I sit looking at him. He comes over - sits near my car looking up at me. My god, he has such expressive eyes. I watch. I don't know what to do. Maybe he's just out and about and has a home. He seems like such a good dog. OK, I make a deal with myself. I'll come back tomorrow and if he's still here I'll see if he wants to come with me. "See you tomorrow." Putting the car in gear I head for home. As it turns out I forgot to buy hamburger. I was so looking forward to a burger. Guess I'll have a cheese sandwich. I can't stop thinking about the dog. What would it be like to have a dog? A restless night in bed - I wake up very early. Still totally dark I start my morning coffee routine - getting ready for work.

The whole day my mind is on this dog. Maybe I should look for him on my lunch break, but it's only a half hour and what would I do with him for the rest of the day if he came to me. And besides, maybe he isn't even there. I'll just wait until the end of my shift. What a slow day at work, but it's finally over. So anxious to see if the dog is at the Marsh I don't go swimming. Stopping at the market for the hamburger I forgot yesterday. Soon I'm at the Marsh. I stop the car and look around – no dog. Damn, well maybe not damn, could be he's home where he belongs. I back up and just before leaving I see him. Stopping the car I get out. The dog slowly walks towards me.

Reaching into the bag I pull out the hamburger I bought. Breaking off some I throw it to him. Down it goes in one gulp. Do animals have taste buds? They must, but they eat so fast. I get out and he comes over to me.

He continues staring at me with his big brown eyes. "Do you want some more?" He comes even closer. I throw him more burger. Again, the same as last time, he devours it. He must be hungry. I invite him into my car. Taking up my offer, he's in the front seat next to me - sticking his head in the bag of groceries. I move the bag to the back seat. What to do. Without thinking, I drive back to my cabin with a houseguest. I've never had a dog.

# TED

Pulling into my place, I stop the car, get out, and shut the door – oops how rude of me, my guest is still in the car. I open the door. What's up with this, he only has a stub tail? He's not some purebred whose owner disgustingly docked his tail. He must have been born this way. Anyway he's awfully cute. "Come on boy." He gets out. Getting my sack of groceries - minus some burger - we walk toward the cabin. Opening the door I call him in, but he sits a few feet away from my makeshift porch - not moving. I ask him again, but still no response. Not wanting the heat to escape, I close the door, and put away the groceries. Looking out the window he's still sitting on the cold damp ground. Well, now what. I brought him here and he won't come in. I've fucked up – I shouldn't have brought him with me. He's probably worse off here than he was at the Marsh. Putting on my jacket, I go outside, and sit in the chair on my porch. Still, he sits away from me. I call him over, but he doesn't respond. Now what? Going back inside I bring out more burger. Holding the food in my hand, but he still doesn't come over to me. I call him again. Then I throw the burger in front of him. He quickly goes for it and in a second it's gone. I do this again – he gets it and down it goes. Even dressed for the cold, it isn't comfortable out. I go back inside. Then this idea hits me. Maybe I can get him inside my house by offering burger. This burger was going to be my dinner tonight, but what the heck. Opening my door I drop some burger. He doesn't move toward it. I close the door and he goes to the food in front of the closed door. The next step – put some burger just inside my door. He doesn't move. The door still

15

open - I step back into the shadows of my house. He slowly walks to the food. He backs away when I come toward him. I wonder why he got into my car since he seems so fearful. No figuring this out. I put more burger a few feet further inside. Stepping back, this time he goes for the food. He must really be hungry to be so brave. Seeing me he takes a step back, but he's still in the cabin. Slowly I go over to the kitchen counter and grab another bit of burger. I drop it on the floor. He looks and looks, then slow step-by-step goes to it. I move - he sees this and looks ready to flee. He is now 15 feet away from the door.

"That's a good boy." He tilts his head slightly - looking at me. I continue talking to him, "Do you have a home? Well, you're welcome to stay here with me if you want." He's trying to figure out what this human is saying. He plops on the floor. Without looking at him I make a wide birth and shut the door.

Here we are. This dog and I.

# TED

This is how we spend our evening - the dog on the floor - me on my couch. When I decide to go to bed I figure he needs to go out and take care of business. Opening the door and still he sits. I call to him, standing by the open door. Slowly he gets up and goes outside. I shut the door – it's cold out. Waiting a few minutes I open the door. I don't see him. Maybe he won't come back – this worries me. Again, maybe I shouldn't have taken him. I wait a few more minutes, open the door, and there he is. Slapping my side I call him in. He comes in.

Days go by. He waits for me when I get home from work. His stub tail wags when he sees me. I have a friend. This is new to me. I've been alone for so long - don't really remember having friends. It all started, wait don't fucking go there – just leave it. What's done is done and there's no way to take anything back.

We get used to each other. I think I should train him. If I'm to take him places, he needs to know he and I are together. So, I start. I'm just calling him dog and this seems to work. I want to see if he'll stay when I tell him to. I could use food to do this, but I want to try without food.

"Sit, Stub." I put my hand on his rear and gently push down. He sits. Oh goodness, I called him Stub. He's got a name. I get up and he follows me. Again, "Sit." Putting my hand on his rear I gently push down until he sits. When I walk away he gets up and follows me. I repeat my sit command until he stays even when I walk away. Then I tell him, "OK." He gets up and comes to me. This could be a fluke so I do it again. He follows my wishes. "Good boy, Stub." His tail wags. Wow, this is a good start.

The two commands I want him to follow are: to sit and stay, and to come every time I call him. It appears he's taken to the first command. I'm very pleased and he appears to be pleased too. I was thinking this would be hard to accomplish, but I'm grateful he learned this so fast.

In the days that follow we work on the other command. I cannot believe how well he's learned them. He now comes every time I call him. He sits and stays until I say, "OK." I can now take him places with me.

# TED

I decide to take Stub to the Arcata Marsh. I'm curious how he'll react. Only a few very white clouds grace the sky – moving across the blue. I park my old beater. He doesn't have a collar – thus no leash. When I get out, he literally jumps out of the vehicle. I hope he doesn't run off. He doesn't. This is a good time to practice the commands. "Sit, Stub." He does. "OK, let's go." He gets up. Again, "Stub, sit." Then I walk about 20 feet from him. "Come, Stub." Getting off his haunches he bounds over to me. "Good boy." Patting his head, his stub tail wags. We begin our walk. He continually stops to smell. By the last pond, birds are out en masse – don't know what birds they are, but they're swirling in a dance in the sky. We're interrupted by this when a bicyclist speeds by. Stub jumps out of the way as the man in his funny tight fitting colorful clothes and silly helmet peddles by us going fast – too fast. Don't think he is supposed to be riding fast in this peaceful spot. "Let's go, Stub. We saunter back to the car.

I've been so involved with Stub that little else is on my mind and this is a good thing. Back home I sit on our couch and my new friend sits right up against me - two peas in a pod.

Waking up in an unusual bright and sunny morning, Stub and I go to Redwood Park. The sun splashes on the grass, ever so green. The redwood forest almost surrounds the large grass area. Kids play on the playground – squealing in delight as proud parents watch. College students play a game of ultimate Frisbee - lots of activity. We go to the trailhead to the forest – hopefully we'll be alone. Along the well-worn path there are huge redwood stumps – these tree were gigantic. Some of the stumps are more than 20 feet in diameter. This area was heavily logged back in the 1800's. At one point a steep gully is filled with ferns – so green against the color of the redwoods and the blue sky that ventures between the trees. We bypass this gully and go up the trail. There's one thing about redwood forests - the forest floor are fairly bare – mostly ferns. There's a lot for dogs to smell in this forest, and smell, Stub does.

"Look Stub." It's the old woman from the pool. She's walking down the trail in front of us – coming our way. She hesitates when she gets close - that look of recognition in her blue eyes. I stop. Stub starts to run off after some random smell or noise that only dogs know. "Stub. Come!" He does. "Sit, Stub." He sits.

This woman smiles, looks at Stub – then looks at me. "What a well trained dog. He sure is smart."

"Yes, he's very smart." Awkward silence. "Have a nice walk. It's such a beautiful day."

"You too," she answers. Hesitating for a moment, she continues, "Have I seen you at the pool?"

"Yes, you have. I recognize you too."

"Yes, that's it." She starts to walk away, but turns, "My name's Amy. What's yours?"

"Ted."

"Nice meeting you ... Ted."

"Nice meeting you as well."

"Guess I'll be on my way."

"Wait a second please." She quizzically looks at me. "I just want to tell you that you're a very graceful swimmer. I admire how well you swim." I've done it now – broke the anonymity.

"Thanks. You're not so bad yourself. See you around." And she disappears down the trail.

"Well, Stub. That was something. Gosh, she even recognized me. And her name, Amy. Come on let's go." Walking the trail - up we go. This trail will actually go all the way up Fickle Hill, past my cabin, and connect to Kneeland. After a while we retrace our steps and go back down. The whole time Stub walks in front, but he occasionally looks back to check up on me. This has been a good day. What a difference having a friend makes - someone to share with - someone to keep me company. We've become good friends. I think he likes hanging out with me. "Stub, you're such a good boy." He wags his tail.

# TED

Back at our cabin we settle in for the night. Old – this is weird. On the trail today she didn't seem so old. This is how it is with me. I'm 70, yet I don't feel old. I have energy from my swimming. Swimming is what keeps me feeling young. Not a lot going on in my life, but the one thing I do have is my health and vitality – swimming makes this happen. I also have peace of mind and heart – as much as I can have when I swim – my one saving grace. One day at the dentist office I was sitting close to the receptionist. She'd ask the patients their dates of birth. I was all ears. When I heard their birthdates I thought wow, I'm older than they are. Do I look like them? No I don't. In a way this confirms that I look younger than I am – or maybe it's that others look older than they are - not walking erect - slightly stooped, or kind of shuffling their feet instead of sure steady steps. So, in this case what the hell is "old"? This swimming woman has sure steady steps and is a hell of a good swimmer.

My god. I'd forgotten about the vignette I made up about her. Need to stop thinking of her as old, but she is a mystery to me – I keep seeing her everywhere. Stub's also a mystery. Why did he get in my car that day? Why was he at the Marsh? There are now two mysteries in my life. I bet Stub doesn't look at me as a mystery and I have no idea what the woman thinks about me.

Already dark when we get home - we're going to have to leave earlier to catch more daylight. On the couch, Stub and I sit. I get a beer, take out my little pipe, and fill it with herb. It's raining. I like hearing the rain on my roof. I just don't like it to rain for days and days and days - too much of a good thing. When it rains for days on end I can feel trapped, but tonight it's very peaceful. Getting one more beer, I fill up Stub's food bowl and check his water. He jumps off the couch to eat. Again, do dogs even taste the food they throw done their gullets?

"Time to go to bed, Stub." He looks up at me as I get up from the couch. This is where he sleeps. Gosh, I forgot to eat dinner. I am prone to do this some nights. Once settled into my bed I'm one of these people who goes to sleep quickly. No screwing around in my mind. Close my eyes and I'm asleep.

> Sun's out - it's a warm day. Everything around me glistens - so bright. A little girl wearing a blue dress and saddle shoes crosses the street. A red Camaro comes screaming into the intersection. "Stop!" Useless. There's nothing I can do other than look at this car – look at the girl. A woman yells, "Amy! just as the car slams into her. She's thrown up in the air like a rag doll. Falling off to the side - the car drives over her – dragging her down the street. This car doesn't stop and the little girl falls away from the speeding vehicle. This cannot be! Rushing to her – she's on her back. Her poor body is twisted in an unnatural way. Her eyes are open - she sees me. Then they close and her chest stops going up and down. I am all alone with the girl. Everything's in slow motion. The leaves on the trees rustle – I hear this. Birds call from the telephone wires. And the little girl is no longer - just a memory in someone's life. Tears rage in me. Deep and terrible cries.

I wake up. Stub is up on the bed helping make me better the way dogs do – licking. I was crying, not just in my sleep, but in the here and now. Putting my arms around him. "Oh, Stub." He spends the night with me on my bed. It's difficult getting back to sleep. The girl's name was Amy. What's with this?

Putting my head into his fur, the interval of Stub's breaths are the same as mine – this helps. I fall asleep.

# TED

**A** day without; without any consequences. I really want to go for a swim. The pool has four others in it, but the old woman - got to stop calling her that - her name's Amy - isn't in the pool.

I sit at the edge of the pool, put my legs in the water, and watch the other swimmers. One swimmer is a very large woman. She does the breaststroke. Doing this stroke her butt comes up out of the water - it's huge. I try to not be judgmental, but how do people let themselves get so large. I imagine how different life would be if I had to carry around an extra 100 to 150 pounds. I enter the water and push off the wall. No matter what happens in my life when I swim my existence is washed in the pureness of the water.

No need to go to the store, so I head straight home. I now look forward to getting there – Stub will be waiting for me. Parking the car, I get out, and go to the cabin. When I open the door, Stub is standing right behind it. His tail wags, I pat him, and tell him how glad I am to see him. Sitting in the chair on the porch - Stub goes around taking care of his business. Maybe he likes to retrieve tossed balls. There's an old tennis ball in the cabin. I get it and toss it in the yard. Stub doesn't run after it - he only walks to it. He smells it, then comes to me minus the ball. Not a fetcher.

# TED

The days drift past like a slow train - nothing out of the ordinary. The rain has stopped. I open my eyes - rubbing the sleep out – then stretch. Amy's face comes into view. I haven't seen her at the gym. Again, I wonder why I'm so interested – she's just some random person who likes to swim. Morning light enters my cabin. Difficult to get up – it's cold. Stub licks his paws – he's getting ready for the day. I am not ready. But forcing myself up, I stagger over to the stove, toss in some wood, and get the water ready for my coffee. Stub's still on the bed. He looks over to me. It's easy to see his eyes hold love for me. Such a new thing, this love - so many years without. In kind of a trance, standing over the stove I need my coffee. Pouring the hot water in anticipation of the warming brew. Stub jumps off the bed and goes to the door. He wants out. When I open the door, the sunrays have reached the top of the trees. I stay on the porch - Stub comes back and we go in. I feed him. All's right in his world.

The dream. Where do dreams come from? I guess I'll really never know. This recent dream was so damn real. What should I do about it? Nothing, but the girl hit by the car was named Amy. How can this be.

My mind drifts to work. This job takes no mental thought; so, I'm free to have my daydreams when working – daydreams - night dreams - I must be living in some strange altered state - a state of denial. This brings a chuckle. I'm good at not delving deeply into things – just like the surface cleaning I do at work - just cover and take care of the obvious. It's time to head down the mountain – my job awaits me. Oh boy.

I let Stub out again. It'll be a while before I get home. He sniffs around. Dogs have big noses. They smell things humans can't. In fact, they can smell if someone familiar has gone past, rubbed against a bush. Though dogs don't think of time the way we do – they use their noses as a powerful tool. Stub comes back - I let him in.

Today is Friday. This weekend I need to do something with Stub – maybe the beach. Kind of on autopilot I make way to the gym. One aspect I like about my job is looking at the women. So many of them wear tights. I like women who are physically active, working up a sweat. But, seriously this is as far as I get. No way could I even approach them. I'm just a damn janitor. But that's not the real reason. Fuck me.

Amy comes in while I'm collecting the trash. She looks at me and smiles. I nod and look away as if I'm busy – feeling shy - feel as if I've entered her life. But this is ridiculous – the dream was probably just a coincidence. But what if...

Getting the last of the trash picked up I take the garbage sack out to the dumpster. Such a scam – this job. The owners have never been janitors and have no idea what it takes. I could do all of my chores in no more than 4 hours, so every day I just mosey along trying to look busy.

# TED

Slept well. No disturbing dreams. Stub spent the night in the bed with me. It's official - it's our bed, our couch, our cabin. He's 100% moved in. A slow morning – no rush to get to work. I love my weekends.

"Hey, Stub. You want to go to the beach?" He doesn't answer. I think he's trying to figure out what I'm saying. He knows I'm talking to him. The sun's rays beam down from above through the canopy of trees. Hard to say if the rest of the sky is like this - my view is limited – that's what I get for living in a redwood and Douglas fir forest. Going to the car, I open the passenger door, and call Stub. He jumps right in. We go all the way to Big Lagoon. The beaches in Humboldt County are fierce, wild and very wind blown. Very few people go out to them. I can get solitude with no interference. Today is no different - bathing in the air - brisk and cool. The powerful untethered waves break against the shore. Just wish the ocean wasn't so cold up here. Clouds, which normally make up most of the sky, are absent, and the sun dominates. But in this part of the world when it's sunny it doesn't mean it's warm. Glad I'm wearing my hoodie and jacket - these along with the stocking cap keep me warm. Stub's fur keeps him warm. I'm trying to figure out what breed or breeds he is. He has German Shepard in him and probably some Black Lab and Huskie. Under his outer coat there's a fine down. I read where a dog has close to 1,000 hairs per square inch, bet he has more than that. Damn, Stub is a forest of hairs. I know, because I am starting to see them around our cabin. He's exploring and has his nose in the sand under a large redwood log on the beach.

His butt's in the air - his tail rapidly moving. Wonder what he's found. How these monster logs get on the beach is a mystery to me. They must have been carried to the ocean in rivers ripped with rushing, fierce water - float around, then get driven up on the beach by another storm - surf – wild - showing no mercy. I walk along this shore empty of people, but I'm kept company by pelicans, godwits, sandpipers, seagulls and other unseen creatures. Stub is still at the log as I continue on my way - leaving him to explore. Soon he runs past me. Not a graceful run. He has a bull chest and runs like a fullback crashing through a defensive line. He's so strong.

Walking down the beach for a mile or so. What's that up ahead? What's with all of the commotion? I now jog along the shore, very interested in what's ahead of us. Stub's leading the way. My god, it's two Gray Whales. They're inside the surf line. Stub and I watch. I'm amazed and thrilled - don't know what Stub's thinking. They roll around in the shallow water. We're only 30 feet or so away from them. Wanting to go in the water so badly I take off my stocking cap, but decide I'll just watch them from the shore. Maybe they're scratching themselves on the sand. They're huge. "Pretty damn cool, huh, Stub." After maybe 20 minutes these whales turn and go out into the ocean - away from the shore. This is glorious.

I once observed an ant crossing the cement – so small – so insignificant – could be crushed at any moment by an unseen foot passing by. Still looking to where the whales were I think of the times I've been in the ocean - the ebb and flow of the earth, breathing in – out - in - out - a living being. Entering a vastness beyond knowing - embracing the mother of us all – the ocean. Feet – knees – waist - a breath - dive into – then under large waves - powerfully crashing – intense. Immersed in this blessed water - calm as the wave breaks above. Up to the surface - the now crashing wave past me - on its way to the beach. In this peaceful moment I'm on the lookout for what's coming next. This is freedom. In the moment - smaller than small - it goes on and on. World without end.

As expansive as the universe is, that same vastness is also into the incredibly small – the minute – the micro. I believe Quantum Mechanics is about this. When I was a small boy around twelve years old, in a quiet moment, I waved my hand, and dust particles danced about in a random fashion. I remember thinking, "What if the earth is like one of these dust particles that just hasn't been swirled about by the hand of a boy somewhere. The earth could be that small." Later I found out scientists observe that comets are fertilizers to the planets they crash into. These comets bring whole new elements to the planets – giving diversity that wasn't there before. Then seeing what sperm looks like traveling on its way to the egg – wow! They look similar. The same truths seem to be for things so immense as to be incomprehensible all the way down to an incredibly small scale, also incomprehensible. And I am just an infinitesimally small creature in the vastness that is the universe. With these thoughts, I brush the sand off my pants. Stub and I go along the beach. It's been a good day for us.

Evening light is accentuated by a full moon. I go outside in the clear night; moon is lurking behind two redwoods. Stub stands next to me. He's not looking at the moon. Don't know if dogs notice things like a full moon. Getting chilled I go back in, Stub follows. I stoke the fire – want to get warm.

# TED

Don't usually get coffee from a coffee shop, but I feel like one. Walking into the Phoenix Café, I get a cup. I like this place because it's on the plaza and I can look out the large windows. The plaza is a special place for me. Just feels ... so old fashioned – a large grass area surrounded by Victorian storefronts. In the center of the plaza is a statue of President McKinley. A Mr. Zender got the statue at a fire sale after the 1906 San Francisco earthquake. So, here's this statue – loved by some, hated by others. I'm on the side of hating it. There's a strong desire to get rid of it – remove it from the plaza. The oddity about the statue is that McKinley is reaching out to shake the hand of the assassin who seconds later took his life. I spent a few years in Hawai'i and came to learn what an asshole McKinley was. He destroyed the Kingdom of Hawai'i for imperialist reasons. It was the time of European colonialism and McKinley wanted the US to be a part. Also, this - the sons of missionaries had become large landholders growing lots of sugar and pineapples. These poor guys had to pay tariffs when their produce was shipped to the US. This cut into their profits. They managed to get a covert US Navy ship with Marines to land on Oahu. With their armed power they dissolved the Hawai'ian Parliament and arrested Queen Liliuokalani. The reason there's the Union Jack in the upper left hand side of the kingdom's flag – now the state flag - was because the Hawai'ians based their government on Great Britain's Parliamentary system. Queen Liliuokalani was a queen in the same respect as England's queen - mostly ceremonial. Parliament made the laws. A higher percentage of Hawai'ians were literate in

Hawai'ian than were literate in English in the United States. President Grover Cleveland sent a US Army General to survey what had happened. He went to Hawai'i and reported back to President Cleveland that this immoral act needed to be reversed and that the US needed to give back to the Hawai'ian people their nation. But McKinley beat Cleveland in the next election and became president. The independence of Hawai'i came to a smashing halt with the overthrow. But not to worry, these expatriate Americans were for democracy. They wrote a new constitution – only in order to vote, you had to own land. This left out the vast majority of Hawai'ians. Still today, the Hawai'ians call this the "bayonet constitution". I go over all of this looking out at asshole McKinley, but have to chuckle because seconds after this portrayal he was dead – and hopefully he'll soon be gone from my sight.

In walks the old – wait – Amy. Looking down, I don't want to talk to her, or anyone for that matter. Hoping she won't see me, or worse yet come over and talk to me. I keep looking down slowly moving my cup in a circle. Damn, here she comes.

"Hi." A warm smile beams from her face. I look up.

"Hi." I quickly finish my coffee.

"Can I sit here?"

"Of course, but I've got to go."

"OK." She sits as I get up. "Hope you have a good day," she says to me.

"Thanks." And I hurry off. Boy that was close. What would I have possibly talked about? I shouldn't have told her she was a good swimmer. This kind of opened up...I don't know - opened up something – something I'm not ready for. I want to look back at her, but don't, and walk across the plaza past my friend McKinley.

# TED

Such an odd life. Thinking about the encounter with Amy I open my cabin door and let Stub out. I wonder how old he is – don't think he's very old – maybe two or three. When I was a young man I felt I wouldn't live to be fifty. So, why did I feel this? No idea, just did.

So, here I am, seventy and not dead. I breathe in and breathe out everyday and I don't even have to think about it - just sort of glide along step after step going in no particular direction – just going. That's how I ended up in Humboldt County - along the fog-shrouded coast - encasing everything in a cold dampness. This fog, in a way, is concealing and comforting to me. I know others often complain about it, but not me.

My cabin is so excellent. It's in the forest of tall ones. Leaving my front porch this morning I walk - free of the fog; sun blasting its way through the redwoods – tall - ancient - with a gift for life that's unique and beautiful. For these few minutes I forget I'm with Stub. Looking around - I don't see him. "Stub. Come. Come here." He crashes through the ferns, wagging his stub tail - eyes bright with anticipation. "Good boy, Stub." Again, I'm very glad to have a friend - one that doesn't ask questions – doesn't demand this or that. He just wants food and to be loved. Oh, and to love back. How lucky am I. "Hey, let's go to the beach." He tilts his head trying to figure out what I want. Back to the cabin I gather my things - remembering to bring warm clothes because of my friend, the fog and my other friend, the wind. It's a lot warmer up here than down on the coast.

Stepping out of the VW, the air is bright. The fog bank has receded off shore. There's only a slight breeze. Stub runs hard along the beach. Seeing a bird – going after it. Giving up on the chase, then sniffing about, as all dogs like to do. "Stub. Come, let's go up the trail." Wow, different world here than down on the beach. The beach - the opening to the vastness of the ocean. Here up on the bluff – trees stand tall - other trees lie horizontal in death - ferns grow in abundance. A trillium breaks out in its white glory on the damp forest floor.

I sit on the leaves and needles. Stub comes over and plops down next to me. And for this moment I'm wrapped in peace and comfort. Light streaming down from above – through the trees - bark reddish/brown. Unseen creatures crawl, eat, and re-create, and die. Fern fronds brush against us as we walk under the trees and make our way back to the edge of the forest on this bluff.

The waves – large – powerful - pounding the shore. What a magnificent thing waves are, never ceasing – this is something you can count on. And seriously, how much in life can be counted on. Step by step, down the steep incline. We get close to the water. I sit - take off my shoes - wiggle my toes, and touch my hand to my heart. What a good day. A feeling of lightness invades me. I could just float up into the vast blue with white clouds passing, changing - drifting, and re-shaping again - in constant motion. Softness prevails as I walk along the shore under the umbrella of blue. Damp sand – cold ocean water touches my feet - air almost warm - soul comforting. So glad to be here with Stub and with an unusual feeling of lightness.

Nearby a young man in a tie-die T-shirt holds the hand of his girl friend dressed in a colorful wrap exposing her legs and they too walk along the shore. Stopping the man turns to his friend. She goes up to him and wraps her arms around him. They sway back and forth not knowing they're being watched. Gently he puts his hands to her face and kisses her. They break from this and walk hand in hand along this beach – under a gleaming sun.

I wander along, find a spot, and drop down on the warm sand. The sand darkens as a lone cloud mutes the sun—and this too passes into brightness. "What a day." Closing my eyes I fall asleep listening to the waves and dreams grace my being. When I awake, Stub is sleeping next to me, his body up against mine. I can feel his body heat. A family is near - children playing. "See Daddy," the girl child, maybe seven years old, in a bright new bathing suit calls out from her castle in the sand. "I see, honey," the proud poppa says.

Another man gets out of his car, walks away, not bothering to lock it—it doesn't matter. Nothing matters. He walks along the sand going up the trail to the bluff. Not knowing where he's going or even why. In the shadows of the tall trees he slowly walks, hands in his pockets, eyes looking down, not noticing anything other than his sorrow. "She's gone." Taken away, maybe he'll never see her again. Family disrupted, separated, and ruined. Nothing can ever be the same. No days on the beach, in the park, or at a matinee with his daughter - thousands of miles away, she's gone. Sweetness of the morning - when still asleep - she would come into his room - morning sunshine in her brown eyes - a smile held only for daddy - a kiss, "I love you Daddy."

"I love you too sweetheart." Everything is worthwhile when she appears. Sad job, sad life are tossed out the window in the expectation of a day in the park. Gone. What to do. A giant spoon has scrapped away his insides re-placed with nothing - large and cavernous.

He trudges along the forest floor. Stopping him in his tracks, a silver explosion of brilliance reflects off a raven's wings as she flies away, and lands in a high branch of a redwood tree. This is a gift, he thinks, but sorrow covers this moment, and he continues walking - looking down. Somewhat surprised, he sees a purple sack on the ground. He reaches down and touches the velvet cloth and to his surprise there's a pipe, lighter, and marijuana inside - a gift. He wanders to a place on the bluff overlooking the ocean, sits down in a ray of sunlight, smells the earth, and sees the ocean - clear, reflecting the brightness of the day. Pulling out the pipe, he fills it, and draws the herb into his lungs. Clouds float and drift across the blue as he releases the smoke and repeats this again. In his mind's eye he sees his daughter - bright loving eyes - wondrous smile. Another raven flies off through the tree branches.

Getting up, he brushes his pants, and soon finds himself on the beach. He takes off his shoes - sand warm from the sun. Lying on the beach, he drifts off, and finds sleep. The water reaches his toes from the rising tide, this abruptly wakes him. A little startled he gets up. Stretching, arms in the air - time to jog along the beach. Barefoot along the wet sand, looking out at waves - giant – crashing – heart beating in time with the waves. Along this beach he glides. He looks out at the ocean and step-by-step goes into the very cold water - startled, body tingles, soul flushed with the ocean that wraps around every inch of him. Only staying a minute he steps out of the cold. A raven is on his towel. "Oh no!" He runs to his towel, too late, the bird flies off with his purple sack with the gold colored drawstring filled with his newfound marijuana.

The raven lands with her booty on a tall spruce tree on the bluff overlooking the ocean. Twirling the small bag, the raven drops down out of the tree, onto the earth laden with leaves, branches and needles. Her beak goes to work - her claws hold the sack, tearing at the gold string that attracted her in the first place. Ripping away the gold string from the purple cloth is hard work. But it pays off and the raven flies off through the tree branches holding the golden string.

Two separate lives. Could be the same, but today they are very different. One, trying to be light against all odds, the other wrapped in a deep sadness. Another day the roles could be reversed and that's how it is – on the beach – on the bluff - in the sun - in thoughts that carry the day.

# AMY

Stepping out on my porch, the moon is setting over the bay. How beautiful. People have been fascinated by the moon since the beginning of time. Our menstrual cycles are moon based; yet it's called the man in the moon. According to some, the moon is feminine, the sun, masculine. The moon gives reflective light, which is considered a quintessential feminine trait. I don't know about the reflective part being feminine. Does this mean that the masculine makes the points and women just reflect on this masculine point? I don't think so.

I adjust my scarf and put my hands in my jacket pockets to keep them warm. A somber mood takes hold. I can't stop myself from thinking-feeling about my daughter. But she's not here and sorrow places itself on my heart. Putting my thumb, fingers outstretched, to the place where my heart resides, a solitary tear falls. Going back inside, I get my stocking cap and go back out. A cloud now covers the moon. It peeks out from this cloud and soon is unencumbered. The years have crept up on me. How does it all fly by so fast. Not sure, other than the beauty of Humboldt, why I moved here. No family, no friends, and hours spent alone, but the wild ocean – aggressively pounding the shore gives me strength. I've always been a water girl, but the ocean here is too damn cold to go in. The pool at the gym is a substitute for the ocean, albeit, not a great one. I hear the rivers are magnificent to swim in. Going inside I decide to drive up to a river tomorrow.

Stopping at the gym, I ask for advice about where to go. I'm told the Mad River at the Maple Creek Bridge is a cool place. The directions seem easy enough. This will be good. I need to get out. The drive is beautiful through the canopy of trees, sun filtering down. I come to an open space – pastures with horses and cows – a barn and a beautiful old ranch house. Oh my goodness it's so beautiful. The river is clear – surrounded by trees – the sun accentuates the clarity I feel. I slowly drive across this concrete bridge – river below. On the other side of the bridge I get out and marvel at the beauty I find myself in. Definitely not L.A. Walking down to the river - looks so pure. It's fall and the air isn't warm, but I've heard it gets very pleasant up here in the summer. Yes, I'll come up here then. It'll be glorious. That is if it's true the air really does warm up. Looking over – a tree's growing on the bank of the river. It's not a large tree, maybe 10 feet high – wonder what kind of tree it is. Its roots travel over a rock reaching down to the river, but don't reach the water. In just a short time the river will be wild with rushing brown water, or at least I've been told. I wonder if the water will reach the roots then. Making a note to return when the rains are bombarding the land and the rivers. Looking forward to seeing this – the wildness. Gosh, the L.A. River is encased in cement, but I do remember at times, water - very high - rushing wild held within the confines by the concrete. Wonder how this will look, standing on this bridge watching the rush to the ocean.

Maybe I should at least go in – even if just for a moment. Putting my hand in the water, yes it's very cold. Need to be alone. Looking around – I am. Dropping off my clothes I walk into the water. Damn cold, standing knee-deep waiting for courage to get to the point I can swim. Hands in front - I dive in. Yes, very cold and in this cold, the bottom – so clear. The tree – I want to swim over to it. I'm so taken by this tree – don't know why – just am. Cupping my hands I draw up water from the river and splash the roots many times. Don't know if it's right, but I think of the tree as my tree.

Very chilled - need to get out. Not thinking - didn't bring a towel. Don't want to go up to my car without any clothes on – what if someone were to drive by.

Funny, back in the day, people went out in the woods, swam on rivers naked all the time, and no one seemed to care. But those days are long gone. Standing by the river's edge shivering, I take my shirt, and dry myself off as best I can. Putting on the rest of my clothes, at least I have my jacket. All wrapped up I walk back to my car on the road above the river. A truck drives by pulling a trailer with a couple of horses in it. Glad I didn't get caught naked.

Feeling good about this little adventure; I am, once again, reassured as to why I moved here from crowded L.A. Could never do what I have just done in L.A.

# AMY

Back in town – at the market for food. Cruising the aisles - searching for something to eat tonight. That swimmer is in the checkout line. What's his name? Never been good at remembering names, however, I do remember his swimming – very graceful. Oh ... Ted, that's his name. He seems to be in his private world. I was disappointed that day at the Phoenix Café when I got up the courage to approach him, only to have him get up, and leave me sitting at the table alone - said he had things to do. I, on the other hand, don't have a lot to do - mostly reading, hiking, swimming, and the occasional movie. Hard to make friends, but I'm trying.

Leaving the store, a bright red car is going too fast up G Street. A little girl is crossing the street. "No!" Screaming, I drop my bag of groceries, and run to the street. The car slams on its brakes and swerves away from the girl, missing her by only a foot. The girl in her yellow dress – looks to be about the same age as Emma. "No! Don't go there". The girl stands in the middle of the street crying.

I rush over to her. "Are you OK?" She doesn't respond – eyes full - glisten with tears. Her breaths are abrupt as she tries to stop crying. The sweet little one clings to me – tears streaming down her face. Sobs, she cannot stop. "That was scary, I know, but you're OK." I walk with her over to a bench and we sit. People leaving the store don't notice us. "What's your name?"

Catching her breath, "Sandy."

"Do you want a ride home?"

"No, I couldn't do that. Mom would kill me if I took a ride from a stranger."

"I understand. I'm just glad you're safe. That car was going way too fast. You have to be very careful crossing streets with people like that driver going so fast. Please be careful."

"I will." Sandy gets up.

"Here." Taking a Kleenex from my purse I hand it to her. She wipes her eyes and face, turns, and starts to walk away. "See you," I blurt out. She turns back and waves - her face showing a shy tentative smile.

I start for my car – wait, my groceries. Luckily the bag is still where I dropped it. Picking it up, the eggs are broken – a mess. Going back in I buy more eggs. Back at my place, I pull the food out of the bag and clean the egg mess. On the couch - tears scream from me - sobs deeper than seem possible escape. "No, not again!" More tears – my body racks with sobs. Getting up – I need a Kleenex, but the flood doesn't stop - falling to the floor. "No! No! No!" Crying until no more tears. I rise up - wipe my face and eyes with the tissue scrunched up in my hand. The tears start all over again. "What's the use. What is the goddamn use."

Emotionally strained - beat – I need to go outside. The car, the one that almost hit the little girl is parked across the street. "Asshole." Ought to break his windshield. But, instead I go down the street. Going in no direction, just walking. "I need to swim." Going back, I gather my things for the pool.

# AMY

Getting to the gym. Still distracted by the near accident I forget to check in. The receptionist asks if I'm a member. "Yes, I'm a member. Sorry. I'm Amy Nelson." The receptionist checks me in. I hope my eyes aren't red from crying. A swim will do me good. Opening the door to the women's locker room. Taking off my clothes, holding my swimsuit, I go over to the full-length mirror. "So, this is me?" Age has taken its course – a still flat belly, but the skin isn't like it used to be. Gray hair – at least it's full. Breasts almost the same as they were, never big, but perky. This isn't so bad. I'm still at the market, watching that damn stupid car almost destroy the little girl's life - nothing to smile about. But, wait; the car missed the girl this time. I sense a smile enter my face – very small, it quickly leaves. Not a lot to smile about. Glad I'm the only one in the locker room. Looking again, eyes still very red from crying. Shit, someone's entered. I'm not at all ready for small talk - got to get in the water. Quickly getting into my swimsuit, please don't talk to me - I quickly go out the door – good, no talk. At the pool I set my towel on a chair. No one else is in the water. There isn't even a lifeguard. Soon a lifeguard comes in holding her lifeguard buoy. She smiles, and I return the smile. Sitting at the edge, legs in the water – yes

Once in the water, I imagine myself in Hawai'i, warm air – warm, clear, and inviting water - not like here. I remember dolphins – swimming hard, trying to get close. They can leave me in a second; I am so slow and awkward. Can't get close. Maybe this will help me get closer - stop with arm strokes – put one arm stretched straight in front - other by my side. That's it. OK, here I go - turning slightly toward the dolphins. My fins help me go fast. Getting closer – God – getting closer – oh my - three feet. I'm wrapped in some kind of peaceful acceptance - with the dolphins in Kealakekua Bay on the Big Island of Hawai'i. And I'm wrapped in that time – even now. I was blessed – maybe I'm blessed now to be here in this water – inside a still healthy body. Yes I'm blessed today.

Not really pushing myself – more like cruising. A young man enters the pool. He's pretty buff. Bet he's a good swimmer. After he enters the water it's obvious he isn't a good swimmer as he tries to pound his way across the pool. He'll get tired quickly swimming like this. He stops at the end of the pool breathing hard, trying to catch his breath. I want to help him with his stroke. It pains me to see people like him struggling so hard to swim when it should be so easy. But it's his life; sure he doesn't want some old lady advising him on how to swim better. Back into myself, I go across the water, pull, glide, pull, glide. I love the glide part. Counting my strokes across the pool – 16 strokes. This is a good way to make sure I stay strong in my swim and don't get lazy. Wow, it'll be so grand this summer in the rivers. I got a glimpse the other day at the Mad River. My tree. It really was a blessed day. Maybe this has been a good move to Humboldt - out of the crowds – people - masses of them everywhere. No space to be alone.

It seems to me many people don't want to be alone – will do almost anything to not be alone. Being alone frightens them - so their time is kept busy. Watching T.V., sporting events, going to bars - putting much of their lives into distractions – filling the void so well they don't even know they're alone – that they have so little depth to their lives. Work - come home - eat dinner - drink too much - watch T.V. - climb in bed, and the next day doing it all over again – on and on and on and on. A song from my childhood comes to mind: the Silhouettes: *Get a Job.*

> *Ev'ry morning about this time*
> *She get me out of my bed*

*A-crying, get a job*
*After breakfast ev'ry day*
*She throws the want ads right my way*
*And never fails to say*
*Get a job, sha na na na, sha na na na na*
*Sha na na na, sha na na na na*
*Sha na na na, sha na na na na*
*Sha na na na, sha na na na na*
*Yip yip yip yip yip yip yip yip*
*Mum mum mum mum mum mum*
*Get a job, sha na na na, sha na na na na*

*-William Horton, Richard Lewis,*
 *Earl Beal, Raymond Edwards – Silhouettes-*

As a girl I really didn't get the significance of that song. Then what happens after you get that job? That job you hate, but so desperately need. Sha na na na, sha na na na na - yeah – that's what life is like for so many. I really liked being a teacher. High school kids are pretty wonderful for the most part. Some kids just sparkled and helping - not just with my class, but with their problems or dreams – helping in their personal lives meant a lot to me. Being trusted filled my heart. Think I'll keep my eyes open - maybe volunteer somewhere.

He's getting out of the pool. Bet he lifts weights – all those muscles, but not muscles made for swimming. Good luck guy with your swimming. I keep swimming.

# AMY

Walking up H Street, I'm enveloped by the old Victorian houses - graced by elegance of a time gone by. I'm fortunate to live in an apartment carved out of an old Victorian. I'm in the back of this old house on the second floor. Interesting, the Milhouse family lives in the main part of the house. They're Quakers and so odd because they're related to Richard Milhouse Nixon.

Arcata isn't like L.A. where everything seems to have been destroyed in the name of progress. What was it like back when these houses were built? When people think of the past it's just a glance at what it was like - just catching a glimpse is all. Yes, life used to be so much better people will say, but not if you were Black or Indigenous. It just depends how you look at it.

It's a shame the huge Victorian was demolished for the market. The near accident flashes in my mind. At least this time the girl is unhurt – still breathing – still alive - my God, a matter of inches. It could have gone that way those many years ago, but it didn't. Stop! The little girl in the yellow dress is OK. Her face, the crying, and her shy smile when she walked away – and she did walk away. Going across the street, I enter the store not knowing if I even want to buy anything – just something to do. Getting a cup of coffee, I decide to sit on the patio. It's well protected from the wind by large windows. It's warm on this patio and the coffee is good.

There's Ted. He's just sitting down holding a newspaper. He seems so shy. The last time as soon as I sat down he got up and left. Getting up from my table, going over to him. He can't say he's got to go - he just sat down. Feeling bold, "Hi." He looks up from his paper, but doesn't respond. "Do you mind?" I don't wait for an answer as I pull out a chair and sit. I desperately want to make friends. If he doesn't respond or seems annoyed I'll let him be. Awkward tension – silence. Finally, "Did you see that little girl almost get hit by the car the other day?"

Putting down the paper, "Yes, I did."

"Pretty scary, huh."

Scratching his head, "Yes it was." More silence.

What to say. "You're a really good swimmer."

"Thanks. It's what I do."

"Me too. I love to swim." More silence. Trying to figure this guy out. Maybe he's married or has a girl friend. Or maybe he just wants to be left alone. His eyes, blue, seem withdrawn. Taking a drink from my coffee – hoping he'll talk to me other than short answers.

Here goes nothing, "I sure like watching you swim. You're very grace-ful in the water. Where you on swim teams?"

Looking at me, he puts his newspaper on the table, "Yes, in high school. But what I really liked was water polo, but that was another lifetime ago." More silence. What's going on? "When that girl almost got hit by the car it brought up a dream I had. What do you think about dreams?"

"What do you mean?"

"Sometimes they seem so real."

"Guess so. But I don't remember a lot of my dreams."

"Can I tell you about the dream I had the other night?"

"OK."

"It was one of those dreams, so vivid – so real. This dream came to me before the girl almost got hit. The sun was out; it was a warm day. Every-thing around me glistened - so bright. A little girl, wearing a blue dress and saddle shoes, was crossing the street. A red Camaro came screaming into the intersection. "Stop!" Useless. I could do nothing other than look at this car – look at the girl. Just seconds before the car slammed into the girl an unseen woman yelled, "Amy!" The poor little girl was thrown up in the air like a rag doll. Falling off to the side, the car drove over her, and she was dragged down the street. This car didn't stop and the little girl fell away from the speeding vehicle. I was in a state of panic. This cannot be! Rushing to her – she was on her back. Her poor body was twisted in an unnatural way. Her eyes were open - she saw me. Then they closed and her chest stopped going up and down. I was all alone with the girl. Everything was in slow motion. The leaves on the trees rustled – I heard this. Birds called from the telephone wires. And the little girl was no longer. Just a memory in someone's life. Tears raged in me. Deep, terrible cries. In fact, it woke me up – Stub was standing over me – licking my terrified face."

I'm cold and angry. "No! ... Who are you?" I slam my coffee cup on the table - coffee spills out. "Who are you? How'd you know this!?" Out of control, "No. Tell me how you know this!" I'm ready to explode.

"It's just a dream I had."

"No it isn't! How'd you know? How did you fucking know?"

"I don't know what you're talking about. It was just a dream."

"No it wasn't! Who are you?" I have no idea what is going on – terribly upset – can't even see straight – look at him like this isn't real.

"I'm sorry. Really sorry." A panic look in his eyes, "Got to go." But before he can make his exit.

"That's exactly how my daughter was killed 26 years ago. Who are you and what are you trying to do to me?" Tears stream down my face. "She had on her favorite blue dress and saddle shoes. How'd you know this? Tell me!"

"I don't know. I'm sorry – I just don't know."

"You know! You're evil! Some kind of devil!" I yell at the top of my voice, "Go!"

# AMY

People are looking at me. Got to get out of here. Getting up, my chair falls over – more people look at me. I don't care – just go. Walking, head down I almost run into a young woman pushing her little girl in a shopping cart. "Sorry." I hustle out. My car's at my place, so I've got to walk. And walk I do, going in the direction of the Humboldt State University campus. Hands in my pockets, head down - tears fall unobstructed on my pants - to the sidewalk. A couple of students walk toward me. I make sure they won't talk to me. They don't and up the hill I go. Not thinking, just walking "No!" I see it all over again – my girl – the red Camaro. Damn. Soon I'm at Redwood Park. Joy oh joy – kids playing in the playground. My daughter, my Emma! The light is gone from my eyes. The light of my life is gone. I know this – have known it for years – then this asshole tells me his 'dream'. Dream – how can it be? And I walk on the grass getting near the forest. I can be alone up there. Step by step until I enter the forest.

Why did this happen? Damn him! Think I've stuffed that horrible day away, but I haven't. It's always with me – never leaves. I carry the weight - doing the best I can. But now, not good at all – just really screwed. Steadily going up hill. If I stop I'll die – and maybe I should. Maybe I could see my Emma again. We could laugh, run, and play – bright – full of joy. Got to keep moving. Wish things would settle down, but they don't. This trail isn't used much – good – I won't run into anyone. Her ashes and my salt-water tears mixed when my Emma's ashes were put into Mother Ocean for all time. Floating, scattered – all one. The massive water and my sweet little darling floated away for all time. Damn! Damn! Damn!

Sitting behind three giant ones, my tears flood the forest floor. "Emma. I love you so. Why did you have to go? Why did you have to leave? Emma. I should have stopped it and I didn't." No words now – just wails – thank God I'm alone in this spot protected by these trees. On and on and on - tears that cannot stop. "Em...ma." I lo...ve you. I miss you my dear Emma." Air comes in gasps between the terror. Lost on this earth in a flood of tears.

Getting up - got to keep moving. So, stuffing my hands in my pockets I take step after step going up the steep hill. No more tears – probably don't have any more tears in me. Maybe I've used them all up. A raven calls and lands on a tree ahead of me. The sun reflects off her feathers as she flies away – silver – almost blinding bright. Wish I could be this raven – if I was, I'd fly far, far away – to forever leave this place.

All those years ago and every detail is imprinted in me like it's today. It is today – it's never left. Yesterday, today – they're all the same. Time is a cruel companion and it wraps itself around me – giving me no comfort as I walk in the shade of the redwoods and Douglas firs. Sitting down – what to do - where to go - what to feel ... with my wasted heart. Eyes closed. There it is, cawing three times. Is this the same raven? Opening my eyes I can't see her, but on the forest floor is a Trillium flower – white velvet in the dark greens and browns of fallen leaves and needles on this forest floor - spongy and soft, and there the Trillium lives in it's brightness. I sit.

Don't know how long I've been sitting. Don't know how long I've been on this trek. Time to go back, but instead I keep walking up Fickle Hill, my feet leading the way. Sun beams bounce and ricochet through the branches of the ancient ones. Been doing this for centuries - shinning down on a lone passerby one hundred, two hundred years ago - walking softly. Did sadness surround and suffocate that person so long ago? The raven's call is far away. Is she searching for her mate? Standing still - the redwoods creak - slightly swaying. A jogger is coming my way. Stepping to the side - he goes past me – ear buds, sweat, and determination carry him down the trail. Yes, running in the forest minus the sounds, abrupt and subtle - kind of passing through - not being a part of. Is this how it is for this runner? Is this how it is for me – not really a part of – just passing through? I wish I could pass through the deep pain I feel. The sun appears to be getting lower in the sky - hard to tell exactly with so many trees on this steep slope.

There's a cabin. I stand in the shade of the trees. An old VW drives up to this cabin. It's him! "Noooo!" He turns at this, but I scoot behind a tree. Quizzically he looks around. I am silent.

"Anybody there?" He shakes his head, goes to his door, and comes out with his dog. Jesus, hope he doesn't smell me and start barking, but soon they're both back in the cabin. This is hell – pure hell. Why is this all happening? Can I not be free of him? His dream brought it all back up – slamming me in my face – in my heart. I want so desperately to be free of that day, but this guy has come along screwing everything up. Damn him. And where was God that day? There is no God directing people's lives – saving them from tragic deaths. There is only the here and now and all of the incidents and accidents that befall us.

Need to get home. The walk back down Fickle Hill is way faster than the walk up, at least I'm not stopping to accommodate my tears - my loss - my sadness. Maybe it's healthy I cried so much – a dam let loose of the sadness and terror that always resides in me – sometimes hidden, but never forgotten. It's like I have a bucket inside filled with grief and today that bucket was emptied, but it's already starting to fill up.

# TED

Driving up the mountain I can't clear out what just happened. Boy, I've been avoiding people so long and this is what happens when I try to talk with someone. I've always been interested in dreams – never have been able to figure them out. What in the hell took place with this dream about the girl in the blue dress and saddle shoes? How can this all be.

I get to my cabin. It looks so peaceful – under the trees – away from the road – no neighbors. Stub comes up to me – stub tail wagging – glad to see me. Not in the mood to play – her face, angry - yelling at me. Not even Stub can clear this from my heart.

What a day. Glad I'm home. I'm just bad news for women. Things seem to be the same. Not really the same, but ... what's the word I'm looking for? Don't know - just damn weird. This is another reason why I should just keep to myself.

Stub - bet he's hungry. "Hey, Stub. You hungry?" He wags his tail. At least I have Stub. He's turning out to be my best friend – my only friend. "Did you hear someone yell No!?" I ask as I put food in his bowl. He doesn't answer my question. Once again he gulps it down in a matter of seconds. He must have heard it too, but he didn't react. Maybe I didn't really hear a voice. Maybe I just imagined it. That's what probably happened.

My dream – I mean how can it be. Did I somehow enter her life? I hope it was just a coincidence. There's no telling what's going on. I don't like it. It's like the old Celtic gods are playing with me - playing in a cruel way - playing with Amy in an even crueler way - bringing back that moment of horror.

It's really cold in the cabin. The fire has gone out. Crinkle newspapers, gather small sticks, put medium sized wood on top of the kindling, and light it. It catches. I soon add more wood - gaze at it, then close the door, checking the damper to make sure it's all the way open. It is. Getting a beer, I go to the couch. Stub joins me. I put on music: a live concert by the Cure – *Disintegration:*

> *Now that I know that I'm breaking to pieces*
> *I'll pull out my heart*
> *and I'll feed it to anyone.*
> *Crocodiles cry*
> *For the lover of the crowd*
> *and three cheers to everyone.*
> *Dropping through the sky*
> *Through the glass of the roof*
> *Through the roof of your mouth*
> *Through the mouth of you eye*
> *Through the eye of the needle*
> *And it's easier for me*
> *to get closer to heaven than*
> *to ever feel whole again...*

> *I leave you with photographs*
> *Pictures of trickery*
> *Stains on the carpet and stains on the memory*
> *Songs about happiness murmured in dreams*
> *when we both of us knew*
> *How the end always is.*

> *Robert Smith, Boris Williams, Lol Tolhurst, Porl Thompson, Roger O'Donnell, Simon Gallup – The Cure*

Need another beer. Wish I had a Vicodin. Reaching over, I grab my sack. On the bottom of this brown sack is the last of some killer bud I have. Not a lot, but tonight is the night for it. Before getting this ready I get another beer. I check to see how many beers I have. Tonight I'm going to need more than my regular two beers. Fuck it. Lots of beer, the second one in my hand I return to the task of filling my pipe with this killer bud. Funny, using the word killer – maybe I'm on some kind of death wish tonight. Just as I brought up awful, beyond awful memories to Amy – it also brings up my sadness and deep disappointment in myself. Damn San Diego.

Does Stub know what I'm going through? He seems to want to be closer to me tonight than usual. Maybe dogs know emotions better than people. I just know I'm extremely grateful he's here tonight - otherwise no telling.

The first hit of the pot. Let it out. Put the pipe down and finish my beer. Another one is soon in my hand. Another hit on the pipe. There, this is better. Not really.

Closing my eyes - warm in my cabin I'm taken back. Moving along the freeway. San Diego nights - so comforting – warm air rushes in my open windows on my way to pick up Edith - a lightness surrounds me. Going to be a small party at the house I'm living in. It's going to be a fine night. Stopping my VW, Edith appears – a light step – a grace in movement - so beautiful - dimples at the edge of her smile. She enters my car, shuts the door, we kiss, and off we go. I've been hanging around Edith for a few months. "This is going to be a fun night."

Edith, smiles and answers, it will. I am actually kind of floating—at least my heart is. This is when I deeply know how much I love her. Heart singing – we cruise along – freeway headlights/taillights glow – busy – we are in a stream – the flow of San Diego. Wow! Can this really be happening - yes it can - wrapped around me - have never felt this way - never felt love like this. Joy as I look over to Edith. We're close to the house. There it is - leaving the car - we enter. Not a lot of people: Frederick, Nick, Russ, Al, and his girlfriend, Peggy. I'm excited about this love I've found. I kept quiet about it in the car - there will be a time later tonight to tell her. I go and tell Frederick my good news. I feel jubilant - feel alive as never before. Frederick has to finish up studying and I go out to the living room. Where is Edith? All around the house - looking. Roaming the entire house – where is she? The bathroom door is locked. Where could she be? BAM! Russ and Edith come out of the bathroom together. Oh my God - she just fucked him in the bathtub.

OK life - fuck me. Heart drops. This cannot be. Just minutes ago I was in heaven. Now there's nothing - a fucking void - no, not a void - but an emptiness – deep – a chasm. What to do; go into my room, toss myself on my bed, and that's where I stay the night of this party. Sometime later, Edith comes into my darkened room, and asks me to take her home. She's unaware I know about her and Russ. I tell her no. Searching and wanting love just doesn't work. This is what I found out at 19 years old.

A third beer - a fourth - a fifth. I can no longer hop up off the couch. Things aren't so steady. I replay Disintegration again.

I'm no fucking angel. I know what I did. Know I'm an asshole. I deserve nothing. Wish I could just leave - leave everything. Edith left me in a horrible place filled with deep sadness covered by hate-anger-madness. Fuck me. I'm just a lousy fucking shit. And then there was the dream about the little girl in the blue dress in saddle shoes. Wish I hadn't told Amy this dream. I've fucked up someone else's life. That's what I'm good for.

Need more beer. The fire's gone out, but it's no concern to me now. What's that saying when you're drunk, 'I feel no pain.' Not true. That's all I feel now. As I get the last beer in the fridge, throw it down, and stumble off to bed.

# AMY

**W**alking up the stairs and into my small studio apartment in the back of the old Victorian I'm in some kind of haze – not knowing what to do. Taking off my clothes I get into my pajamas. What the hell just happened? Plopping down on my mattress on the floor, I close my eyes. Want to sleep, but know sleep won't come – at least not now. I want to get away - any way possible. Questions rise to the surface – need to be answered, but I have no answers - never have. I've been pretty good at shoving my memories out of my head. Then today! Going over the events. Feeling optimistic about this guy. Maybe we had a lot in common. I do know he loves to swim as do I. Feeling his shyness, I intruded on him, taking a seat at his table - could see he was uncomfortable.

I was still optimistic about meeting him. Small talk, then he tells me his dream – the dream of my life – of my life without Emma. It took me by total surprise – devastating - listening and at the same time seeing it all over again. It took years to lose this nightmare and what I mean by losing it – stuffing it away - unseen and sometimes not even remembered. My baby, Emma. Now it's wide screen in my mind rushing into my heart that took so many years to build up - never completely full, but enough to have a positive life. I loved helping the high school kids. This brought a fulfillment that sometimes covered the loss of Emma. Now this. Tears falling - thought I had no more tears to give today. How stupid to think I could put Emma in a place that wouldn't cause pain. Those days in the classroom were good, but deep down a flood of tears always waited. And today they didn't have to wait anymore. Damn.

My tears now aren't like earlier today – they're subdued gently rolling off my face onto my pajamas. No need to wipe my eyes or face.

I see his face – shocked as I laid into him - turning it so Emma's death was his fault - not just in telling me his dream, but his fault that Emma was taken from me. I couldn't take this – confronting the person responsible for my loss. If I had a mirror I wouldn't want to see my face at that table - twisted, angry, hate filled eyes - my whole being ready to explode. And explode I did. Screaming at him right there on the patio. Out of control - what must people have thought of me? I took my despair and threw it at Ted. Is he evil or the devil? No, he isn't. Why did I act the way I did? Why did I attack him? I certainly know he wasn't responsible for Emma's death, but rational thought wasn't there for me.

At the table, sitting with that man, Emma's death snuck up on me - blasted me. I wasn't at all ready to deal with it. Like I was protecting myself from the harm he was causing. But I can see now, he too, was devastated – not by the dream, but by me. What must he be thinking now? His dream and my life have merged in a very strange way. There is no way to describe this and if I told anyone they wouldn't believe me. But it did happen.

I've been seeing him at the pool and at the market. Why do I keep bumping into him? Then the walk up Fickle Hill and arriving at his cabin. I know he heard me yell, "No!" Wonder if he knew it was me. But I do know one thing - this is all beyond my understanding.

I'm so ashamed. Think I'll drop my membership in the gym. There's a community pool I can swim in. I do not want to see him again. I'll start shopping at the Arcata Coop.

Emma, sweetheart – I didn't take care of you that day when the Camaro took you away. The flood starts up again. Crying, wailing, I cover my face, and lie down. I want to die.

# TED

It's been around two weeks and I haven't seen Amy. Maybe she moved. In a sense I'm glad about this, but as always I have dual feelings. There is something about her that, at first, I thought was pretty cool. An excellent swimmer - a person who takes care of herself. At least this is what I was thinking. Many times in my life I've tried to make connections, but it's hard as nails for me to do. Maybe I've never made any connections of consequence. The only thing that keeps me going is my world of oceans – rivers - lakes - pools. My love of the water.

I'm very sad I caused her so much harm. I certainly didn't mean to. Just thought I'd bring up an interesting dream. First thought – she's crazy – a mad woman. Then when she told me about her daughter – what was her name? Emma, that's it. When she told me about Emma getting killed by the Camaro it changed what I thought. Not that instant, but moments later. In my car on the way home, tears rolled down my cheeks. I was so sad for her – for her loss. Children are supposed to outlive their parents and when this is reversed it has to be devastating. I cannot even imagine the pain of this. I hate that dream and I hate even more that I told it to her. It's impossible to know what goes on inside of another person. Hell, I barely know what goes on inside of myself – let alone others. I'm wrapped up in confusing threads of thought – hard to make sense of any of them. Wish I could be quiet inside - how to do this. Only one way I can figure. Leave the planet. I have no children and in a sense I have no family. I do, but so many years without seeing or talking to them – they're only a faded memory. So, what would be the loss? Stub is licking himself clean. Who would take care of him if I were to leave? More contradictory thoughts. That's me.

Tomorrow's a workday. Should do something with Stub. "Come on, Stub. Let's go somewhere - do something - get out of this place." The weather has gotten colder with more rain. I gather warm clothes and get a water bottle. Reach for my marijuana, but decide to leave it. Out the door - Stub in the lead. Car starts. Look at the mileage. I try to keep track of the mileage on the full tank of gas – so I don't find myself more than 30 miles from a gas station. I'm OK, there's a good amount of gas in the beast. She starts right up. Instead of heading down the hill, I go up the mountain. Don't have any plans - just see what transpires. The clouds are high in the sky - we probably won't see any sun today. The road is enchanting with redwood and Doug fir needles made shiny by the rain – almost red in color - actually a brownish/red. Anyway, it's pleasant driving under the canopy and over the fallen debris from the trees. Stub sits in the passenger seat looking out the window. "Good boy, Stub." I pat him on his head. We come to a fork in the road. Going straight we'd eventually get to Bridgeville, a small place with a general store/post office and not much else. I turn left. This will take us to the Mad River at the Maple Creek Bridge. I drive past the Butler Valley Ranch. Many years before, the county wanted to build a dam in this valley, flooding the ranch. Somehow people in Humboldt voted this down - a good thing. The bridge will come up very soon. There it is. Can't see the river from here. I wonder what it'll be like. Oh gosh, it's rushing, swollen with brown wild turbulent water screaming past. This is how the giant logs get to the beaches. Stopping the car, Stub and I get out, and walk out on the bridge. This scene is so powerful. When I look up river the water is speeding towards me. Turning I walk to the other side of the bridge and the turbulent water is leaving me. So weird. It's as if it's the sex act. When looking downstream the river blasts from me, like the sexual explosion. When I turn and look upstream, the water is coming at me. I'm accepting it in as if I'm a woman.

This comes to mind watching the rush of water of the Mad River on this cold blustery day.

This is the place I usually go in the summer – I love swimming here. Water, unlike today, will be clear. Don't get me wrong – it's swift, but not turbulent like today. Stub and I walk to the trail that goes down to the river. We stop farther away from the river than in the summer and sit. I pick up a stick and toss it for Stub. He just looks at the stick fly over his head. He stays. Again, not a fetching dog. I pat his head. He wags his tail. We walk to the edge of the river. Very carefully, Stub takes a drink.

We stay here a while. I'm trying to recover from my dream, telling my dream, and the intense pain it caused Amy. The sun is low in the sky - rain starts its fall. "Time to go, Stub." Just before entering the car, Stub shakes off the wetness.

# AMY

A week or so has passed since the incident at Wildberries. Glad I haven't seen Ted – so embarrassed – so shamed. I like the community pool and there's even a small gym. Whereas the Welcome Gym has lots of gym rats and heavy lifters, the community pool is way more focused on swimming. It's fun to see the families – all having a good time. Sometimes when I'm swimming I hear the squeals of children going down the small water slide. It's a good place. Besides swimming everyday I'm reading lots of books. When I was teaching I didn't have time to read. An English teacher has massive amount of papers to correct. I was very conscientious – wanted the best for my students. The library sees a lot of me. I also go to movies at the Minor and Arcata Theaters. As it turns out the Minor is the oldest continually operated movie theater in the US. It was built in 1911 as a movie theater. Others are older, but they were built as live theaters then turned into movie theaters.

I guess I've been pushing myself for my whole life. Even though I loved teaching I was very pleased with the prospect of retiring. Right after retirement I was befuddled as what to do. So much time on my hands. I'd always swam, but not everyday. These were casual swims. I bought a T.V., but that wasn't right for me. T.V. is numbing – no need to think – just let the T.V. do it for you. This lasted a month until I gave it to Community Against Violence. They help and protect abused women - help them get back on their feet. I thought about volunteering with them, but to be truthful I wasn't ready to jump into any endeavor that would take lots of time and energy. I wanted to rest. Like the down side of a breath

– so many years 100% involved with my students. I didn't want to do anything. I sat around day after day. I knew this needed to change, but change to what?

Before I gave the T.V. away I saw a program about Humboldt County - it seemed so beautiful. A wild place wrapped in stunning scenery. All of my life in L.A. I never thought about moving. My family was one of the first Anglo families in Los Angeles – all the way back to the 1850s. I started to research more about Humboldt. The more I found out the better it looked. That's it – go. It was fairly easy to do since I only rented. Got a new car and started to organize this phase of my life. Sixty-five and going to start all over – brand spanking new - a new me. Well, not really a new me, but I had no idea how it would turn out. I got down to only a few possessions – didn't want to be burdened by material things. I was going on a quest of sorts. The past is the past. I said good-bye to my few friends. I got maps of California from the AAA and then drove off in my CRV. On a whim I decided to go up Interstate 15 - travel through less populated areas. In a while Interstate 15 turned to US 395 a two-lane highway. For sure, not many people.

When I got to Owens Lake I was surprised how tiny it was nestled in the small Owens Valley. I remember reading about how the city of Los Angeles took the water from this lake - from this valley. It was devastating for the farmers and ranchers. Los Angeles had to send up armed guards to watch over the aqueduct taking the water all the way to Los Angeles. This water was necessary for Los Angeles to grow to the humungous metropolitan area it is today. The value of this small place had no chance against monstrous L.A.

I know I was headed to Humboldt on the coast about 300 miles north of San Francisco, but I kept driving north on US 395, a sparse place with few people. Only the occasional town – all of them very small. Tired of people everywhere – congested and harried. I stayed at small motels built a long time ago. Not up to modern America's motel standards.

Just past Lone Pine, California I came to Manzanar. What was this place? A guard tower standing over a very high chain link fence. I stopped and turned into the parking lot. Inside the visitor's center there were photographs: 'Japs not allowed', people going on busses, people lined up outside of buildings at this despicable place. My god, this was an "internment camp" for people of Japanese ancestry. In World War II the wisdom of the time was that these "Japs" were a threat to national security even though most had been born in the US – were US citizens. They had been farmers, owned small businesses, and did what every American did - trying to do the best they could to support their families – raise their children. They were only allowed one suitcase, put on busses, and transported here. I cannot even fathom the despair they must have felt. They would lose their farms, homes, and businesses. How very, very sad. When trump bellows, Make America Great Again – yeah right. What a fascist asshole.

Looking at the map I figured I could make it to Humboldt in a couple of days, that is if I didn't stop along the way. Which was quite possible since I wasn't on any schedule. Nice not having to be somewhere doing something. In this relaxed mode I continued. The skies were clear and the weather was warm - very pleasing. After eating breakfast in a small café I gassed up and continued driving. I was amazed how stunning this land was. The Sierra Mountains to the west - ragged massive rocks on the backside of California. California was named after a dream in some book by a Spaniard long ago. California is still a dream to many people - remembering the hippies who moved to California, San Francisco in the 1960s and early 70's.

A lot to ponder as I continued my drive into exile. Many hours later, stopping the vehicle, at a sign: Bodie, 13 miles. What was this place? Why not. I turned and drove on a small paved road then on a bumpy dirt road surrounded by high chaparral and sage. No trees here – wide expansive sky - very blue, accentuated by a few clouds drifting along – as I drifted to this place wondering what I'd find. Oh my God, it was a ghost town - a gold mining town that at one time had over 10,000 people, then the gold ran out, and people left. Now it's a state park at 8,000 feet and very dry. The state of California maintains the roofs on maybe 100 buildings - this keeps them from falling down. Other than that they're left alone. I wandered for hours, trying to imagine what life was like when it was thriving. And how in the hell did they find gold here in the first place? Well, they did and now it's gone. Only the gold of the tourist entrance dollars and the gift shop are left. Driving away from Bodie I was amazed at what I had just seen. Spent the night in Bridgeport, a pleasant town sitting in high meadows on US 395 far from the madding crowd.

I'd already learned so much in this new life of mine. Did not know of Manzanar – well, vaguely I'd heard of these camps, but not the details. Then Bodie. This exile was turning out to be very fine. I turned onto US 299, the highway to Humboldt County. I came to a large lake - actually a reservoir – Whiskeytown Lake. Thousands of trees surrounded this lake. How different the landscapes are in California – high deserts, coastal wetlands, huge expanses of forests – so varied. There was a place in the lake marked off with large buoys. Inside the buoys was a circle of swirling water – looked like it was going down a large drain. God, what if some poor soul got caught in this swirl - they'd surely die. I stopped at the visitor center. This lake takes water all the way down to California's Central Valley – the great agricultural center. Thousands and thousands of acres in fruits, vegetables, grapes for wine and raisins, cotton, rice, and nuts. Water is what runs California and it's taken from pristine places to be transported to cities and to corporate agriculture. That's what the swirl of water was. It's the place the water left the lake going to the canals – a massive endeavor getting this water to the dry central valley.

Whiskeytown Lake covered the native people's land who had lived here for centuries - forced to leave when the government turned their lives into a lake. The powerful in California didn't give a damn about the people's lives callously disrupted and destroyed whether it be Owens Valley or the people here displaced by this massive dam. With these thoughts on my mind I continued on my way to Humboldt. I'm now heading west. The sun directly overhead, warm – the water drew me. I took a small road off US 299 looking for a place to swim. In short notice I saw a spot. I was by myself as I walked to the lake's edge. Put my foot in the water, it was warm. Glorious. Looking around, I took off my clothes. The water was clear as I stepped in. The bottom was visible. Once in, I swam across this small inlet. This was heaven – clouds drifted overhead – trees lined the shore – water – the gift of life. So enamored in this soft moment - a smile emerged. I stayed in – floating on my back watching a couple of clouds drift above. Swimming back, I dried off, put my clothes on, and entered my car – ready to continue.

Not many miles west of the lake I arrived at Weaverville. This was an old gold mining town, but unlike Bodie it seemed to be thriving. Two story brick buildings – very quant. People were walking around. Weaverville looked like a happening place. Gosh I could live here. I wondered if there was a swimming pool. Looked like it was the county seat – an old two-story courthouse to my right. The junction to California 3 was in the historic district. Looking at my gas gauge – I had a lot of gas and without looking at a map I turned north on this two lane highway to find what I'd find. After all I was on an adventure. This road ran alongside of Trinity Lake – another reservoir. The water in this reservoir was low with bare earth between the trees and the water. California's drought the cause– not like the full Whiskeytown Lake. I stopped to eat lunch looking at the water, but decided to not go in. After a while I found myself at Fort Jones. An old town, again, no corporate monstrosities. The air was light – matching my mood. I walked around window-shopping with no intent on buying anything. I decided to spend the night there. Got a motel room and relaxed on the bed. After eating dinner I wanted beer, so I went to a bar. It was quiet in this bar, country music on the jukebox.

The next morning I looked at my map. Scott River Road would

eventually take me to Happy Camp. What a name. I wondered out loud if the place was filled with happy campers. Had to chuckle at this. This road twisted and turned as I went north. Not exactly the most direct route to Humboldt. I wanted to resettle on the coast and here I was going through mile after mile of dense forests far from the ocean going north instead of going west to meet the ocean. I got to this place, very small. Nothing new in the town of Happy Camp, a couple of old motels, and just a few businesses - very beautiful and very isolated. Needed to look at the map again. I could either go down California 96 or go on the Indian Creek Road to O'Brien, Oregon. What the heck – I went north. I'd never been to Oregon. This road out of Happy Camp wound like a snake. And if the road to Happy Camp was small – this was even smaller – at times only one lane. Not in a hurry, so all was good. Once on US 199 – even though it was only two lanes it almost felt like a super highway compared to the road I had just been on. Holy cow I ended up in Oregon. O'Brien was on US 199. I surprised myself. Good thing I wasn't on any schedule. At least it was on US 199 – the road to the California coast.

I spent that night in another old motel – small cabins and a carport besides each of the cabins. The air continued to be warm and dry. Had a good nights rest and without eating breakfast I continued my way. I was soon in California and arrived at the small town of Gasquet. There I ate at the She She Café. No McDonalds, Wendy's or WalMarts. This town like all the other small towns I'd driven through hadn't been invaded by corporate America. About 5 miles outside of Gasquet my gas light went on. Should I continue? No. I went back to Gasquet and filled up. No worries, I wasn't in a hurry, but I have to admit I was anxious to get to Humboldt.

After Gasquet US 199 twisted under massive trees. I'd never seen trees so large – so many. As it turned out this highway wound along next to the Smith River. My God, so clear. I saw some cars parked, so I stopped. A trail led to the river, the water, clear – so inviting. There were a few people in the water. I went back to my car, got into my swimsuit, and returned to the river. Once in I couldn't believe how incredible it was – large rocks and the river making its way around them ... and I was in this. I stayed in until I got a bit chilled. Lying on the bank I closed my eyes and listened to the families enjoying their day on the river. Felt blessed. Finally back in my car – on my way.

From here it didn't take long to get to Crescent City, California. It's right on the coast, about 90 miles north of Arcata – my destination. Good, the ocean. A large crescent beach was just to the south of this town. Guess that's how the town got its name. This was the largest town I'd seen since leaving Interstate 15. I stopped and took a walk on this beach.

Close to dark traveling down US 101 I finally made it to the Humboldt County line. Soon after crossing in Humboldt County there was a sign, Gold Bluffs State Park. Why not. It was a few miles on a dirt road. The car handled this well. I soon broke out of the forest. Sand dunes, some covered with grass graced this place. The Pacific Ocean literally yards away from the campground. I smelled the ocean. Only a little blue appeared between the dense clouds - muted colors – grasses weaving in and out of the wind. Walking to the water's edge – pelicans flew by. Waves, large and fierce, crashed against the sand. I walked along this beach – thrilled where I was – thrilled to be on this adventure. This place was glorious. In all of my life I've never seen such unique beauty. Small – only about a dozen campsites – almost empty - I picked a spot. I hadn't brought a tent or even a sleeping bag. Duh. I moved things around in my vehicle for a place to sleep. Knew then I'd have to get camping gear – especially since my new environment was so incredibly beautiful. I had never gone camping when I lived in L.A. Took out peanuts, crackers, cheese, and a beer. I had a feast listening to the ocean waves on this glorious and isolated shore.

The morning was shrouded in fog. Before leaving, I gathered my things, then walked down to the ocean, sat, and watched the waves. The seagulls were talking, pelicans were flying and diving – this was a magical moment. Slowly I went back to the car. Knew I'd have to come here again.

# TED

When the letter arrived I didn't think much of it. In fact I didn't open it – almost threw it away. It sat on my kitchen table for a good part of the day. Just junk mail to be sure. Standing at the table I rip it open and after a few sentences I sit down. This can't be for real. I start reading it over again from the beginning. An uncle, who I never met, just died with no will. The letter states that if I am an heir these lawyers will take 10% and I will get the rest. I carefully re-read the part that says if I am not an heir I won't be charged. There is a return envelope. It doesn't say how much I'll inherit. Damn. Setting it aside, I go outside with Stub.

Images flow over me as I stand on my porch. Gathering my chair, I sit, and watch Stub looking, better said, smelling all that's new in the yard. An animal probably crossed by earlier and Stub is checking it out.

If it's enough money I won't have to push a broom anymore at the Welcome Gym. If it's a lot of money I can travel – no limits – no boundaries. This is wild. Any doubt about the letter has left. I'm definitely going to respond. The possibilities are limitless. I can travel wherever I want - Hawai'i, Ireland, The Isle of Man, Greece. Yes, Greece. I could swim in the beautiful water I've seen in magazines and videos. Yes, Greece. Stub saunters up. Wait, I can't do extensive traveling. Stub. I can't possibly leave him behind. That's not what you do to your best friend - no matter. All of this is just conjecture anyway – not knowing if this will turn out to be true. "Come Stub, I've got a letter to mail." At the post office in Arcata, I buy a stamp from the stamp machine, and stick it on my possible future, as short as it will be at my age. I tell myself not to have too high of hopes. Maybe it'll be a thousand dollars, which will be nice, but not extravagant. Kissing the envelope for good luck, I drop it in the mail slot. Today's Sunday - the mail won't go out until tomorrow. Anxious, no don't be anxious – things of great fortune happen in books and movies, to other people, and now maybe for me. Money has never been a motivating factor in my life. I've only worked when it was absolutely necessary. People my age usually have Social Security or some other retirement. Drifting as I have, getting money from, let's say, unconventional ways. Growing herb certainly didn't pay into Social Security – that's why at seventy I'm still working. Fortunate I guess that I'm still able to work. The irony is my job at the Welcome Gym pays into Social Security that I'll never receive.

All aspects of my life are moving slower now that I've received the letter. A week goes by, no response. Another week passes. I don't think about the letter as much as I did after first receiving it, but I am going to the post office everyday. Into the third week I stop going to the post office everyday – given up on the idea of instant unearned wealth.

At the market a muscle car drives by - loud grumbling engine - the driver with his baseball cap on backwards. At the stop sign he guns his engine hoping to impress someone – especially a girl. He pops the clutch and lays rubber down the street. People stop what they're doing and watch. I do the same, only it brings me to the dream. To Amy - to Emma. Still so damn fucking sad.

Any optimism about the letter has dissolved. On my way home guess I'll check the mail. Pretty soon this letter will completely leave my mind and I can do just as I do everyday – practically nothing – just keep busy at my job - go swimming - hang out with Stub - have a few beers and some smoke. Everyday, everyday.

The guy in the muscle car is parked in front of the post office. He gets out – a short skinny guy. His exaggerated jockey strut takes him out to the plaza. I walk into the post office. In between the junk mail is the letter. Tossing the junk mail in the trash, I leave the post office. This letter weighs heavy on my mind - almost afraid to open it. Stub is waiting for me in my car. He wags his tail as I sit behind the wheel. Turning the envelope over and over in my hands I decide to go to the Arcata Marsh - I'll open it there. It takes only a couple of minutes to get to the Marsh. We get out of the vehicle. Walking along the ponds with my letter. There's a bench overlooking one of the ponds. An egret stands in perfect stillness waiting for his food. A blue heron lands on the opposite side of the pond. Still turning the letter around in my hands I finally get the nerve to open it. Don't really read it, just looking for a money figure to pop out. It does. $10,000. Oh my god. There's a final paper I have to sign, then the money will be mine - so many possibilities.

A time to celebrate. We're close to the Arcata Coop. Think I'll buy some salmon for me and a steak for Stub - why not. The Coop is crowded as it often is. This Coop started out in a 200 sq. foot storefront next to the Arcata Theater. It's grown into this large grocery store. Perusing the aisles looking for food for Stub and me. My hand basket has a few things when I get to the fresh meat and fish counter. I get my salmon and Stub's steak.

Walking back to my car – Stub is patiently waiting for me. About to get in. "Ted." What? Again, "Ted." Looking around, it's Amy. What to do. Feel like running, but don't. I wait as she approaches. What does she want? "I'm so sorry. The other day I was completely wrong. I had no reason to talk to you as I did - to yell at you. I'm really very sorry. I've been hoping, as embarrassed as I am, to see you - to apologize."

Her eyes show these feelings she's telling me. Still don't know how to respond. I stutter, "...Oh, it's OK. I have no idea how that dream came to me. No idea at all. I just wish I hadn't told you – wish I hadn't had it." Wanting to look up, I don't seem able to, "Please forgive me."

"There's no reason for you to be forgiven. I'm the one who needs forgiveness. I was the one totally out of line. Please forgive me – please." She shuffles her feet.

"We've got to be going." Pausing briefly, "I accept your apology." How to feel about all of this – I've got to get away.

Turning, I'm about to enter my car. "Wait." She walks over. "I'd been wanting to meet you, that's why I sat down at your table at Wildberries. I saw you were uncomfortable, but I did so want to meet you – talk to you, and maybe become friends. I'm new here and I don't know anyone. But after how I treated you I wouldn't blame you if you didn't want anything to do with me." She stops and waits for my reply. I am so damn awkward and silence is my reply. Amy continues through my silence. "Maybe we could go on a picnic."

"Oh, I don't know. I'm pretty much a hermit." I think about Stub - the letter - maybe changes are coming my way. In regards to money – things have already radically changed. Is this also a change?

Sadness envelops Amy's eyes. "OK." Turning away from me, she starts to walk away.

"Wait, Amy. OK. A picnic sounds nice."

"Really?" her eyes wide open in anticipation.

"Yes, really."

"Where do you want to go? Being new here I don't know many places. Recently I went to the Mad River at the Maple Creek Bridge. It was stunning. I'm from L.A. and I've never lived in such a beautiful place. You choose. OK?"

"OK. Let's go there."

"When."

"I have two more days before the weekend. How about Saturday or Sunday?"

"Shoots, Sunday then?"

"OK, Sunday sounds good."

"I could come up to your place."

"You don't know where I live."

"Yes I do."

"You do?" How can this be?

"That day at Wildberries I was so distraught I had to walk – settle my heart. I went up to Redwood Park and just kept going up Fickle Hill. I walked for a few miles. I saw you drive up to your cabin. I yelled out, 'No!' I just couldn't believe it was you. Please don't be mad."

"Oh my God."

"I had no idea I'd see you, in fact you were the last person I wanted to see. I was still in a state of shock and it just slipped out. I wasn't stalking you. Do you still want to go on the picnic?"

"I wasn't even sure I heard a real voice. Since Stub didn't react I figured I'd only imagined it. OK, a picnic sounds nice."

"Sunday, around 11?"

"Sounds good. I was really down on myself for what I did to you. Thought you'd forever be pissed at me. This is a surprise. Thanks."

"OK, see you then."

"I'll bring lunch." Amy starts to walk away - she turns, smiles, and waves.

Holy cow. What's happening? "Can you believe this Stub?" No he can't. He's just trying to figure out what's going on. His tail wags. He's happy. And at this moment, so am I.

# AMY

I'm very pleased. He could have ignored me or told me I'm a bitch and to leave him alone. Is my life changing? Maybe. I mean, what did I expect moving over 600 miles from home. It's not that I had a plethora of friends in L.A., but I did have a few.

I wonder what he's like. Will I continue to like him after I've gotten to know him? Or, will he like me? And there's a good possibility that nothing will come of this. It certainly didn't get off to a good start. My heart has never let go of that day. I have tried and tried to lead a life without pain. At times I think I've succeed. Moving here I've carried all this with me - an extra suitcase. What did I expect?

The heart is such a mystery. It can lead to the strangest of places. Or, just lie dormant inside, protected by a rib cage of sorrow. That's it. I want to try. I don't want my remaining years to be shrouded in loneliness. If I'm honest with myself I'd realize that even in L.A. my friends were superficial. Sometimes we'd met after work for a few drinks, never really shared of myself. Neither did these people I hung out with. No one, but no one knew of Emma. I wasn't open, just hid. Guess I never really thought about this. Just figured that's how it was. Not just for me, but for others as well. How many people have close friends? How many people are close to their families - have someone to talk to - someone to hear their problems? That's why there's T.V, filling the void. Then there's Facebook. "I have 437 friends," someone will say. The cute animal stories – I've always been into stories ... and animals. The at home – the lonely - show everyone what they had for breakfast – how good or rotten they feel. A few are magically funny. This has become a life ... and what a life this is. So, that kind of funny – slightly angry person could be dying inside – heart trapped – unable to break free. And the artificial connected world brought to us by a handful of extremely wealthy white men dictates what and how we feel - continues with or without me. You wouldn't know these "friends" if you literally ran into them. "Friends" – what a joke. But many people, myself included, spend hours every day on Facebook with their "friends". Not now, though. I didn't bring my computer up here. I lived without a computer for most of my life – we all did. Now the addiction has taken control of our lives. It's been an adjustment, that's for sure. At first I'd pace my small apartment not knowing what to do. I bought a radio. No way was I going to buy a T.V. The library's became my friend and I go to a lot of movies.

So, this Sunday - taking a giant leap. Gosh, lunch. Don't know if he's a vegan or a vegetarian - what to make for lunch. Wonder if I should bring a couple of beers. Hey, don't stress about this – cheese, crackers, and some salmon will probably be just fine.

I know what to do – go swimming. Packing up my swimming gear I walk to the pool. That's another benefit of the community pool – it's within walking distance. There are swim lessons taking place, so not a lot of open lanes. I have to share a lane with another swimmer. This swimmer doesn't know the prodigal of sharing lanes. No worries I'll just have to be careful. Soon she leaves the pool and I have the lane to myself. I like that there's a sauna just outside the pool. The heat, sweat in the dark sauna, I start singing a song I made up years ago. A song I sang to Emma. I see her smile and this brings me some happiness. Damn! Someone's in the sauna and because it's so dark I didn't see her. I've embarrassed myself by singing. I stop. Soon the woman leaves the sauna and I'm alone, but I don't resume singing. Guess I'm good at embarrassing myself, though this is nowhere near as bad as screaming at Ted.

On the walk home I stop at Wildberries. I want to check out what I can possibly bring for the picnic. It hits me – a picnic. This feels good – the prospect of making a friend. Maybe my life is changing and if it's to change, maybe I'll need to change – don't hide inside of myself. But it'll be hard to hide since I've already exposed my greatest sorrow to this man – no going back. I take a breath in the bread aisle and release it. Yes – a new beginning.

# TED

Sunday morning wake up, let Stub out, and get the stove pumping – it's cold. So, this is the day. Hope it doesn't rain – rain on our parade. I have to laugh at this. Things seem to be changing. First Stub comes into my life, then the 100% surprise of the $10,000, and now getting invited on a picnic. When was the last time I've been on a picnic – can't remember. Years of just ambling along – can't really say ambling, more like trudging through life. I think my basic nature is a light one – like to laugh – see the humorous in everyday occurrences, but heavy clouds of deep disappointment have covered this lightness. Wouldn't it be amazing if the curtain of despair could be lifted.

Stepping outside under the canopy of trees, no clouds. This is good. Stub is still making sure everything is OK - such a good boy. "Come on Stub, let's go in." We do. He gets fed and I work on my coffee.

Is it really possible to find companionship and care at my age? I see Amy's face when she asked me about the picnic. Sitting with my coffee, Stub comes and sits next to me. I think he loves me. I know I love him. Love, the heart opener sitting next to me. Pat his head – he wags his tail. Maybe people should have tails to tell everyone how they feel. No, not a good idea for those of us who hide away.

I was first attracted to Amy watching her swim. Maybe nothing more beautiful than a woman graceful and fast in the water and that she is. And her broken heart on display – covered with anger and hurt. She wasn't hiding away that day at Wildberries. It took a lot of courage to come up to me after how she treated me. She seemed genuinely sorry. I wouldn't have tried to talk to her. I wasn't ashamed, but I was extremely sorry I brought up that damn dream. Can a person be sorry for an accidental screw up? Maybe so. I know I was and still am for that matter.

Dreams. What a mystery. Taken out of this thought - Stub stands, goes to the door, and barks. "What is it, Stub? What's going on?" Getting up, I go to the door, and open it. I see what he's barking at – three deer stand under the trees to the left of the cabin. The male looks to be a 12 point, the other his mate, and the third their offspring. "No, Stub. Let 'em be." He's still barking. "Stub – No!" He looks up at me and stops. "Good boy, Stub." Stub shakes, then joins me on the couch.

What are dreams anyway? Tons of theories, but no one really knows. Stub dreams. Two nights ago his legs were twitching and he was making almost whisper grunts and barks. Hope I never bark in my dreams – hahaha. I've read some about dreams – maybe I should look into them some more. The sun makes itself present in my cabin. It seems the sunrays are intensified sneaking in my window like a prowler. Not a prowler - a welcomed guest this morning. Hope it's going to be fine day - just don't know – it's a huge question mark. I wonder how Amy feels about this upcoming picnic?

I shouldn't put too many expectations on this – that's very clear. If I don't have too much hope, then it can't be dashed. I listen to more tunes on the computer. Hey, I can get a small keyboard now. In the past I've played a keyboard along with some others in improvisational jams. Yes, a keyboard. Wow! That $10,000 is going to be a great asset even in my old age.

So strange. When I was in my twenties I felt I'd never live to be fifty. My God, I passed that twenty years ago. Even when I was forty I thought I wouldn't make fifty. Why I thought this I don't really know – just did – an accident most likely. Just goes to show how little I know.

It's 9:30. The wood supply in the cabin is nearly gone. "Come on, Stub." I let Stub out and go to the shed. Lots of wood, but it needs to fit my stove. Setting pieces on the chopping block I go to work. Soon there's enough to take inside. Good, this has taken up time. I'm very nervous about today. Maybe, just maybe, my life is changing. Changing for the better. Hope so. But again, keep it under control.

And it's so weird that Amy made it all the way up here that day. Why is all of this happening. I have no idea. I don't believe, as some people do, that they are somehow directed in their lives by some outside source – God or some angels. I'm more a believer in what happens, happens – no cause – not directed by some cosmic force. Never been a New Age Hippie.

My clock says, 10:30. Pretty soon.

# AMY

OK, check everything. Got the lunch packed. Oh, need to grab a couple of beers. Make sure I've got warm clothes. Before leaving the door I get my umbrella – though it's sunny out I don't want to get caught. I've been up for a long time, but I've been messing around, and now I'm probably running late. I do this all of the time. Damn the gas warning light is on. Need gas. I'm going to be late for sure now.

It's a steep climb up Fickle Hill under the redwoods and firs - light piercing in streaks through the giant trees. Why'd I leave so late? I roll down my window and smell the air. It's funny – no one in L.A. wants to smell the air. What have we done to our environment that no one wants to smell the air? In L.A. you can't help but to smell the air – foul as it is. Hell, you can even see it. L.A. sunsets are beautiful because of the pollution. I'll never again live in a place with polluted air. That's what was so spectacular about Hawai'i – the air. And it's the same here – clean and pure. Moisture abounds in the air here, so sometimes it is visible – fog. I love the fog, but I hear people complain about it all the time. For now, at least, I relish it. It hides the distinct landscape - makes things mysterious. Certainly have to be careful driving in it. But today the fog lies offshore in the fog bank. It seems the fog - if not present in the day - will roll in before sunset. Cruising up the hill – steep – I go. Going to something I'm not at all sure about. His blue eyes were so hurt – hard to hide. Hiding out – that's me. I wonder if my eyes give me away.

From no one knowing about Emma in L.A. to meeting Ted and immediately giving it away – this is so different. A big change for sure.

Then walking and walking until I came to his place – saw him drive up. His dog was very happy to see him. Hiding behind the tree I felt I was intruding on his personal life - that I had no right to be there. But, of course, it wasn't planned. So, why is this all happening. I don't believe in fate – don't believe that God intervenes in our lives. He's got to be very busy – no time for individuals. It makes no sense to me, for example, in a tsunami a person will say. "Thanks be to God, I'm alive." What about the thousand others who died? Does this person really think God came down – so to speak, and saved his life over all of the others? I'd say he was lucky, not God intervening.

Oh, there's his place. Driving until I can make a turn and go back. Nerves on edge – is this really the right thing to do? Just suck it up, Amy. You're acting like a teenager. Yeah teenager times four. You'd think I wouldn't be so anxious. Quick – take out all anticipations - toss them aside - just a picnic – no big deal. Stepping out of my car, the dog comes over to me. He wags his short tail and sniffs me. Should I reach down to pet him? I do. He lets me and seems to enjoy it. "Hi, Amy." Stepping out of his cabin, Ted comes over.

"I've never had a dog, our family had a dog, but he ran off shortly after we got him. My parents really didn't know anything about dogs, so consequentially I don't know about dogs either. You have him for long?"

"No, he's only been with me for a month or so. He jumped into my car at the Arcata Marsh. I'd seen him there for a couple of days. I gave him some hamburger and that did it. When I invited him into my car he jumped right in. Hamburger can create miracles." He pats his dog.

"What's his name?"

"I'm not very creative – the name Stub just came to me after a few days. He was born with a stub tail. He's such a good boy – very smart." We stand in this thought for a moment. "Want to see my cabin?"

"OK." We go in. It's very basic. Guess you could call it rustic. He's nailed fruit boxes for shelves. A wood stove – I can feel the warmth. A small refrigerator – no stove. "How do you cook?"

"On the wood stove. I don't have an oven. I eat pretty simply. Actually I don't really eat that much. I have a simple life up here."

"I see you have a computer."

"Yes. I listen to music on it. I've created a music station, so to speak, on YouTube. Ready to go?"

"Yes."

"Can Stub come along?"

"Of course."

"Then let me drive. Keep your car dog hair free."

"I don't mind, but sure, you can drive. Let me get my things." I get the lunch, extra sweater, and, my stocking cap. I remember my umbrella - no I don't bring it.

We get settled in the car. "Stub usually sits in your seat." He's in the back seat.

"Want me to sit in back?" This is a joke. Hope he gets it.

He does. "Well, just for today you can take his place." He grins. "Sad, but true it's parked on this little hill because sometimes it doesn't want to start in the mornings and I have to jump start it. Let's see if it'll start today." It does.

Driving under the canopy of trees – sun rays blocked – don't make it down to the road as we drive up an up. "It's so beautiful here. It's almost hard for me to realize I live in such beauty."

"How long have you lived here?"

Hmm, how long have I been here? "Let's see, about three months."

"Where did you come from?"

"L.A."

"Goodness, a lot different here than L.A. I've never lived in L.A. What made you come up here?"

"When I retired I was kind of lost. Didn't want to continue as I had been all of my life. Saw a video about Humboldt – then I looked up as much as I could. On a whim one day I decided to leave - in short notice I was on my way.

"You have any ..." No don't go there - know she had a daughter. Recouping from this, "Any friends you'll miss?"

"Not really. All the people I knew where from work."

"What did you do?"

"I was a teacher - high school English. Did that for thirty or so years. Watch out!" A deer crosses the road. He sees it and comes to a stop. The deer also stops, turns her head to us, and stares - then with a quick motion she hops away into the trees – so graceful. "Boy, didn't see this in L.A."

Quiet on the rest of our journey up the mountain. The pavement ends. If I remember correctly we'll come to the fork in the road soon. I'm right. At this point, not a lot of trees and the sun brightens up our surroundings - brightens my heart. The beauty here is stunning.

We drive through a little valley that is a ranch. This is how life was many years ago. I feel like I'm traveling back in time. The bridge is very near. "Wow! Look at the water." The river is wild – churning – not like the time I came here. A small tree is chaotically tossed about. The place I was before is now under water. He stops his car just before the bridge. We get out and walk on the bridge. Facing up river, the water rushes at us. Walking to the other side, the water screams away from us. It feels sexual – the accepting in and the powerful flow out. Think I'll keep this thought to myself. The other thing I'm keeping to myself is the dream. I still have no understanding of it. In this silence we watch the flow of the river from the bridge.

"Let's move the car. We can park over there." He points to the spot where I parked when I came up here. Walking a little ways, we find a fairly level spot and sit. The ground is a bit damp. Think it'll be OK. He goes back to his car and brings a blanket. This will be better. Come prepared has to be the motto up here – the weather can change so rapidly.

# TED

On the blanket. This spot is sunny, but who knows if clouds will come. Hope not. This is pleasant. She seems nice. I'm at a loss as what to say. Swimming? Maybe that's something we can talk about. The dream – hope this doesn't come up. We made small talk on the way up, but the last part of our journey here was silent – soaking in the beauty of the place. This all must be strange to her – how different than her past.

Both of us on the blanket. Stub sniffs around. He's thoroughly enjoying himself. He starts to wander off. I call him over. He comes right away. "He's pretty well trained isn't he?"

"Yes he is. He comes every time I call him. He sits when I say and he stays until I release him. Watch." I get up and walk away. Stub follows me. About 40 feet away. "Stub. Sit." He does. As I walk away from him, I turn, "Stay!" Back to the blanket. He's still sitting. "OK, Stub. Come." He runs over.

"That's impressive. How'd you get him to do these things?"

"I just kept saying these commands over and over again. I could have used food as an incentive, but decided I wanted him to follow these commands because of me, not because of food."

"Where did you learn to do this?"

"I didn't. I just thought about what I wanted from him and that's what I did. He really is a very good boy – so smart." Stub looks at me. I get up again, walk a few feet away and give him some cheese and salmon.

"Why'd you walk away to give him food?"

"I don't want him to beg for food. I don't fed him from the table, or from here for that matter"

Sitting in this serenity, "See that small tree over there?" Amy points to a small tree on the other side of the river.

"Yes, I do."

"Well, the time I came up here, the rains hadn't really started. It was brisk and the river was really cold, but I got the courage to go in. I swam over to that tree. It's such a beautiful little tree - its roots weren't reaching the river. I cupped my hands and threw water on the tree and its roots. This next feeling I know is odd, but I thought of this tree as my tree and I was helping it with water. I know this is strange. Now look, the water covers all of its roots. It's getting much needed nourishment. Do you think I'm strange to think this?"

She has a special look in her eyes. One of kindness – at least this is what I perceive. "No, I don't think it's strange. You know, this is one of my favorite places to swim in the summer. I've seen this tree many times. No actually I think it's very sweet that you and the tree are together. Maybe the tree knows you and it are kin. I just never gave it any relevance."

The salmon, cheese, and crackers hit the spot. I break off a piece of salmon. Stub looks at me – when I return his look, he looks away.

Glad I brought the blanket. Actually I didn't bring it – it's always in my car – just in case. Amy hands me a beer ... and a bottle opener. A Cerveza Pacifico.

"See that snag over there?"

"What's a snag?"

"A dead tree. You see it?"

"Yes."

"For a couple of years on the top was an osprey nest. It was fantastic to see the osprey pair going to and from the nest. Never saw their babies, but I know they were there. I would have loved to have seen the little one take off from the nest. There's a word for it, but it escapes me." Amy looks at the old broken tree. "The salmon is good. Thanks for bringing it. Cerveza Pacifico is my favorite beer. How'd you know?"

"Thanks. I didn't know you even liked beer. Cerveza Pacifico is my favorite too. I also didn't know if you are a vegan or vegetarian. I took a chance with the food. Glad to see you can eat salmon."

"I eat most anything. Put food in front of me and I'll eat it. I'm an eatatarian."

"An eatatarian?"

"I made it up. It's someone who eats anything put in front of him." She smiles. And in this smile there is a deep beauty. They say the eyes are the key to the soul. I don't know about that, but her smile comes from within her - deep and caring. Stop this, Ted. Don't get carried away.

She breaks this spell. "So, I shouldn't have been so concerned about what I brought. This is good to know."

We sit, listening to the sounds that surround us. The breeze against the leaves. The river, loud in its rush to the ocean. No need for words to break the awkwardness of the silence, but this silence isn't awkward. Gives me a chance to revel being here - being here with Amy.

We sit in its mesmerizing glory. No matter how many times I come here I'm always taken by its beauty. Still, and in silence, we sit immersing ourselves in this grandeur.

Out of the blue, "Can we talk about dreams?"

This sets me back. The last time it was awful. I don't know how to answer. After a moment of hesitation, "OK I guess. You sure?"

"Don't worry it won't be like at Wildberries." She takes a deep breath and continues, "I've always been fascinated by dreams. When I was a little girl, my mother read Alice in Wonderland to me. She told me it was a dream - this fascinated me. I tried to remember all of my dreams. When I was in college I knew this guy who told me dreams were real – as real as our waking world. I put this aside – thought it could be true, but I really didn't know. I mean who really knows. He moved away and I didn't think about what he told me. One night I had a very vivid dream that Don was painting large paintings in a cabin in the woods. Like I said, this dream was so vivid - seemed so real. I had never seen him paint. He never said anything to me about being a painter. About a week later I was surprised to get a letter from him. You know back before email when people actually wrote to each other. I think he liked me. Anyway – in this letter he told me he was living in the Berkeley Hills in a small cabin under Eucalyptus trees painting a mural. How could this be? Maybe what he told me about dreams being real was true. How else could it be explained. I have an idea that people can meet up in dreams. Kind of like their spirits are traveling in dreams through the cosmos – or whatever it's called, and people connect in them. There have also been incidences when a mother was startled awake at night in complete dread – only to find out her son had died that very minute. Dreams are a mystery for sure.

"Then there's your dream. It doesn't fit any of these ideas." She looks down and is silent. God, I hope she doesn't explode at me again. Don't think so, but she could. Amy continues, "I don't think there is any way your dream is understandable. I hope this doesn't freak you out, but maybe it's that we're somehow connected. When I walked up Fickle Hill and came upon you I was terrified seeing you at your cabin. It was like I couldn't escape you. I can't now, but someday I'd like to tell you about my girl. That is if you want to know."

"Yes, I'd like to know." Her eyes and face are soft – open – vulnerable. She's very sweet. Continuing, "Dreams are such a mystery and have been since the beginning of time. Stub has dreams too. His legs move and he makes small grunting noises. He's actually quite cute. I love him so."

Lightning breaks our mood. The sky is no longer blue and is covered by dark clouds. I've been so entranced with Amy I didn't even see this coming. Another crack of thunder – the lightning bolt is close. No need to count the seconds to determine how close – it's very close. "Lets go!" We gather our things and rush to the car, as the rains – heavy, falls on us.

We're soaked to the bones by the time we reach my car.

Pushing the front seat up, Stub gets in back. He shakes and rainwater is tossed all around my car. Amy and I get in. I fumble for the keys. Amy turns, looks at Stub, and pets him. "Good boy, Stub." And we drive away, only stopping on the bridge for a minute or two – catching the last glimpse of the river – high and wild.

# AMY

Ted's old VW pulls into his yard. He turns around and backs into the place on the small hill. I'm drenched to the bone as is he.

It's still raining - the wind blowing hard. Just as I get out a gust bashes into me. Stub's in the lead as we go to his cabin. "Wow. That was something."

"Yes it was. It certainly caught us off guard." He goes to the stove and looks in. There are embers. He collects some small pieces of wood and puts them in. It's clear he knows about wood fires. I don't have a clue. I'm glad he's taking care of the fire. It's cold in here. "You look very cold and wet." He gathers sweat pants, socks, and a flannel shirt. "Maybe you should change." I accept the clothes and stand holding them – not knowing where I can change. "Oh, the bathroom is behind that door. Sorry it's pretty small and dumpy."

I'm not the most observant person, but I see there's no paneling in the bathroom. I can see the 2x4s. Primitive. Maybe in all of L.A. there's not a single place like this. I use the towel hanging over the shower door, dry off, and change. I run my fingers through my hair - damp and most likely very wild. When I come out of the bathroom he's changed as well. Men change a lot faster than women – we have so much to pay attention to. He takes my wet clothes and drapes them over the two chairs at his table.

"Want some coffee?"

"That would be sweet."

"Do you take cream and sugar?"

"No, black is fine."

"Sorry I only have one filter. I'll make yours first."

The rest of the cabin is like the bathroom, no paneling – 2x4s visible. Going over to the stove I hold out my hands for warmth. The whole cabin appears to be warming up. This wood stove does a good job. I wonder if I'll ever heat by wood. There certainly are a lot of trees up here. He hands me my cup and I go to the couch. Stub with his wet fur is at one end of the couch. "Stub, you want some coffee?" He doesn't. I like this dog. He's polite and is certainly well trained.

"You offering my dog, coffee?" he says with a twinkle in his eyes.

"I was just playing with him."

He finishes up with his cup, goes to the refrigerator, pulls out a small carton of cream, and pours it in. "You sure you don't want cream or sugar?"

"No thanks, this is good. In fact this is excellent coffee."

"Thanks." He sits next to me – we're like three peas in a pod, Stub, Ted, and me – silently sitting. I like it that every moment doesn't have to be filled with talk. The rain pounds on the roof – the occasional crackling of the fire can be heard – all so peaceful. This is so nice. My coffee is half-way done. Looking over to him I smile, but he's looking at Stub. What a pair they make.

I finish up my coffee. What to do next. I could stay here – peacefully wrapped in contentment. Will he want me to stay? I can't even guess. He's friendly and damn, his eyes are so expressive, but there's reluctance in the air - I can feel it. So, I say it, "I think I should be going." Getting up with my cup I put it on his counter. "Wow, your counter is awesome. Where did you get it? Was it here when you moved in?"

"No. I made it from a virgin redwood slab I found under a house in Eureka."

"It's beautiful." I get my clothes from the chairs and start to go into the bathroom.

"They're not dry yet are they."

"No, but it'll be OK. Do you want your clothes back?"

"No, your clothes are still wet. It's cold and wet out. You can get them back to me later. OK?"

"You sure?"

"Yes."

"OK." At the door I turn, he's still on the couch with his buddy, Stub. He gets up. Stub stays. "I had a very good time today. I'm glad we did this." What else is there to say? He comes up to me. Hug me – I want you to hug me. Standing for a moment that seems to be stretching.

"I had a good time too."

Wanting that human touch, but not going to get it. "Yes, I hope to see you again."

"Me too. And besides you've got my clothes."

"OK, bye." He's still at the door looking at me. I wave and he returns the wave - I drive off. I ponder about what's happened today at the Mad River – in his cabin. It's been really good. I've met a gentle and kind soul. I think we're becoming friends. At least I hope so.

# TED

This has been a good day. Amy seems very nice ... and very pretty. Not in a glamorous way - down to earth. Her soul seems so sweet. Gosh, what's going on. I do know if she hadn't come over to me the other day I would have never tried for a connection. Set in my ways I guess. But it's true that our encounter at Wildberries scared the bejesus out of me. She was so distraught and angry. I sit down on my couch. "Hey, Stub. You have a good day?" He looks at me and wags his tail a couple of times.

This is crazy. I picture her in the pool swimming – graceful, long, lean. And when she looks at me her eyes have an intensity to them. Because of me? No! It's just how she is. What will become of this? Probably nothing. But she does have my clothes. If the recent past is any indication she'll contact me to give my clothes back. Damn – part of me is excited and another part – probably a bigger part of me wants to be left alone. I've been torn for a long, long time. I've casually met other women, but I never followed through, and they faded away. Sometimes when forced to make a decision between two opposing actions I'll usually choose the path of inaction. There have been times this was the right decision, but sometimes I take the inaction route and it doesn't feel right, but I do it anyway. And after a while it all just fades away. That's my life – just fading away into old age.

A day to stay inside and read a book. I want to lie on the couch and read. "Hey, Stub – you gotta move." Looking at me he stays. I go over and nudge him off the couch. Damn he's all wet – now the couch is wet. A towel – he needs a towel. The towel Amy used is in the bathroom. I use it to wipe off Stub and put it on the couch. I'll read in bed. Stub goes back to the couch. And this is how the rest of the afternoon goes.

Tired from reading, I set the book aside, and close my eyes. Sleep quickly sneaks up on me. When I awake, the sun is nearly gone. Thankfully I didn't have strange or obtrusive dreams. It was very intriguing what Amy told me about dreams. Dreams being real, as real as our waking lives. The dream she had about the painter – how could it be. Or the people who wake in the middle of the night in terror about a loved one, only to find they died at that very moment. You know, it just might be that people do meet through the cosmos in dreams. But that doesn't explain my dream about her and Emma. Maybe it doesn't matter about dreams. What is - is what is. This is a frivolous thought. Dreams have been considered important throughout history. Will I ever fully understand them? No I won't - just peeks and glimpses. Oh goodness. I had a dream way back in high school that changed my reality. I had a Spanish teacher, Mr. Laris. He used to pick on one student in class. Called him Rotor Rooter. Rotor Rooter was a company that cleaned shit out of septic and sewer lines. I, along with most of the students, knew this was wrong, but we remained silent and this poor kid took the humiliating cuts by himself day after day. In this dream it became clear to me what an asshole Laris was. The next day I told him what a jerk he was. Actually I was almost yelling this. He kicked me out of class and for the rest of the year I had the other Spanish teacher. Dreams can enlighten, or in this case clarify a situation. But, once again, where did the dream I had about Emma come from? Getting out of bed, stretching, I check the fire.

# AMY

Driving down the mountain my windshield wipers barely clear the rain from my windshield - makes it hard to see – it's that intense. A road crews has sawed a tree that fell on the road. Wow, what if a tree fell on my car. Well, no worries that won't happen. It's nice up here on Fickle Hill. I like that Ted has no neighbors. I'm in the middle of town, which has its advantages. Everything is close and I can walk wherever I want to go. Well, not to the rivers. Today – wow! Rushing wild, standing on the bridge, and my thoughts watching the water rushing away, and toward me. Sex. I must be awfully lonely for this thought to come up. What role does sex have to do with loneliness? I think what I miss most is having the comfort of another person – being close. I remember when it was good with Tom how I looked forward to sleeping with him. Cuddling together throughout the night. Not necessarily sex, just feeling the body heat of his skin against mine. That was heaven.

A dog. Ted's dog keeps him company, maybe I should get a dog. My apartment is so small. A dog Stub's size would never fit here. There certainly are smaller dogs than Stub, but I've never liked small nervous yappy dogs. But I won't be in this place forever – something to consider.

Gosh – it's after 5 already. Feeling restless – want to go out. Goodness, I'm still in Ted's clothes. The rain has stopped as I change into my clothes. A thought - I take off my clothes and put his clothes on again. I'm going out wearing his sweats and flannel shirt. Why not, though it does seem a bit strange.

Walking by the Minor Theater - a movie's showing tonight that was filmed in Humboldt: *Escape In Time*. Think I'll see it. The first showing is in an hour. I go home, eat some food, straighten up a bit – then go to the theater. I sit very near the front of the theater. I want my movies to be bigger than life and this helps. After a few trailers – it starts.

Leaving the theater I'm carried away by it. This is what I like about a good movie – it takes me to a whole new world and this movie did this. The cinematography was stunning - it captured the beauty of this place. The attraction to water and how important it was to Jon. My connection to water – Ted's connection to water. This aspect parallels mine. But what got me the most was the story line. Dreams played a big part of the story. Well, maybe not dreams, but something took place between people outside of the norm - people somehow connecting. Jon, a janitor at Humboldt State University, somehow merged with John Anglin – a convict incarcerated at Alcatraz – trapped. Both of them trapped – one in prison and the other by his own making - a life going nowhere. I was and still am trapped in my life - another strange coincidence. It wasn't a movie where everything was explained. It was up to me, the viewer, to figure it out. And the irony was that I wasn't able to figure out what happened and why – just as in my own life. Movies can take on a life all their own and this one has given me more to think about regarding dreams. Emma's face. My dear beloved, Emma.

Outside in kind of a daze - glad it's not raining - I feel like walking. Streetlights reflect on the wet sidewalks and streets. It must have rained when I was in the theater. The neon signs for the bars create wonderful patterns on the wet cement. Walking along - the movie as my companion. People are out and about - I go into a bar: The Sidelines. Turning, I quickly leave. It's a sports bar - multiple T.Vs blasting sporting events – very loud. I go to another bar, Toby & Jacks – much quieter. I sit at the bar and get a Cerveza Pacifico. Twirling the bottle mindlessly - the day's events pop up. The good time I had with Ted and Stub –gosh he's a good dog. Lightning – sharing stories – just the general good feelings of the day. And seeing my tree getting all of the water it can use. I wonder if the water gets much higher will the tree get ripped away - probably not. It must get through the raging winter rush of water - it's still there. I'm looking forward to swimming on this river come summer.

Back home, I look around for something to do. The bed seems to be calling me. I take off my shoes and lie down still wearing Ted's clothes. Ted's a mystery - maybe not, but he's entered my life - the dream - seeing him at his cabin. These coincidences are hard to figure out. Just like in the movie, we're connected - a dream is playing a big part. Soon I'll be asleep and who knows where this will take me.

# TED

I haven't seen Amy for weeks. Maybe she's forgotten all about me. Maybe she just doesn't want to see me again, but we had a good time - at least I did and she told me she did. This could be for the best. If I'm honest, I was starting to fall for her. Seriously, probably better I haven't seen her knowing my track record. Not that this has anything to do with San Diego. Stop! Everything has to do with San Diego. This all circulates in my mind as I sweep, clean, and look busy. I do like that my mind can drift on this no think job. My mind drifting in and out of thoughts – what good does it do me.

"Ted to reception." What now. Someone broke a glass on the pool deck. Grabbing a broom, dustpan, and a towel, I go to clean up the mess. There's a sign that says to not bring glass to the pool area. Some people don't listen or pay attention. Either this or they don't give a damn. Have no idea. Oops, I don't pay the best of attention at times myself. Not to judge – just go clean it up so no one gets cut.

I can't help but notice one of the swimmers in a red swimsuit. She is very fast. No matter, got to finish up with my chore. She ends her swim, takes off her swim cap, and shakes her head – brown hair flying about. Getting out of the water she has a swimmer's physic – broad shoulders. This woman is trim, but not skinny. I'm terrible at guessing people's ages, but she looks to be in her 40s. "Watch out, there's broken glass here." Stopping, she looks down and makes a detour around the glass, smiles, and nods at me. My eyes follow as she goes to the woman's locker room. I really admire people who swim fast and to be honest, women who swim fast are very attractive. Sometimes when I'm swimming and a woman is in the lane next to me going fast and smooth; I look at her. Not to be a creep, but it's only a matter of three feet or so - a close-up look. This is one of the hidden advantages of swimming. I wonder if women look at men? Probably not. Bet they don't know a man's admiring them as they swim. Soon she's out of my view. Nice. After this minimal break I finish picking up all of the glass, but as I walk away I see a piece of glass glitter on the deck. Better look everything over again. This piece could cut someone. I get down on my hands and knees and search for more glass. I find three more pieces. OK, think I'm done here.

If I was fifteen years younger I'd want to know this swimmer in the red swimsuit. I'm too old now. I can say this, but even if I were younger nothing would come to fruition with her. This is how it's been all of my life. Fuck me. Well, not necessarily true. I did go on a picnic with Amy – had a good time – so, this is different. I'm taking trash to the large trash bins behind the gym. Pausing, I look up the hill. Is that snow? My goodness it sure looks like it. Maybe snow at my cabin. Very cool. We don't get a lot of snow here, but it does snow sometimes. I've seen snow covering the beaches. Yes, it's on the coast of California, but most people view California being like Southern California. They couldn't be more wrong. It is so different. We're 276 miles north of San Francisco.

Amy's just moved here from Southern California – L.A. She's seen the difference. Amy – I wonder what she's doing now. I can moan about myself – poor me. But Amy has real reasons to be sad. My discontent is of my own making – my own damn making. Shut up, Ted. Better get back in – don't want to be missed. Missed, no one looks at janitors – we're just background in people's lives. I slowly wander back inside – there's no hurry. I put my broom and such away. Kathy, the receptionist, thanks me.

Just before quitting time I step outside to see if the snow is still there. It is. Good thing Stub has all that fur. His downy fluff under his outer hair will keep him warm. I smile. The drive home is fun. I know some people wouldn't look at driving up a mountain in the snow as fun, but I do. Volkswagens are actually very good in the snow. The engine is over the driveline so there's weight and this helps with traction. Two cars are on the side of this narrow road unable to go further. No one is in the cars or beside them. Guess they're back down the mountain. Snow covers my place - maybe 2 inches or so. The snow makes it so quiet. My footsteps are marked in the snow. I appreciate anytime I have peace and contentment. Gosh, my cabin looks so quant. Stub comes running out of the cabin, then stops. Looks at the snow. Oh my, he puts his nose in the snow and takes off running. A nose snowplow. This is hilarious. Sometimes Stub makes me laugh. He's good this way – need to laugh. Now he's running full bore in circles – so excited. He gets so much joy out of life. I could learn from him. I'll try.

The cabin is cold. There aren't any hot embers in the stove. Working diligently I get the stove going. Letting Stub out again, I go to the window and watch him. There's that nose again sniffing. Getting a book, I put it on my chopping block end table. Start to sit, but don't. Need to let Stub in. Opening the door he's still out and about. Stepping outside I close the door - don't want the cabin's warmth to leave. Some snowflakes, lazily make their way to the already white earth. Stub comes running – we go inside.

Lying on the couch I get my grandmother's quilt and crawl under it. I love the stories of Barbara Kingsolver. I get completely caught up in them. This one is about a young woman who has a baby dropped off to her. I don't really know how she does it. How she can create such strong characters - their thoughts and feelings are powerfully shown – amazes me – takes me into the world she's created. Wish I could write like her. I've tried numerous times to write a story, but my imagination doesn't go to places Barbara Kingsolver's does. After a while I let the book slip - my eyes close - a short nap sneaks up. Stub, cleaning himself wakes me. I tend to the fire. Soon the cabin will be toasty warm.

Time to feed the dog. Again it only takes seconds for Stub to eat his food. I let him out. Stub has a good outlook on life. He has a good place to live, plenty of food, he plays and explores, and has me to love him. So, I look at my life. I have a good place to live, all the food , beer, marijuana I want, a job that pays the bills, and a new best friend, Stub. Sometimes all is doom and gloom with me. I'm not jumping with joy now. Wish I could say content, but pleased will do. Don't want to get carried away – hahaha.

In this space I think about sadness. Hate that word depressed. Some-one will say, "I'm so depressed. When will it ever get better?" It's a poor me attitude. Damn I hate this. It's exactly what I feel a good lot of the time - poor me - fuck me. Not fuck me because I'm so sad – no, fuck me for what I did.

# AMY

**W**hat to do today. Many years this question seldom arose. So busy grading papers, setting up lesson plans. Not a lot of free time. I do remember thinking on the first day of summer vacation that I'd have months and months of free time. Not really, because I wanted my lessons to be fresh. I'd take a couple weeks off, just being lazy - then I'd work on lesson plans. Then all of a sudden the calendar would slam me with the realization that school was going to start up soon – too soon. That one summer I went to the Big Island of Hawai'i was a thrill. It's like Hawai'i isn't even a part of the United States. I was on the Hilo side. The makeup of the people – let me say it this way. If the majority of the people aren't white then the culture won't be white. I reveled in this. Thought about moving, but decided that visiting it was good enough. That was maybe 10 years ago. Haven't been back since.

Back to what to do today. I've still got Ted's clothes. He must be wondering about them. Maybe even wondering about me. He seems so shy. No, that's not the word. Hmmm – withdrawn that's more like it. I wonder what his life's been like. He seems intelligent, so I doubt he's always been a janitor. A real mystery and, of course, there's the dream. How and why is this all happening? I'm drawn to him that's for sure. Standing on the bridge watching the water rush away from me, rush to me – a sexual act in my mind standing next to him. Wanting a hug so badly when I left his place. OK, I'm lonely.

How odd that word lonely is - many varieties. In my marriage to Tom it got to the point that I was very lonely. Being lonely because no one is around is one kind. I think the loneliness of a person living with someone, but separated from that person is the worst kind of loneliness. Closing my eyes I can see it all.

Silence invades the house. Clock ... ticking – breeze against the window, I wait ... inertia of the weary. Slowly moving – stretching - sitting up - my feet on the floor, I stare out the window – still dark. Wanting all to be still ... and in this there is refuge. Floor slightly creaks, my first footstep is announced. Please ... no noise – nothing disturbed - not a thing – be a ghost – unnoticed – invisible, and I walk lightly out of my room – as if on air – so quiet – barely there. How has this happened? Lower than low with no importance at all I make my way to the kitchen. How to make coffee without making noise? Water in the kettle, turning on the flame – dancing in the early morning dark world. The sun makes its appearance through the windows – diffused by dust – a softness - a sort of glow.

Damn! The kettle screams – quickly turning it off. Listening for sounds ... there are none – good. Pouring water over the coffee, it drips into my cup. Then, as if almost on tiptoes I, without a sound, walk back into my room – arrange the pillows, and sit holding my coffee – warm in my hands. A new day and what it'll bring is the same as yesterday and will be the same as tomorrow. And here I sit, slowly drinking my brew.

I wonder when Tom will wake up. Listening – intent - for any sound – wanting the stillness to last. Again – how did it get this way? And this morning is followed by another, and another, a week, a month, a year – and so it went.

Now, from a distance the years have given me, I remember how it was - in the house – in the marriage – all alone - where anger ruled – tossed around just like my dad's photo, the chair, the small ceramic bowl we got in Mexico I so liked - just thrown in a fury as far as they could go – just get rid of them. Anger thrown was the thread that bound.

Now I know what took place – wished I had known back then – would have saved heartache, desperation, depression, and a deep, deep sadness – a whirlpool sucking me into torment – an abyss of tears. And how, at times, I just saw myself swimming far out into the ocean – miles – never to return – just disappear into Mother Ocean, the creator of us all.

Not angry with him – at one time he did love me, but a strangling rope of anger does not hold love together. I'm just deeply saddened that I didn't see – didn't realize the truth. But damn it, I had seen - just had refused to recognize the symptoms that the patient was dying – a little bit every day – every day the same. I only wished, without hope, that maybe the love we once shared could somehow return – the joy return – the hope return. No, this is all wrong. It was me who withdrew – who hid. The love of my life had been cruelly taken from me and I didn't know what to do. Tom just reacted to me. I wasn't capable of love – didn't think I could love. No matter - all this is long gone - nothing can be done about it now. These thoughts come up occasionally, but I'm not wrapped around them anymore. Actually I'm surprised they've come up now.

After Tom left I was frozen – unable to move – just hoping my world would fill with the always around the corner, elusive love - appearing for a moment or two – only to rush away. What was going on? I had a loving heart – cared – was kind – or so I thought. Probably not, why else was I shuffling along – out of view – people holding hands walking down streets. My hands – holding on to nothing. And now in my small apartment – I don't tiptoe - not wanting to disturb the peace. I am surrounded in solitude of my own making.

Three high school girls walk past jabbering away on their way home from school – fresh with so much to look forward to. Hope for the future. No other way to describe it other than lively and energetic. Talking about boys - talking about friends – all with hope. It's a funny, when I was young I too was full of hope. When an in idea would pop up I'd think – what a good idea. Gosh, I'm so busy. But, no worries, I can always do it later. Some of these ideas I did do later. Others I simply forgot about or on further inspection felt they weren't such good ideas after all - glad

I didn't do them. So, this is how it was. And for sure when I got my teaching job it took up most of my time. I didn't reflect on things to do other than teach. After Tom, I spent most of my life alone. I did have my students who, for the most part, I dearly loved. My fellow teachers were often times kind and caring - good people. I was surrounded by people all of the time, so I wasn't lonely, but outside of work I spent my time alone. I didn't mind this as I told myself I had plenty of people time at work. My family was far, far away – in actual distance and in closeness. But, I wasn't lonely. It's only recently come to me that my life is different than way back then. Maybe it's because I'm not so busy – have time to reflect.

I now realize I don't have all that much time. It's not that I'm going to die soon, but realistically there aren't that many years left for me. But then again, I feel healthy and alive – thank God for swimming. I see people in and around my age - stooped shoulders, shuffling their feet as they move along in their lives. I stand erect and have a jump in my step. Good for me, but realistically my years on this earth are limited.

Loneliness has crept up on me. I miss the company of my students. Not dreadfully so, I just do. Ted comes to mind. I'm I being stupid wanting us to be friends? He seems so withdrawn. I wonder what his story is. His clothes – I still have them - the perfect excuse to see him again. He seemed interested, but who knows. I'll put his clothes in my car, so if I see him I can return them - the least I can do.

I guess I'm a dreamer now. I do quite well, being by myself daydreaming. Daydreaming is different than having dreams, but they are somehow connected. What dreams do I have now? Good question.

# TED

Feeling restless. The moon is out. "Come, Stub. Let's go outside." I wrap up. Stub doesn't need to get dressed – he has all of that fur – thousands of hairs per square inch. Don't know why, but I chuckle at this thought. Stub's such a good boy. Outside looking through the trees - the moon's light accentuating in a stream through this dense forest. Too cold to sit, I walk around under the trees.

"What's going to happen to me, Stub?" He doesn't answer, but he does come up to me - I pat his head - there's that tail – wag, wag in comfort and happiness. He's easy to please because he loves me so – and I him. We're good for each other.

Nothing unusual – everything is in place. My heart is inside beating away. One day this too will stop. Won't be bad, probably be a good thing considering. It seems I'm wrapped up in the past. San Diego was many years ago, but I can't seem to let it go. No! Don't go there – damn me. Fuck this – I'm going to bed. Know it's early, just need to get away. And sleep will bring this.

*"Stop! Please! No! Oh, God, help me. "I'm sorry, really I'm sorry. Please, I didn't mean to hurt you."*

*"Hurt me? You fucking cunt. I'll show you hurt!"*

*Ripping my blouse – hands too strong to stop. "Oh, God, please don't"*

*"Don't what?"*

*"Don't do this."*

*"Do what? You fucking bitch - I'll do anything I want. Maybe you should*

*have thought of me. I loved you ... and you didn't give a shit about me – you just used me – didn't give a damn. Now you're going to pay."*

*Struggling – no chance to escape. The door. Maybe someone will come. He's too strong. What to do? Nothing. There's nothing I can do. He's ripping of my bra. His face – twisted – eyes dead - dead to any humanity. Rising up – quickly shoved back down. Light streams in the window – freedom. This can't be happening, but it is. I have to make a break – the window – just jump through it.*

*"Struggle and it'll be even worse. You like to get fucked and that's what's going to happen to you." Steel eyes. Trying to keep attached to the floor so he can't take off my pants. Pulling on my pants - there's nothing I can do to stop him. My panties clawed off me. Shoved in my face – hard to breathe. "Smell this." Can't smell anything, can't breathe. Panic. I'm going to die. He's going to kill me. His hand, holding my torn panties, pulls them from my face. Gasping for air. "Don't worry, cunt. I'm not going to kill you. You're going to feel the hurt you gave me. Look at you, you pathetic bitch!" Laughing. "Kiss me." I don't move. He screams, "Kiss me!" I lean up to do that. His hand slams me down. "You piece of shit. Kiss me? Fuck you. I don't want a kiss from you, you sick bitch!" He stands up. I start to move - his foot on my face. He takes off his shirt. "You try to move again and this foot will stomp your ugly self-serving face. You won't be so pretty anymore. Won't be able to use it to hurt anyone else. Even your tight ass won't be able to seduce and use men. I fucking hate you." Standing over me, naked with a shit-eating grin. "Ready?"*

*No use. Closing my eyes, I whisper, "Please."*

*"Yes I will. You asking for it? Thought you'd like this." A laugh straight from hell. Open my eyes for an instant. His face distorted, twisted – I can't look. Turning my head – his hand snaps it back. "Open your eyes! I want you to look at me while I make love to you." I can't look at him. "I said look at me!" I want to disappear – go inside myself. Can't stop him – there's nothing I can do. I open my eyes to his awful-hate filled grin. "That's better." Thrusting angrily again-again-again. Hot burning pain inside me with all the hate*

*he can muster. My eyes open - this is what I see.*

"No!" Eyes - startled - open. Not again! Stub stands next to me – trying to figure out what's just happened. This Goddamn dream has come back. Fuck me. I close my eyes - to sleep - to disappear.

# TED

It took a long time to get back to sleep and a fretful sleep it was. Rubbing my eyes, stretching, I'm not ready to face the day. It'll be hard to toss the dream out of my mind. It's in my heart, that is, what I have of a heart. Damaged goods. Stub looks at me. "OK, I'll let you out." Let Stub out and prime the stove. Don't know what to do. I call work and tell them I'm sick. Think I'll just stay in bed all day - I mean, why get up. I remember Stub. He's at the door. He doesn't bark or scratch, just sits patiently waiting for the door to open. After feeding him I go back to bed – looking at the ceiling. This is going to be a long day. Trapped in my emotions - on my bed - in my own hell. Why am I like this? Why can't I break out of this? It's always been and still is. Why? I don't want this. What am I going to do? No answers. I don't want to be like this. How can I ever forgive myself? But I'm in too deep.

Stub jumps up and lies down beside me. He knows I'm hurting, but has no idea why. He puts his paws on my chest, snuggles up, and gives me a lick. "Oh, Stub." When will this ever end? It never will. And this is how I spend the day until night finally arrives, have some beer, smoke my pipe, and hope dreams don't destroy my sleep.

# TED

Waking up – it's dark. Stub is up against me. Don't want to, but I go over the dream again. It's as clear as I am now in this cabin - that real. This idea of not being withdrawn – of being open has met head on in a crash of my life. I guess it shows the futility of changing how I am - being open. Stub feels I'm awake and he wakes up too. Dogs don't have despair. Yes, they can have great sadness, but they don't have despair. "Thanks for helping me, Stub." His beautiful dog eyes show love, care, and concern. "Love you, Stub." Wag, wag.

I've tried stuffing this all-away like it never happened, but it did happen. I've never forgotten. I've spent these years doing what I do – mundane – without much value. How I live with these demons is to shove them aside. This works for a while, but then they come back – they're always there. Damn these memories. Hey, don't get mad at the memories. I'm the one who did it. I'm a fucking sick, sick asshole.

So I sit. Directionless. Wrapped in darkness - more than lack of light – no guide. No where to go – motionless – can't step back – can't go forward – there is no forward. The body breakdown – I can feel it coming - a train that can't be stopped.

I'm trapped in my own making - just fucking tired of... really need to leave the fucking planet. Stub, next to me. He loves me deeply and what love is in my heart is for him. Lying next to me I feel his heat. Reaching over I gently place my hand on him – feel his breathing – he looks at me. Stirring, he lifts his head – expressive dog eyes. Without him I would ... don't want to think about it. If I left who would take care of him?

Who would love him ... and who would he love? The rope holding the tetherball, that's Stub. Cut the rope as the ball goes around the poll and it screams off – gone.

No fucking longer. The world passes me by – I mean, who was he anyway.

I don't want to get trapped in this thought. The escape. I'm going to have to be strong to make a break from how I am – this bullshit attitude – can't be good for the heart and again, the heart is a person's engine – both physical and in care. I want both parts to be strong. That's what I want – to be healthy and alive. My resolve for this has certainly weakened. Not so sure I can. There I go again. Stop! Torn with anger and remorse. A new way – there's got to be. The one thing I do know is that Stub loves me and I love him. Having this love is new. So fortunate Stub came into my life - maybe he can be my anchor. Can love be contagious? I'm learning a life lesson from a dog. This is good news.

When I'm slammed – thrown to the ground, sometimes I'm strong, fight back, but most of the time I'm not strong and just want to hide – see no one - to have this "thing" disappear – go away. What I want – to be light – tired of carrying all of the weight around day after day week after week year after year. I'm going to need strength if I'm to break from my past. And how to do this? I've tried ignoring, pretending. You'd think after all the times they've surfaced, causing pain in my heart that feels like death that I'd learn to do something different, but what. And I've certainly thought about ending everything, but I'm still here. Some people are slow learners – that's me. Hard to get clarity and reason. Hard to break free.

Stub's by the door. He wants out. Getting out of bed I let him out. I go outside as well. The trees slightly sway in the breeze. They creak, groan, and moan in an otherwise silent moment – and there I stand. And for now I'm only here – nowhere else.

When I swim I'm also in the moment – pulling, gliding through the water. Maybe that's one reason I like swimming so much. Takes me away - sometimes far, far away.

Stub returns from taking care of business. I pat his head and we go inside. I work on the fire and feed Stub. I try to think of ways to be strong, but can't. Still too much confusion.

Going over what's been thrown my way recently. No need to go into the murky past. Just pay attention to the now. First, Stub, then Amy, and the almost forgotten $10,000. Are these signs? Maybe they are. If I deal with them as signs maybe this will help. "Hey, Stub. You some kind of sign?" He doesn't answer. For the heck of it – I go to the shelf where I put my checkbook. Fumbling it open, the balance is far greater than it's ever been. I start contemplating about it. No. This money will not take me to a new place – a new place in my heart. Putting it back, I make my coffee. That first taste is always so good. I sit on the couch – mind swirling about trying to grab something solid. Then Stub jumps on the couch. He's definitely solid.

It's been quite a while since I gave my clothes away. Maybe this opportunity with Amy has escaped me. I should have done something that day she left my cabin. As to what I don't have a clue – just something other than standing by the door waiting for her to leave, and leave she did, and she hasn't come back. So, this is how it's always been. Do I like it? No. Then I need to do something different – need to make a change. This swims around inside. Hopefully something will come up I can grab onto. That's what I want – that's what I need. Nothing comes up – no ideas. I'm still in a state of confusion. No matter – I put wood in the firebox – at least I can be warm. I crawl in bed.

Under the blankets – Stub by my side. Maybe a dream will come to clarify – though usually my dreams do little to clarify – mostly they confuse. Thunder breaks this thought. Damn, I think I left the window down in my car. Slip out of bed and go out barefooted – feet squishing on the damp ground. The car window is up. Lightning and thunder simultaneous - white blinding light. Quickly retreating into my cabin. Stub is by the door. "Wow, that was close, Stub." Soon sleep surrounds Stub and me as thunder and lightning bash away at the forest I'm in.

# AMY

Drying off in the locker room. It was a good swim – then, of course, all swims are good. What was I expecting, moving here. Grandstands of people all yelling, "Good for you!" What I didn't truly expect was the grandeur of the place – wild – the openness of it beyond my dreams. The two times I've been to the Mad River show me this. It didn't really show me – I was in it – I was part of it – not some movie. Ted, he didn't exactly open his arms to me, but I don't blame him. My God, I brutally attacked him. Should just give up on this – get his clothes back to him and move on? Regardless of what I do, his dream lays heavy on me. Where can someone find out about dreams like his? Nowhere really. No one knows – though some people pretend to know. I guess it really doesn't matter; Emma's gone and has been for years. I seem to be grinding to a slow halt - just wish I could be open, make friends, and have a good life. Now my life as a teacher was good, but I want there to be more. And this more is ... don't know - guess I was really expecting something dramatic. Give it time, I mean after all there are many years inside of me and this is all new. Need to be patient and the Mad River was damn wonderful. It'll be glorious to be immersed in it come warmer weather – something to look forward to.

On G street near the Arcata Marsh, I park my car, and get out. This is where Ted got Stub - such a good dog. Walking along, I take a few steps off the trail, and continue. Oh my! A very old redwood log has been carved with faces - it's so powerful. The log has turned a bluish/gray with age. The figures – angst shows on their faces. They appear to be floating in air – ghost like. It's bewitching. Off the trail - very few people have ever seen this - the sculptor probably knew this, but did it anyway – out of view except for the wanderer like myself. I sit, look at it, scoot up to it, run my fingers along the faces, and turn around resting against it. Leaving this precious log I wander to the ponds – reflecting on what I've just seen. I go down to the edge of Humboldt Bay, sit on a rock, and look out at the sun, low in the sky, the bay water lapping at my feet. Closing my eyes – this thought comes to me. "I am a good person." I repeat this to myself over and over again. Eyes still closed, "I am a swimmer, powerful and strong" I repeat this as well. Then I go back and forth between the two, "I am a good person. I'm a swimmer powerful and strong." It feels good saying those words to myself. Affirmations – that's what they are. Maybe I'll get into the habit of saying them. Tomorrow when I wake up that's just what I'll do. Take pleasure in the small gifts that surround me.

Opening my eyes, an egret lands maybe 20 feet away. She looks at me slightly tilting her head - so beautiful – long and elegant standing in the shallows absolutely still, patiently waiting for her food provided by a luckless frog. After a short while she leaps up and leaves me. My spirits are lifted in the air with her as she takes off. I feel light and so lucky. Take beauty and peacefulness where you find them. Recognize them, relish them, and this is what I'm doing. Thinking back to L.A., people there like to be in crowds - lots going on - Disneyland, Knott's Berry's Farm, etc. I wouldn't trade this spot for those in a million years. Maybe I've found my place. Getting up, the sun starts its departure from the day. The fog bank is close to shore and will soon cover this place with its protection. There's a softness in the fog – softens the edges.

I walk away from here with, "I am a good person. I am a swimmer powerful and strong." These words – these thoughts surround me – give me comfort.

# AMY

Sitting on my bed I get up, open the curtain, then sit down again. Oh, yes, the affirmations. I don't sit like I've seen meditators do; rather I sit straight, back against the wall. Closing my eyes, I take some slow breathes gently releasing them. "I am a good person. I am a swimmer, powerful and strong." A gentile wave covers me this cold damp winter morning wrapped in a blanket of serenity. Opening my eyes I smile.

I picture Ted sitting on his couch with Stub. I'm going to go to Ted's and return his clothes. Could go to the pool, but I want to return his clothes. It'll be a drop off and nothing more. This way it'll give him an opportunity to talk if he wants to. I'll do this later today. If he's not home, so be it, I'll just drop them off with a thank you note. That decided I continue my regular routine. After coffee and breakfast, I'll take my walk around Arcata. Windier than I thought when I step out, I return for my jacket and scarf. It's taking some time getting used to the colder weather up here. L.A. was so warm compared to this place. Gigantic white clouds – some seagulls fly under them making their presence known. The sky here is so clear, strong. Not the crowded air molecules thick with pollution that's L.A. I'm very grateful for this. What we take for granted. I am grateful for this air and wonder how I lived so many years in that over crowded – over stimulated place.

Guess it's earlier than I thought, not many people out and about this Saturday morning. A homeless man, thin, skin dry and wrinkled. I look down as I walk past. "Say, can you spare a dollar?" I keep walking. Stop, reach into my pocket, return, and give the man a dollar. His almost tooth-less grin thanks me. I continue along. When I started this walk I thought it would be a quick one – just around town, but my feet carry me to the Marsh. Glad I dressed for the cold, because that's what it is – cold. I make my way to the far pond. The narrow path is on the buffer between the bay and the pond. A very large flock of small birds in the air - swirling in mass - surprises me – a jolt – the good kind. Their hue changes from black to white to black again as they twist, turn, rise and fall in unison. They make a path under the clouds in and out of the blue and white. Quick turns all in a choreographed manner. Mesmerized I watch. Maybe I should get a camera – so many wonders. But no matter, I'm seeing all of this with my own eyes. More beauty in this short time up here than I could have ever imagined. The birds fly off and settle on the ground. I sit on a bench looking out to the bay, "I am a good person," rises to my lips. Eyes closed, the wind hits my ears, sound changing from far off to immediate. On this bench for quite a while – sometimes eyes shut - want to hear the sounds without sight. I'm pleased I'm hearing so much. Birds – some close and some far off - want to learn their names. Off in the distance I hear the wind. It gets louder and louder as it approaches. Then it sweeps to and past me. How odd, the wind has actual boundaries. Never thought of this before - experiencing moments I never even knew existed. Slow easy breathing. Opening my eyes - the sun is out and about, but not very warming. More seagulls about, scavenging – quite a racket. It seems some birds have beautiful sounds – seagulls make more of a racket than a beau-tiful sound, but I do love hearing them – seeing them above fishing boats coming into the harbor. This brings me to a song from my childhood: Quiet Village by Martin Denny. I remember how it carried me away into a paradise I had yet to see – only imagined. Anyway, I read later when they were trying to record seagulls for the studio version of the song, they had no luck, the seagulls refused to cooperate. They gave up; as the sound guys were pulling their equipment - ready to go - one of them threw down the uneaten portion of his sandwich. The gulls flocked to it screeching - trying to get a piece of the food. The sound guys realized this is what they needed to do. They set up again and threw food on the beach. So, what sounded like peaceful tropical birds was, in reality, seagulls fighting and posturing over food. Our perceptions are not always accurate. With this thought, I gather myself, and start my walk back to town with the song in my head.

I wonder if the library is open yet. I need to get a book and that's where I head. It shares a parking lot with the City Hall, Police Department, and Fire Station. All are new modern buildings. Good, it's just opened up. The homeless seem to hang out here – warm, dry, well lit, bathrooms, and of course, lots of reading material. I walk about looking at books. I should be able to remember good books I've read and who the authors were, but this is difficult to do. I continue looking for books. I gather four, check them out, and leave. I stop at the Phoenix Café for a cup of coffee and look further at my new books. They serve good coffee here; it's warm and friendly. I live just three blocks from this café and soon I'm walking up the stairs to my place.

I open *East of Eden* by John Steinbeck and am immediately taken to the place and people in the book. On my bed I read until I get sleepy, close my eyes, and take a snooze. Waking up - time to swim – not in a rush, but I find myself moving quickly - almost staccato. Taking a deep breath and slowly letting it out - a lot better. Gathering myself, I go back down the stairs, but before I descend I stop and look out at the bay. Damn near magical – the vastness of it. Love the ocean, because it goes on forever – no limits. I knew of this in L.A., but here I can have it everyday.

Sitting on the edge of the pool. I soon go in. I pull and glide – watching my hands enter the water, how bubbles rise to the surface, and I remember the ocean – especially Hawai'i. Swimming brings me a peacefulness that covers every inch of my skin - of my being. In the sauna after my swim I am even more relaxed. Not to regret my life, but I should have moved here years ago.

Time to head up the hill. Looking to make sure I have Ted's clothes I begin the short jaunt up Fickle Hill.

# TED

I remember thinking as a boy, when I got old that I'd have life figured out. I mean, I'd have my whole life to get things right. Not true. It's as if what I've done and not done have all piled up, can't get the suitcase shut even after sitting on it. I haven't had that dream in a long time – good reminder that I'm a piece of crap.

Please, what am I going to do? Guilt still wraps itself tightly around me like I can't get a breath. I wish it would keep me from breathing – then this all would end. But what about that Greek pushing that stone for all eternity. Are we punished after our deaths?

Is that a car? Stub's on alert, I get up, and go to the door. It's Amy. She gets out holding what looks like my clothes. She smiles and waves walking up to my door. "Hi. Sorry, I still have your clothes." She stops, looks down, then back up again to meet my eyes. Silence. This is a huge jump from what I was just thinking about. Don't think I'm ready for this – the smile and general good feelings she apparently has. "Here." She holds out my clothes. My hands don't reach for them. My whole being is still, not able to move. Slightly shaking my head to get back in this moment I reach for my clothes. My hand touches her hands. What to do. What to say. Barrier of emotions backed up - unable to get out. How long will this go on. "Well, anyway, I wanted you to have your clothes back." She turns back toward her car.

"Wait." Turning back, she looks at me. I can't catch what she's feeling – never been good at that. "Thanks."

"Just sorry it's taken so long."

"No worries." Hesitating, "Want to come in?"

"You sure?"

"I'm sure." No I'm not, but I say this anyway

"OK."

She ambles over to me. I realize I'm standing in the doorway. Awkwardly I move out of the way and she enters. Standing in her coat, stocking cap, and scarf for what seems like a long time. "Just throw my clothes on the bed." She does. "Coffee?" Pointing to my couch, "Have a seat. Black, right?"

"Yes, black." She takes off her stocking cap, coat, and scarf and lays them across her legs.

My back turned - making coffee – this is good, a respite from her eyes - from what she may want. I can't make up my mind. I'm in complete turmoil, glad she's here, but what I'd been feeling before she arrived has a strong hold over me. I also wish she wasn't here. Could have let her go. Winds of confusion reign over me - I don't know what the fuck I want. Wrapping my hands around her cup, I take it to her. Our fingers touch. "Thanks." After making mine I also sit on the couch. "Where's Stub?"

"Oh, he must be outside." He is. Standing patiently at the door. "Sorry, Stub." He comes in and shakes.

"You're lucky to have Stub." Amy pets him.

"Yes, I am." Turning to Amy, "I think he likes you."

"Hope so." He presses up against her leg. She smiles. Stub wags his tail.

Silence – what to say. Clumsily searching for words. Does she see this? Probably. Her eyes – expressive and clear, seem to be seeking – mine must be filled with bewilderment. OK, say something. I stumble out with these words. "I had a good time at the river with you."

"Me too. I want to swim there in the summer. I did briefly go in before the rains hit. The water was cold, but it felt grand. That's right. I already told you this."

Stub jumps up barking. "What, Stub." Getting up, I go to the door, slightly opening it - a large deer is in the yard. "Amy, come look." I'm not going to let Stub out. "Stub, quiet. The deer needs his peace." Amy comes up next to me and the three of us look at this magnificent animal. I'm aware Amy's up against me. Closing the door and settling again on the couch. This time Stub's on the couch between Amy and me. She pats his head; he turns, and looks at her. "He definitely likes you."

"You really think so?"

"Yes I do." This isn't going well. Can't talk about Stub forever.

"Where you ever on a swim team?"Amy breaks the silence.

"When I was in high school, girls weren't allowed on the swim team, but I've been swimming most of my life."

"And that was where."

"Los Angeles."

"I forgot, did you tell me how long you've been up here?"

She looks up at the ceiling, then answers, "Just over two months."

"Do you like it here?"

"Yes, very much. I can't believe the beauty. Just yesterday I saw an old redwood log at the Marsh. It was off the trail and there were faces carved in it. The redwood log was a blue/gray. The figures looked like ghosts. It was stunning."

"That's so cool. I go to the Marsh all of the time, but I haven't seen that log."

"I can show it to you. How long have you lived here?"

"Hmm. Lets see." How many years has it been. Using my fingers. "About fifty years."

"Then I feel good I can show you something you haven't seen. Fifty years is a long time. It's odd how life is. Turn around and you're already old. How does this happen so fast. And you moved up here when you were how old?"

"Nineteen."

"My, you're old." A glow in her eyes, then a smile.

"Hey, that's not nice."

"So?" A broad grin graces her face – sitting on the couch with Stub and me.

"So, how old are you?"

"You're not supposed to ask that. We have our secrets huh, Stub." Thrust up against her, she pets him again. He does like her. "Want to guess?"

"No I do not." Smiling. I'm having a good time. The initial awkwardness is gone. Just Stub, Amy, and me. "I'm lousy at people's ages."

"Oh, come on."

She could be sixty – that's what I think. "OK, fifty."

"That's a guess," a sly smile.

"Well, aren't you going to tell me?"

"I don't know. Why do you want to know my age?"

"I don't. You brought this age thing up." She lets out a laugh.

"Are you laughing at me?"

"No I'm not." Hesitating, she continues. "I'm laughing because of you." Another laugh escapes from her on the couch with Stub and me. This girl has a sense of humor. I don't laugh much at all. This is so different. Here it comes - a laugh. Both of us giggle on the couch and this turns to full on laughter. Oh goodness. Slowly it settles.

It's 6 o'clock and dark. Now what. "You want a beer?"

"OK."

I grab two. I start to take a drink. Amy, holding her beer, "Wait. Let's make a toast."

"OK."

"Hmm. To all us swimmers - may we always swim on."

Clink – the toast is made. I want a smoke, but not now, maybe she'd be disgusted by this.

"Sixty-five"

"What?"

"I'm sixty-five."

"No. you're not."

"Yes I am."

"You don't look it. And your swimming. You look fabulous in the water – sleek and graceful." I've embarrassed myself saying this - hope I haven't been too forward.

She smiles, then looks down. "You're too kind." I get us another beer, check the stove, and add a few pieces of wood. There are moments of silence, but not awkward moments – just peaceful.

Stub gets up and goes to the door. I follow and let him out. "Amy. Come see the moon." Standing in the doorway the moon looks to be resting on a branch of a redwood tree. And just then an owl, silent in flight, flies past us, and lands on the branch with the moon as a backdrop. No words for this. The owl turns her head and flies off. We go back to the couch, but before sitting, I get my clothes from the bed, and put them in my chest of drawers. Maybe she'll take this as a sign the evening is coming to a close. Where will this go if she stays? This makes me nervous.

"This has been fun, but I think I need to go."

"Yes, it has been fun. I haven't laughed like tonight in a long time." Maybe I shouldn't say this.

At the door, I open it, but remembering the last time, I put my hand on her cheek - slowly - ever so slowly - gently - almost whisper like - I kiss her. Softness enters me. Amy's eyes are moist with emotion. No hug, no embrace, just this sweet, sweet kiss. She steps back – our eyes seemed locked on each other. Turning, she walks to her car - looks back to me. Something is going on. "You want to get together again?" Not waiting for an answer, "Let's go swimming."

"I don't see you at the gym anymore. You swimming real early?"

"After I was so mean to you I thought you wouldn't want to see me – so I quit the gym and joined the community pool. Let's meet up there. OK? How about tomorrow around noon?"

Amy is so sweet and kind. She seems to care for me. This is all so new. I stumble a little. "Yes, that sounds fine."

"Bye."

"Bye." She drives away. I close the door, making sure Stub's in the cabin.

# AMY

The drive down the mountain seems motionless – like I'm not even driving the car. A deer jumps out; I slam on the brakes, stopping maybe a foot from the frightened animal. With a leap she's gone. Too close - need to pay attention.

Resuming my way. What's the deal with Ted? He seems to have entered my life in a big way. In a way I don't understand. How does stuff like this happen? I know this sounds absurd, this isn't some movie – it's real. *Escape In Time* comes to mind, it had a lot do with dreams. It twisted reality and dreams so the character didn't know what was real. Dreams. Ted's dream about Emma. Finding myself at his place after my craziness at Wildberries. His love of swimming. Our ages. Our loneliness. Well, maybe he isn't lonely – I'm only assuming this. So many similarities – they seem beyond coincidence. Glad I missed that deer. Then there was the deer and the owl I saw tonight. And Stub. I think he does like me. Never had a dog, he's pretty damn wonderful. So many dogs are yappy, not controlled – only by a leash - seem like a bother, but Stub has a calm, loving, and inquisitive nature.

Though I vowed to pay better attention to my driving I'm in town before I know it. I'm very deep into my thoughts. I want another beer. Driving to the plaza I park, but decide that a beer at home will be much better. Pretty sure I've got one in the fridge.

Walking up my stairs, I enter. My apartment is cold. I turn on the stove and open the oven to let heat out. This will be faster than my weak electric heater, which I also turn on. Sitting on my bed I can almost feel the warmth of Stub against me. Warmth of bodies against each other. Not against, but in unity.

I've had a few boyfriends in my life, both before and after Tom. The marriage to Tom was a benchmark. After our breakup I didn't see anyone for a long time and when I did I'd compare the new guy with Tom. More talkative - less talkative - seemed to listen better or not really listen at all. Drank less than Tom - drank more. Everything was a comparison. Years after the breakup I was still wrapped up in him even though we were apart. And in reality had been apart – in our own worlds - even when we were together those last couple years. Strange I'm thinking this. I truly believe he is completely out of my heart. My God, after all these years he should be gone.

Reach over to pet Stub. He's not here – wish he was. Also wish I had somebody to talk to about what's going on, but this would be new for me. My deep innermost thoughts are just that - inside - not to share. I'm going to have to figure this out myself.

Tomorrow, what will this bring? Beer empty, getting up for another. All the way up from Mexico, here in my hands. Slightly turning it - condensation drips down the label. I rub my fingers on the bottle creating pathways for the condensation – a distraction from my thoughts. I'm good at finding all sorts of ways to divert my thinking, divert my feelings, but on my bed tonight I focus on why I moved up here - needing change – not a lot of thought put into it. Now it's hit me hard - this place is not only physically different, but somehow I am changing as well. You'd think at sixty-five a person would be settled in their thoughts – on how they feel.

Hand on my cheek, slowly with the greatest of care moves closer and closer – our lips touching in the softest way. Have I ever had a kiss like tonight? No. I was and am still surrounded by some sense of ... sense of what - I don't know. Words are escaping me. Feelings can have words attached or not. Words can define the feelings, yet because they are only words they are limiting. So, no words here, just sit in the glow of that moment. And with this sweet thought I lie down, get under the covers and close my eyes.

# TED

Kissing Amy? It's confusing - what must it be for her. Seems like I really care for her and I do. But how can I go from the deepest despair – knowing what I did - feel like dying - to a light feeling. No, it wasn't light. What was the feeling? Just felt very special. And now turbulent winds batter my soul - deep-seated feelings of worthlessness have been thrown in with feelings of belonging. Which is it? It can't be both. The fight is on. Before Amy drove up I was clear that my life has and will always be - led by my past – that my past directs me – that I'm encased in a horror of my own making. Then tonight - enjoyed her company – felt free. It wasn't a distraction. And while she was here – often held thoughts of my past disappeared. It was good to share and how the owl landed on the tree branch. And laughing at her funny attitude. A smile creeps up on my face.

Wait! Don't get carried away. This cannot last. It was a hundreds of years ago, or so it seems, when I felt love only to have it ripped from me. Am I defined by this? No. It's what I did about it - twisted my spirit - anger and hate and this manifested in the cruelest way and this is what's stayed with me - more prominent than anything else. My partner all of these years and what a fucked partner it is. It'll never go - never stop telling me what a worthless piece of shit I am - that's my partner - that's why I'm alone. All of these years it's been a constant - too awful – too big to say it never happened - because it did happen. Goddamn me. So close to going over the edge.

Stepping outside with Stub, the moon is now hidden from my view.

Stub walks around sniffing, finding the right spot to pee. He does - then he scrapes his paws on the dirt masking his scent. His scent protected from a predator. My scent is hidden. No one can know.

Still standing on my porch. Why in the hell did I ask to see her again. Tomorrow, the pool. This was a big mistake. The war is on. Go. Don't go. Well, I can't do both. Back inside on the couch, Stub jumps up, and plops against me. He did this with Amy. Stub, you like her I know. Once again, "Stub are you guiding me? OK, Stub – I'll go tomorrow."

# AMY

Checking the time. It's 11:45. Getting out of my car, I walk to the pool. I don't see his car. It's cold out, but at least there's no wind. I've noticed the wind often comes up in the afternoons. Oops, forgot my swimsuit. Turning, I retrieve it and once again, head towards the pool. Not many people here – good. I don't mind sharing a lane, especially if the other swimmer knows pool etiquette, but it's way easier to get carried away in thoughts and feelings if I don't have to be concerned about another swimmer, but this isn't the case today - there's only one swimmer.

What to do – should I wait here by the pool, go out and wait, or just start my swim? I think I'll wait by the pool. It's warm here. No matter how cold outside, the pool area is always warm. I change and bring my daypack with my clothes out to the pool deck. Watching the clock, getting somewhat anxious. I could be putting way too much into how I feel and especially about how he feels, because I have no way of knowing, though the kiss was pretty wonderful. It's after 12. Putting my legs in the water, gently kicking. Lowering my head I thank the water for the blessings it gives me and ease myself in. Up from behind me, "Hey, Amy."

Turning around – he's standing by the lane next to me. "Hi, Ted." He does what I did – sits and swirls his legs about. Awkward, does it have to be like this - what to say. "What kind of workout do you want to do?"

No answer – he's still looking at his feet in the water. "I don't know. What do you want to do?" He licks his goggles and rinses them in the pool. "I kind of do the same thing every swim. I swim 64 lengths half free

– half backstroke."

"Do you have a hard time remembering what length you're on?"

"Yes I do. I have a method with my fingers to help keep track, but I do lose count sometimes."

Wavering - what to say. "Let's just swim what we want. I've never done a coordinated workout, especially with someone else. This OK?"

"OK, just curious though. What do you usually swim?"

"I swim for 45 minutes or so." Putting on my swim cap. He doesn't have a swim cap.

"Do you swim all freestyle?"

"Yes."

"Not butterfly?"

"Butterfly? Yikes. No."

"Me neither – it's an impossible stroke. Many years ago at this pool a guy swam over 200 lengths, without stopping - all butterfly."

"Wow!"

"We were doing a lap-a-thon the raise money for the pool. The pool only used to be open during the summer. In fact, the city was contemplating turning it into a roller-rink. That's why the lap-a-ton. We wanted the pool to be open all year."

"Did you swim in the lap-a-thon?"

"Yes, I did. Crazy, I swam over 700 lengths of the pool – only stopping to get out and pee. I drank a lot of water."

"700 lengths without stopping. How long did that take?"

"Just over five hours. I won't ever do that again. It was tedious, but I did it. I figured it was about ten miles."

"I could never do that."

"I think you could. I have this funny attitude that if the water isn't too cold I can swim forever."

Swim forever? That's a thought. I think I might be capable of this, just never thought about it. He's got his goggles on and looks ready to go. I put my goggles on. "Let's get started." And off we go. Swimming freestyle he's somewhat faster than I am, but when he swims backstroke we are close to the same speed - this isn't a competition. It's fun to look at him, not as a stranger, but as a friend. A friend? I hope so. I've never made a time to be with someone swimming. Looking at the clock, I realize I didn't make a note of the time when we started. Back and forth – long pulls, smooth glides. Stopping to adjust my goggles, a woman is in the lane next to me. She licks her goggles, and swishes them in the pool. She looks at me and smiles. I return the smile. Don't see a lot of red swimsuits. Putting on her blue swim cap she looks at me - I nod - then proceed with my swim. She's also a good swimmer, we are close to the same speed, but when she swims the breaststroke I pull ahead of her. I don't swim the breaststroke. I have two people to watch today in this swim.

Ted stops his swim and hoists himself on the deck. I'm on the other side of the pool when he does this. Maybe I should get out too, but soon he's back. "I had to pee." I know if his usual workout is 64 lengths of the pool, he's probably done that. Hope he's OK with me swimming longer. Maybe so - he's back in the water. Oh my goodness he's spinning in the water. I've never seen this before. He spins around all the while moving across the pool. I stop swimming as he goes past. Head under water I watch – this sure is something.

The woman in the red suit is at the end of the pool and turns to me, "You swim here much?"

"Yes. I try for six days a week. And you?"

She takes off her goggles and rubs her eyes, "I try to do the same. I've never seen you here before. Do you come really early?"

"I just started here. I used to swim at the Welcome Gym, but this is a much better pool."

"I agree. What's your name?"

"Alice Humphrey."

"Nice to meet you, Alice."

"Likewise."

"I'm Amy Nelson."

Before Alice can respond, Ted comes to a stop by us and, he too, takes off his goggles.

"Alice, this is Ted. Ted this is Alice."

Oh goodness I don't know Ted's last name. "You guys want to take a sauna?"

Alice says she's got things to do in town and needs to go. She pulls herself on the deck – turns and says good-bye. Turning to Ted – he's watching Alice leave. "So, you want to take a sauna?"

"Sure."

The cold whips me - the pool water still on my skin. The sauna's in a small courtyard. I shiver as I make my way. I open the door and we enter. Always dark in the sauna. I look around to make sure there's no one lurking in the shadows like the time I was singing. Gosh, that was embarrassing. Thinking about being embarrassed. "Ted, I don't know your last name."

"Lewis. And yours?"

"Nelson."

Getting comfortable. There are two levels. The closer to the heat source the hotter it is. This is where he sits. I'm on the lower bench. "Why don't you swim here now?"

"I don't have to pay to swim at the gym – a perk for working there. Haven't swum here in a long time. This is a better pool though. Glad I came. What was her name – the woman next to you?"

"Alice."

"She a friend of yours?"

"No, just met her today. She's a good swimmer."

"Yes, I noticed."

My eyes have adjusted to the dark. His eyes are shut; he's leaning back against the wall. More used to the heat now, I go up on the level he's on, lean back, and shut my eyes as well. It's not too long before I want to go. I can only take so much of this intense heat. Almost whispering, "Ted." He turns to me. "I need to go."

"Do you mind if I stay?"

"No, I don't mind. I can only take so much of the heat. This has been fun." Getting up, "I've never done this before – made a date to go swimming." Looking down, "I liked looking at you swim." I'm slightly embarrassed saying this. What the heck, why not. "You want to do this again?"

"Yes I do."

"Maybe you could call me and we can set a time."

"If I had your phone number." I tell him my number. "Sorry, I am terrible at remembering phone numbers. Maybe you can leave it for me at the receptionist's desk."

"OK. I will." I tootle off leaving Ted in the heat.

# TED

This has been special. Maybe I've made a friend. She said she's never made a date to go swimming. Is this what this was – a date? The sweat is rolling off my face. I scoot to a lower level and close my eyes. I'm glad I'm by myself - alone in my thoughts.

What if. "Ted?" She stands by the sauna door - doesn't move - looking at me – eyes inviting - beckoning. Getting up – moving in front of her – she puts her arms around me. Sweet sweat mixes - slick - skin on skin - smooth – we embrace. Reaching up, she puts her hands to my face-heat-sweat-eyes in softness and kisses me gentle and delicate. Pulling back, she puts her hands on my chest, then moves them along my skin up and around my neck and head - hands in my hair she draws me to her and kisses me again - a strong kiss. I'm brought back to my cabin and the sweet kiss we had. This fantasy is not so far off base.

Shaking my head at this. Time to go. As I leave the sauna three teenagers enter. I leave, quickly shutting the door.

Still early in the day, I go home to my friend. He rushes to me, standing on his back legs. It's like he's hugging me. "Good boy, Stub." His tail wags vigorously. I let him out and stand on my porch watching him. We re-enter our cabin. Stub is huge in my life. It's no longer my this, or my that. It's become ours. I grab a book and lie on our bed to read. Stub jumps up and lies next to me. After a while drowsiness approaches, I mark the page, close the book, and shut my eyes.

Waking up, I'm a slug. I often take naps, but they're short - 15 minutes or so. I must have slept longer – the sun is making its departure. Stretching, maybe I should make some coffee. I do.

On the couch holding the cup, the woman in the red bathing suit comes to my mind. Something about her. Not a clue as to what, but a vague feeling swirls around me at the edge of my awareness.

And so the next couple of days pass – Amy on my mind. I should call her. OK, I need to get that number and call her. Just got to take a breath and do it. Get my wallet. It's not there. Check my pants, search the pockets – no paper – no phone number. I look again, still no phone number. Go over in my mind when I got home from the pool – what did I do with the phone number? "Stub. You see what I did with Amy's phone number?" He doesn't answer. Damn it to hell. I walk across my cabin in a methodical way - go into my bathroom. It's nowhere to be found. I wonder if she's waiting for a phone call - what to do. Well, whatever I do it will have to wait until tomorrow. Grab a beer, get my pipe, turn on my music, and soon I'm in bed.

The morning is unusually cold. I look out the window to see if there's snow. There isn't. Stoking the fire, feeding Stub, and letting him out, I prepare for the day. After coffee I try to figure out what to do about Amy. I drive to the pool hoping to see her. Actually the pool isn't open – some maintenance issue. The next day I go to the pool before work. I even go during my lunch break to no avail. God, I'm stupid – can't even hang on to a piece of paper. After work on Tuesday I have an idea. I go to the Phoenix Café – maybe she's there – she's not - only a couple of people sitting at the tables with miss matched table clothes. It's a funky little the café, but it's clean, just not like any other café I've ever been to. The woman in the red bathing suit is working. What was her name? Searching a little – yes, Alice. At this café you go up to the counter to order. I do and Alice comes over. There's a hint of recognition in her eyes. "Ted?"

"Yes. And you're, Alice?"

"Yup. What can I get you?"

"A mocha." Waiting, Alice brings me my drink. "I'm trying to get ahold of Amy, you know, the woman you swam next to the other day. She gave me her phone number, but I lost it."

"Isn't it in your phone?"

I pull out my flip phone. "I don't put any numbers in it."

"Oh." She straightens her apron. "You know, I saw her yesterday at the pool."

"I've got an idea. If I give you my phone number, maybe the next time you see her you can give it to her?"

"OK." She then hands me a small piece of paper and pen. After giving her my phone number I take my coffee to a table by the window that overlooks the plaza. A seagull has landed on McKinley's head. Hope it takes a shit.

# AMY

I wonder if Ted picked up my phone number - it's been five days and he hasn't called. Alice is here. I wonder where she works to have random times off to swim. She's nice. We get out of the pool at the same time. In the locker room, drying off, "You want to get some coffee?" she asks me.

"Sure. Where do you want to go?"

" I don't know."

"How about the Phoenix Café?"

"No. It's a nice place, but it's where I work and I don't want to hang out there on my day off."

"I can understand. Let's go to the Silver Spoon."

"OK. Meet you in a couple of minutes."

We arrive at the same time. I order a mocha and Alice gets a regular coffee and a bagel. Her hair is still damp from the pool as is mine. She's very athletic – easy to see she's a swimmer, broad shoulders. She's heavier than me - smooth skin over her muscles. She has curves I don't have. I've always been a Skinny Minnie. Her eyes sparkle and show a curiosity. Taking a bite from her bagel, "You're a really good swimmer."

"Thanks. So are you. Have you ever been on a swim team?"

Alice answers, "Yes. In high school."

"Where?"

"San Diego."

"And you? Where you on a swim team?"

"No. When I was young they didn't let us girls on swim teams."

"Oh come on. How old are you?"

"Sixty-five."

"Wow, you certainly don't look it."

"But I am. How old are you?"

"Fifty."

"And you don't look fifty."

"Thanks."

I take a drink of my sweet chocolate/coffee drink. "How long have you lived here?"

She ponders for a moment, "Ten years. And you?"

"About three months."

"And you're from?"

"L.A."

"What did you do in L.A.?"

"I was a high school English teacher."

She wipes her mouth with one of those weak café paper napkins. "I wanted to be a teacher, but I was too messed up in high school to get good grades. The idea of being a teacher left me."

"What did you do?"

"Actually, I dropped out a month before I graduated. Mom was sick - I needed to help her. She was pretty out of it. She didn't even know I dropped out."

"Was your father there?"

"No he wasn't." Saying this in a harsh tone. It's clear she doesn't want to talk about her father.

"Must have been very hard on you."

"Hard on me? It was extremely hard on Mom." A tear appears in her eye, followed by a rush of tears. I wish this hadn't come up. This is obviously very difficult for her. She can barely get the words out through her tears. "Yesterday would have been her birthday. She died ten years ago" She gets up. "I've got to go."

"Alice, I'm so sorry." I get up and hold out my arms. Crying, Alice goes into them, holding on to me. We break from this embrace; she turns, and goes to the door. Opening it, she looks back at me, with a small brave smile she tentatively waves, and leaves. I can't finish my coffee – take our stuff to the self-service bin.

There's just too much sadness in the world. Emma. Walking away from the café I find myself crying. They say time heals all wounds. How much time does it take? I head to the Marsh. Sitting on a bench overlooking the bay - this place has become my safe spot - a place to gather myself. When I see Alice's eyes – her hurt and pain, my tears rise up again. A young couple – hand in hand walk by. They pretend they don't see me, but I know they do. The tide is out - the bay is all mud and in this mud there are rivulets of water going out to the open ocean. Pilings from what's left from an old dock stick out of the mud. Egrets stand completely still waiting for food to pass in front of them. Gulls overhead, and a line of pelicans fly over the horizon. This isn't a distraction. Not some stupid thing to take away the pain. No, it's recognition that all is not lost – that all isn't sad - that I am so very small in the grand scheme of things and despite all the pain and sadness there is beauty. Bless this new place for showing me this.

# TED

This is crazy. I'm looking for Amy wherever I go - for her car – for any sign of her. The odd thing is I don't know what I'll say when I see her. I'm sure I'll eventually see her. This isn't a large city – small, around 12,000. I finish my day at the gym. Instead of swimming I go to the community pool – maybe she'll be there. Driving up I see her car. This is good and at the same time nerve racking. I seem driven to find her. Hope I'm not considered a stalker. My intentions are good, though very scary - to be open – to have a friend. Be honest, more than a friend - someone to be very close to. Am I capable of this? Don't know, just driven. I pay, enter the locker room, change into my swim trunks, and go out to the pool. She's not in the pool - what to do. I always feel like swimming, but now I have something else to do here - find Amy. Outside, I go to the sauna. Dark I'm adjusting my eyes – on the look out.

"Ted." It's Amy.

"Hey, Amy." Can't see her – only a shadow.

"You go swimming?"

Tentatively I answer, "No."

"No?"

Embarrassed, I tell her, "Actually I was looking for you." I stumble in my thoughts. "Is this OK? I lost your phone number - this is the only way I know I might see you."

"Glad to hear this. I thought you were ignoring me."

Still standing, I make my way to sit beside her – close, but not too close. Don't want her to think I'm a creep. "You've seen Alice?"

"A couple of days ago. We had coffee at the Silver Spoon after swimming. She seems very nice."

"I saw her a couple of days ago as well. She works at the Phoenix Café." Should I tell her about giving Alice my phone number? Going over this. I'm such a social dweeb. "I gave her my number to give to you."

"You did? Gosh, she must have forgotten, but it was an emotional time for her. The day before would have been her mom's birthday. She was very sad. It seems no matter how old we are when our parents die it's a great heart ache." Too dark to see her expression. "I hope to see her again. To be honest I've never had a lot of friends. Work friends, my students, but for the most part I've been a loner." She adjusts herself on the bench. "I'm going to move to a lower bench. It's too hot up here." I remember her comment last time about the heat. I don't want her to leave – so I'm glad she's moved. I follow her.

"I spend my time alone too." No way am I going to tell her why. I wonder why this is for her – I certainly know why it is for me. Opening up with another person – almost unheard of.

"I was and am not able to let Emma go." A minute goes by – sitting in the heat of the sauna. "Her death is my life. I can't erase that day. It's always in me – no matter how I try - it just doesn't ever leave." Stumbling in her words, "Sorry to lay this on you – it's just so damn sad."

"Don't be sorry." I can't imagine what it must be like to lose a young child. I don't have any children.

Again. "I'm sorry." Softly, "I'm sure you don't want to hear about it."

My eyes have adjusted to the dark. Her blue eyes – sad - look down – her arms wrapped around herself. She's holding on in the dark heat of the sauna - sitting beside me. I want to reach out and hold her, but don't. "No. You're wrong. I do want to hear about Emma - about you." I take deep a breath.

Releasing herself, her hands rest over her legs. I can see – we're that close. She doesn't respond with words. Once again I'm socially inept -

socially stupid.

She surprises me. "Thanks. It means a lot to me."

I surprise myself and take ahold of her hands. In doing this we are partially facing each other. Tears rise up in her – she cries. I feel terribly sad for her.

Her words are soft. "When you told me your dream it brought to the surface all the horror of that day. So many years I've been able to stuff it away – get on with my life. But I realized at Wildberries that it's always near the surface and it came back with a vengeance. I want it to go away - just go away. Not the memory of my daughter, but the remembrance of that Camaro tossing and taking her life - that's what I don't want to remember."

Rubbing her hands, "I'm so sorry I told you that damn dream."

"Don't be sorry. And why you had that dream is a mystery. How did it come to you? It's beyond knowing." Taking her hands away, she rubs her eyes.

Maybe somehow we were meant to run into each other, but I don't say this – too strange a thought. I've never been a person who believes that everything happens for a reason. Sometimes shit just happens – no spirit or God making it so.

"I need to go." A small almost smile is on her face. "Thanks for listening. I'm glad you tracked me down. Let's try this again – I'll leave my number at the desk."

"And I'll try not to lose it."

Amy gets up and leaves me in the dark heat. She's a wonderful person - my heart goes out to her. So, this means I must have a heart. This is good news. Maybe it's possible to have a heart even after what I've done.

# AMY

**N**ice to find someone – a man who listens – who cares. At least it appears he cares. I've now found two people who could be friends - not superficial, self-indulged.

I need to find a way to have peace about my Emma. I've always just stuffed it - it's very apparent this hasn't worked. My God, all of these years and I still don't know what to do. I did have six wonderful years with her. How can I realize this joy and not be overwhelmed by sadness? I've got a few photos of her. After she was gone, I took them all down, and stashed them away. I tried a few years ago to bring them out - to set them up so I could see her. It was too sad – couldn't do it, so I took them down again, and hid them. I'm going to try this again, but somehow I have to feel differently than I did the last time. One photo comes rushing at me. She's in her yellow dress, saddle shoes, and that blue ribbon in her hair. She loved that dress - and her smile - the biggest - most loving smile in the world. That's it – I'll get it out. But this time it'll be different. God, I hope so. I need to be free to love. That's what happened with Tom. I didn't know how to love anymore.

Looking for the small box with the photos, I finally find it in my old suitcase. Shouldn't have been too difficult finding the photo – I don't have many things with me. Wiping the dust off the box, I bring out this photo, kiss her, bring her to my chest, and hold tight. Sadness tries to enter, but I refuse to let her in. Holding my Emma in my hands - tears flow. Not tears of sadness, but rather tears of the overwhelming love we had for each other. Where to put it? Looking around my small place. I put it at eye level on the window in the door. That way everyday when I leave I can take her image with me. Glad I'm doing this.

Getting ready to go out – I need food. Grabbing my cloth shopping bag and out the door. Oops. Forgot something. Go back inside – look at Emma, "Love you my sweet girl." Then go out. No tears – our love still strong - won't let the sadness in - an umbrella of protection - lightness in my step going down the stairs. I need to make a birthday cake, Emma's birthday is tomorrow. Chocolate was – no – is her favorite. At the store I realize I don't even have a cake pan. I get one of those aluminum ones. Gosh it's been years since I've made a cake. About to leave when I remember to get candles - then I remember sparkles - Emma loved sparkles. All set, I leave for my apartment with the goodies for a cake - for my Emma's cake.

"Amy." Alice is just going into the market.

"Alice."

She turns and joins me on the sidewalk. "I'm so sorry. Ted gave me his phone number to give you. He'd lost the paper with your phone number, but I forgot to give it to you at the Silver Spoon." She reaches in her pocket and hands me Ted's phone number, "Here."

I take the paper. "No worries. Ted actually tracked me down at the pool."

"Good. I feel bad forgetting to give it to you."

"Well, it was a rough time for you."

"Thanks, it was." Looking at my sack, "Say, what's in your sack?"

"Stuff to make a birthday cake."

"Birthday cake?"

"Yes."

"Is it your birthday?"

"No. I don't really celebrate my birthday." Feeling proud, actually standing a bit more upright. "It's Emma's birthday tomorrow."

"Emma?"

"She's my six year old daughter."

"Didn't know you have a daughter. Does she live with you?"

What to say. Be proud. Be strong. "No, she doesn't." In a stillness of thought. "Why don't you come to my place – help with the cake."

"OK. I was going in for a bottle of wine. How about I get it then we go to your place. Is it far?"

"No, only a few blocks." She goes in and comes out with a bottle of red wine, some ice cream, and what looks like a gift. Can that be? We walk together and down the alley I point to my apartment. "That's my place. It's small, but I like it a lot." At the top of the stairs we look out at Humboldt Bay – light fading and gold appears to abound in the water captured in the bay that will eventually go out and mix with the ocean.

Alice, stopping before entering my apartment. "Wow, what a view."

Standing in the kitchen, me with my sack, and Alice with her wine and ice cream. Putting the ice cream in the freezer and the cake fixings on the table. "Oh, we'll need a corkscrew – I think I've got one." Rummaging in the silverware drawer, I bring it out, and hand it to her. Alice quickly opens the bottle. I'm not that good with corkscrews – don't need one for my beer. I find a glass for Alice and pour the wine. She turns, "Is that your daughter? Emma, right?"

"Yes."

"She's beautiful. What a smile."

"Yes, she is." I show her my bed; there aren't any chairs in my very small bedroom/living room. We sit.

"How old is she. The photo looks fairly old."

This is going to be a test. Can I tell Alice about Emma and not cry - not get so sad I want to die? Can I? "She would be thirty-two tomorrow." I can tell this has come as a surprise to Alice; her face shows it. "She was taken from me when she was six years old. A car ran her down. She died in my arms." Tears want to rise up – No! No! No! One tear does manage to escape from my soul. I want to be strong, be joyous – make a cake. A whisper of a smile. "Come. Let's bake that cake."

I get up and so does Alice. "I'm so sorry, Amy. God, I'm sorry." I cannot stop my tears. Tears fall from her face as well. Alice puts her arms around me and hugs me in the deepest way – love pouring out of her into me. We break from this hug. "Can we invite my Mom?"

"Of course." I remember she died ten years ago. What to say.

"Can I tell you more?"

"Of course."

In this moment of openness a very sad Alice, "She took own life. She'd been so sad for so many years - she finally couldn't take her sadness anymore."

"Oh, God. I'm so sorry." Standing in silence, I continue, "There's just too much sadness in the world." I pull her to me and we hug once again. No sense in trying to stop our tears.

"Hey, let's make that cake for our party." I get some napkins and we take care of our used tears. Making the cake brings us to the moment - a moment between two friends. This is going to be an excellent birthday party. Thanks, Alice.

The cake is done and I pull it out of the oven. It cools on the kitchen table. Alice gets another glass of wine. My beer is almost finished. Quickly draining it I get another. The cake has cooled off. "Time for the party to really begin." Holding the candles, "How old would your mom be?"

"You don't have enough candles. How about putting six candles on it." I do. About to light the candles when Alice sings and I join her. "Happy birthday to Emma, Happy birthday to Emma. Happy birthday dear Emma, happy birthday to you." I begin to sing a happy birthday to Alice's mom, but stop. "What's your mom's name?"

"Edith." Together we sing happy birthday to Alice's mom. Mood is bright. I blow out the candles all the while remembering Emma doing the very same thing those many years ago.

"What was your wish?"

"You know you're not supposed to tell." Actually I didn't make a wish, just pretended.

"I didn't know, but I got Emma a gift. Hope it's OK." She gets it out of the bag. It's a weaving kit for young girls."

I am so touched. What an incredibly thoughtful thing to do. "What a wonderful gift, thanks."

The cake and ice cream are delicious. I put the dishes in the sink. When I turn around, Alice has grabbed a piece of the cake. Oh my God, she smashes it in my face. "You can't get away with this!" I grab a piece, she turns, but I reach around and put it into her face. A cake in the face mess. We giggle and this turns into full on laughter. I fall to the floor and have a hard time catching my breath. Alice is in a chair - tears of laughter mix with the cake. She sure looks funny. Slowly I stand, take a deep breath, and sit at the table with Alice. "You're a silly mess"

"You're one to talk."

Remembering the sparkles, I get them, rip open the package, and throw them all over Alice. Before I can stop her, she grabs the sparkle package from me and I'm now covered in sparkles as well. We're a cake/sparkles mess.

"Let's go to the bathroom and look in the mirror." We start laughing again.

"Just a minute." Alice returns with her phone. "We need to record this for posterity." Taking the photo – she shows me. It's funny as can be. What a mess.

"Amy, I've got to go to work soon." She looks at the clock. "Wow, I have to be there in a few minutes."

"You better clean up. But, then again, maybe you should show up like this. It'll be a conversation starter for sure." She ignores this goes into the bathroom and cleans up.

When she's done, "Thanks so much for inviting me to the party. I think Mom really enjoyed herself."

"We enjoyed ourselves too. Best birthday party in years."

"Yes, in years." Alice leaves for work and I bathe in feelings of companionship and joy.

# AMY

What a grand time. The party was fabulous - so much fun and laughter. Maybe, just maybe I've turned a corner. I go to Emma's photo. Her beautiful face shines - warmth rises in me. Warmth of a love so deep that it'll never disappear. And, Alice, bringing the weaving kit. How did she know what a truly wonderful the gift it is. Going over, I pick it up. That's what I'll do tomorrow - make a potholder.

The setting sun, not covered by the fog bank streams light in my place. On the window, Emma is basking in the sun, strong, light, and beautiful. I do love the fog, but here in this moment I'm glad for the sun on my daughter - on my life. Profound happiness - not like the laughing at the party, but an inner glow. That's it – the glow is within me. It's my glow.

So much to consider. I know I've said this to myself a few times, but it's worth repeating. Kind of like my affirmations – the beauty of this place – the Mad River, the Arcata Marsh, and even from my porch - Humboldt Bay. The solitude I feel - then meeting two people – one a friend for sure and the other, maybe a friend - maybe beyond friendship. Holding my hands in the sauna, comforting me. I want to comfort him, but I don't know if I can. Ted's a mystery.

All those years in L.A. wanting a close connection with a man. Trying, but then just giving up. Egos can be so destructive. We need egos, but not having them be a bull in a china shop. Not exaggerated, beefed up, not so vain as to not see or care for others. I know I've just been up here for a little while, but that L.A. ego – look at me – I am pretty damn hot. Got lots of dough - great house - great car; yep, that's me. I've got it all. Maybe it's because there's less money running around here than L.A. - maybe the push for wealth pumps people up to feel they are so damn important.

Time for a walk. Sun low in the sky creates shadows as I walk down my alley with no particular destination. Some kind of action on the plaza. Police cars – red, blue lights flashing. Don't want anything to do with this. The Marsh is pulling me, but it's getting late. I'm definitely not a fan of the sun going down so early. I turn around; avoiding the plaza I make it back to my apartment. I grab a beer, sit on my bed, and turn on the radio. KHSU sometimes plays some pretty cool music at night. This is also where I get the news – NPR. Ted listens to music on his computer. I'd like to have tunes to listen to other than the radio. I'll look into this. How to get a computer, yet not get hooked on it.

Getting sleepy, I turn off my light and in this darkened silence I go over the party, Emma, Alice, her mom, and me. We were all there - all having fun. Hope Alice's night at the Phoenix is going well.

Then I remember the dream I had when I was six. Was it a dream? I call it a fever dream, but it was so much more. My family was in a cabin on a mountain lake. (Lake Arrowhead). I got an intense fever. I remember when I woke up – my mother came over and asked me if I knew how long I'd been out. I didn't know – she told me a day and a half. She handed me my brother's Red Rider comic book. I was thrilled to have it – though I couldn't really read all of the words – just some – that's how I know how old I was. When I was in this incredibly high fever I entered a gray void – fog like place. I started moving through the void going faster and faster. As I did I started to lose my body. The faster I went, the more my body was fading away – just kept getting smaller and smaller. The best part was that I was in a complete state of bliss. I did not want it to end. Then when I was nineteen I read the Tibetan Book of the Dead; it stated that before entering the next existence there's a gray void like place. This has stayed with me all of my life – a huge impact. I truly believe my body was near death with that very high fever. All these years, in a sorrow led life, why didn't I put Emma in that state of bliss. She must have traveled like I did - blessed and joyous. Comfort my dear Emma. Travel on my sweetness. I fall asleep in this sweet repose.

On this new day the sun is out – most mornings the fog bank wraps around the land connecting it to the ever-present ocean. Today the sunrays seem to reflect how I feel. Don't want to hide – want to be in the moment. This morning there's a brightness in the air. A brightness beyond the sun. A brightness inside me. I make my coffee and return to my bed. Slowly the hot liquid warms me up.

Breakfast eaten, dishes put away - Emma's weaving kit calls me. I get it and return to my bed. The instructions, even for this old English teacher, are simple. I can do this, but before I start, I set it aside, wrestle my back to the wall, close my eyes, and sit in peace. "I am a good person. I am a swimmer powerful and strong." Repeating slowly. On the in breath, "I am a good…" on the out breath, "person." On the in breath, "I am a swimmer." On the out breath, "powerful and strong." Don't know how long I'm sitting with my affirmations. Slowly I open my eyes. A glow surrounds me. Not an actual glow, but a very strong feeling of peace, kindness, and love. I want this to stay with me. It will stay with me. I will be strong. I will be accepting.

Sitting on my bed I make the potholder. It's a bright red, blue and yellow – I can smell my little one. Treasuring this time I continue to sit. I take the new potholder and bring it to Emma's photo – to Emma - hold it up. Gosh this is so her. She'd be so proud. I'm so proud. "Love you sweetheart."

Hard to describe, but there's a lightness to my soul so many years hidden away - dragging footsteps – head down. Despair was my friend and not a very good one. Bye! I just know this is going to stay with me – not leave. Even with these positive feelings I start to get down on myself. No! That cliché enters me, 'better late than never'. That's me all right. An enormous opening as large as the ocean has exploded in grandeur inside me. I have a grin for the ages. Getting up I do a little dance.

# ALICE

A lot of chaos tonight. Some asshole tried to rob Toby and Jacks. There was a standoff, but thankfully he surrendered. Usually Arcata is a safe place. But this certainly did bring a buzz to the café. Jon isn't usually around at night, but tonight he's stopped in. While he's in the office this homeless man comes up to me. "Could I work for some food?" I go ask Jon. He tells me it's too difficult to have someone do chores for food. I go back and start to go tell him no, he can't work for food, but Jon follows me out to the gentleman waiting at the cash register. Jon tells the man he can have a burger, salad, and fries. After he gets his food, Jon pulls me aside. "This is what I do. Anyone who asks to work for food, I give them some food – usually what I gave this guy. We can afford to give out some food." My admiration for Jon soars.

"I'm glad you told me this. I've been asked before and I didn't know what to say." Jon starts to walk away. "Jon." He turns to me. "You're a good person, Jon" He smiles and is soon out the door. Yes, he really is a good guy.

It's a slow night, but just a couple of minutes before closing a couple walks in. They look inebriated. This is one aspect of closing I don't like - when people come in just before closing. They take their time ordering. It's a big order. Cooking it up, I take it to them. They've apparently got all night to eat. Slow and maybe it's because I want to leave. I do what closing chores I can while they're at the table. I remember to hang the 'closed' sign on the front door. Jon tells us if we forget to put the sign up and someone walks in we are to serve them. My God, these two are going to be here all night. Then I do the dramatic - put chairs on top of the tables surrounding the couple hoping they'll take the hint. They do and they don't. Finally done, they leave. No tip – damn them.

While doing my chores, and because they're so routine, my mind drifts. The party. It really was something. The laughter, the silliness, the cake in our faces, throwing sparkles. I think Mom really enjoyed it. I think Amy likes the gift I brought for Emma. Don't know why I did it - a spur of the moment thing. Walking up the stairs, I had my doubts about the gift. If Amy hadn't come out to greet me I probably would have taken it back to my car. In my mind's eye seeing us - I haven't laughed like this in a long time – in a really long time. Amy is so nice - we seem to have a lot in common. Maybe I've got a swimming partner. She sure is a good swimmer, maybe a better swimmer than I am, and not to boast, but I'm a good swimmer. Then on the deeper side, the pain of losing her daughter. This has to be the worst possible tragedy – losing a six-year-old daughter. To see it happen and to not be able to stop it. To hold your daughter in your arms – dying. Sitting down I can't stop the tears. Poor me – Not. Anything I've experienced pales in comparison.

I'm taken out of this when someone knocks on the door. I get up and point to the closed sign – they leave. What were they thinking. Back to my chores. Finished with what I have to do, I get a glass of wine, and sit looking out at the now peaceful plaza. I don't want my sadness to overtake the joy I felt at the party. I will not let it take over. Finished with my wine I go out the back door, making sure it's locked.

# TED

As nervous as I am, I need to call Amy. It's too early to call her now – a little later. I know exactly where her phone number is – taped to the bathroom mirror. What to say. Oh well, just do it. Something will come up. I let Stub out and go with him. Very early - the sun is still in the east behind the mountain. Stub comes up to me. I know he's hungry, but I want to go on a little walk. "Come, Stub." And we go in back of the cabin. There's no trail, but it's easy walking under the giant ancient ones - so still. I bet the trail going from what is now Redwood Park up to Kneeland was used by people centuries ago. I'm in awe with this thought. There's a tree on the Maple Creek Road about a half a mile past Korbel that has a multitude of arrows in it. This site is said to have been used by Indians to commemorate an important peace treaty. In memory of the treaty, each tribe, on this trail, would shoot an arrow into the bark. How modern man makes trails – huge eight lane concrete pathways. It was way better in the old days. What have all of the modern advances actually meant for our souls? Very little. But I live here with my best friend and we can be mesmerized in a trail sort of life. Good riddance southern California and your mass pollution and distracted lives.

Sitting, Stub comes over and plops down next to me. I love how he does this, just kind of falls to the ground. I pet him. In silence, this forest world consumes me. So much to see. So much to smell. Putting my hands to the dirt under the moist leaves and needles. Bringing it up, the earth clings to me and enters me - earthen, moist - life giving. Shutting my eyes and when I open them the sun is making its presence known. Streams of light between the ancient ones - Stub and I - not ancient - sit still in the magnificence of this moment. Stub gets up, shakes, and puts his paw on my leg. "OK, Stub, let's go eat."

Glad I remembered to take care of the stove before we went out – the cabin is warm. Stub fed, my coffee made - I sit. I can call Amy now. Holding my flip phone in my hand. Funny, I've memorized her number. OK, Here goes.

"Hello."

"Hi, Amy – it's Ted."

"Hi, Ted." Silence. "How're doing?"

"OK. And you?"

"Actually I'm doing quite well."

"That's good. How about … hmm … doing something today?"

"OK. What do you want to do?"

Now what. "How about swimming."

"Sounds good. What time?"

"I don't know - around 4?"

Not much of a phone person. "OK. See you at 4."

"OK. See you then.'

"Bye."

"Bye."

Can't believe how nervous I was, but it seemed to go well.

# AMY

Walking onto the pool deck – there's Alice. She's getting out of the pool, stops, and comes over to me. "Wow. Wasn't the party a hoot?" Holding her swim cap and goggles – she shifts her feet. "I've thought a lot about it. I hope my gift for Emma was appropriate?"

"No. It's a fantastic gift. I made a potholder with it this morning. I love it. It's ..." Hunting for words, "Thanks so much."

"You're welcome. Say I've got an idea. Why don't we set up some times to go swimming together - I'd like that." Alice, smiling, "Maybe I can become as good of a swimmer as you."

"You are."

"No I'm not, but hey – I think we're both pretty good in the water."

"Yes, let's do swim together. Since I'm retired and have nothing but free time. You set the day and time."

"I'll ask Jon if I can have the same schedule every week. I'll give you a call Thursday – that's the day the schedule comes out."

"Swell."

"I've got to go." Alice looks at the clock. "I dilly dally so much that many times I have to rush. That's me. See you."

"Yes, we'll talk on Thursday." Alice walks to the woman's dressing room. What a sweet person. Sitting at the edge of the pool – kicking my legs slowly back and forth in a meditative state when Ted walks up.

"Hey, Amy." He licks his goggles and swishes them in the pool. "Ready? Race you to the other side. No, just kidding." He's smiling.

There's a lightness in the air – good feelings abound. I shove off and glide, hands in front. He's still at the edge of the pool watching me. In the gravity free water I feel clean and whole. He drops in and begins his swim.

I've slid into his lane right behind him. Reaching out I touch his toes. He stops. Smiling, "Race to you to the side!" I jump out and rapidly swim to the side. He doesn't catch me – of course I had a head start. At the end of the pool, "I beat you – knew I could." Joy is evident here in this water. We keep swimming - both of us in the same lane. I have to admit I like looking at him – so close in the water – he – gliding in a graceful rhythm. Wonder how he sees me in the water. Now he's doing that turning in the water routine. I've got to learn it – looks like so much fun. I stop and he comes over and rests as well.

"You want to come to my place? You haven't seen it."

"Yes. I'd like that. Glad I fed Stub before coming here."

"See you in a few." Both of us get out and go to the locker rooms. He's kind of a Skinny Minnie himself. But he does have broad shoulders – oh, and yes a slight paunch. Looking down - I'm free of this. Beer, maybe it's the beer, but he looks good to me.

When I'm done I walk out. He's waiting for me. Men always dress faster than women. I've walked here - know he's driven. "I don't know where you live. Did you drive?"

"No, I walked. Everything is in walking distance for me. Well, not everything, the beaches, the Mad River, but in town everything is close."

"Come with me. You can tell me how to get to your place."

We get in his VW. "This is a really old car isn't it?"

"1957." He tells me the oddities of the car – like not having a gas gauge.

"Times sure have changed. You can't buy a new car today that doesn't have GPS – no hands phones – cameras - devices to tell you if it's safe to change lanes. This technology is wasted on me. My CRV has some of these." I have to stop talking – we're getting close. "Here - stop anywhere around here." He parks his car, we get out, and go to my alley. He's looking around. Pointing, "Up there." We walk up my stairs and pause at my door. The bay is golden again in the late day sunlight.

"Wow."

"Yes, that's what I feel every time I'm on my little porch." We enter.

"What a nice place.

"Yes, but it's kind of small, but it suits me just fine. Here, look." I sit at the kitchen table and reach out and touch the stove, the refrigerator, and the kitchen sink all the while sitting at my table. "See what I mean – small. Want a beer?" I know what his answer will be.

"Yes." He's standing in the kitchen with me. Maybe he's trying to figure out where to sit. He sits at the table. I walk past him and signal him to follow. He does. I take my pillows and prop them up against the wall and we sit on my bed. Turning the beer in my hands, that first sip is always so refreshing.

"I'm going to practice that spinning you do in the water. Looks like great fun."

"It is. I first discovered it swimming on the Trinity River. Eyes open seeing the sun distorted through the water – going very fast with the flow of the river. I'm a funny guy. I remember in first grade spinning around on the playground. Got myself so dizzy, fell and hit my head. Maybe that's what's wrong with me." He smiles. All in fun.

"Where's the Trinity River?"

"It's on the Hoopa Reservation about 10 miles east of Willow Creek. Can I tell you a story about the Trinity River?"

"Of course."

He settles back and closes his eyes. "I love swimming on the Trinity River—pristine—can see to the bottom of the river - so clear. It's swift and strong, to make it up the river I swim up the eddy - too swift to swim up the middle of it - pulling myself against the powerful water flow making its way to the ocean. Slow - pulling hard. On one of these swims I felt I was being watched. This was a very strong feeling - perhaps a bear, mountain lion, or some other animal. I continued until I got to a place too shallow to swim. I rested in the grandeur that surrounded me – then I swam down river in the middle - so swift - so fast. Maybe nothing is this freeing. Spinning around and around like some kind of twister - under water looking up through the water - on my back - seeing the distorted sun. This is freedom beyond anything else I know. I got to a wide spot in the river. There were these incredible granite rocks in this little cove. I stopped, did egg beater kicks to stay above the surface of the water, and took three photos with the underwater camera I'd brought. Soon I was back where I'd left my clothes, got dressed, and went home - still feeling I was watched. When I got my photos back there was something incredible about them. In one of the photos it looked liked white cloth or white feathers. It was very dark in back of the white image I'd captured. I looked at the negatives – they were fine. I've done everything possible wrong from time to time—shooting full rolls when there was no film in the camera - crimping the negatives—putting my finger over the lens. Do it wrong - yes I have, but there was nothing wrong with these negatives. When I showed Chuckie Carpenter, a Hoopa fisherman, he was flabbergasted. He told me that many years ago, there was a bastard in the tribe named Potato Boy. Bastards weren't valued in their society, but through hard work and good morals, Potato Boy rose to prominence in the tribe. Then Chuckie told me Potato Boy's animal spirit is a white bird. My camera shot at 1/800 of a second and to this day I believe I caught the spirit of Potato Boy. So, when I felt I was being watched—I was, in fact, being watched. I'd love to show you the photo. I still have it."

"Wow! I want to see it. See this place. Swim - do spinners – see everything - experience it all."

"You can – we'll go there this summer."

I feel like I'm spinning now. My emotions are a swirl. "That'd be wonderful." Bathing in this thought, "I haven't told you, we had a birthday party here yesterday. There's still some cake and ice cream."

"You did. Who all was here?"

"Alice, her mom, Emma, and me." I see his confusion. "Really we were all here. Alice even brought a gift for Emma. Wait a second." I get up and retrieve the potholder. "Alice gave me a child's weaving kit and I made this potholder with it this morning." Still confused – maybe he thinks I've lost my mind. "Let me explain. Alice's mom would have just had her birthday. She died ten years ago and in this sadness she moved up here – to get away – just like so many of us. I invited her mom to join us. We put six candles on the cake and sang Happy Birthday to Emma and Alice's mom. We ate chocolate cake and ice cream. Then without any warning, Alice grabbed some cake on smooshed it in my face. I took a piece of cake and not so delicately put it in her face. I got the sparkles and threw them at Alice. She grabbed the bag of sparkles and got even with me. The laughter was out of control. I laughed so hard it was difficult catching my breath. Seriously Ted, it was the most fun I've had in years. You know it lifted me beyond sorrow – sorrow I've held inside for all of these years. Just a second." Getting up I get two more beers. Look at Emma shining in the window. Carefully I take Emma's photo down and bring her and the beers over to Ted.

"She's beautiful - what an infectious smile. My God." He is getting sad, I can tell.

"Ted. I feel like I've turned a corner in my life. There's a glow inside me. It was like the party opened up my heart. And yes, I know Emma and Alice's mom weren't here, but they were in our hearts, and we shared this. All four of us shared. I hope this also happened for Alice. She's such a warm spirited person. Seriously, my life has changed and I know it will stay this way. Not at all sure why all of this is happening to me. The beauty of Humboldt, making friends with Alice. Did I tell you, we're going to set dates to swim together. I am glad beyond glad I moved up here." Hesitating, should I say this? "Then there's you." I'm trying to peer into his soul.

This was a bold thing to say. But maybe this is the new me. Not really new, but changed.

His eyes show a depth. I can tell he's touched by what I've told him. He sets his beer down, moves Emma's photo, and comes close. His hands on my shoulders – he pulls me to him. Skin tingles – heart explodes as he hugs me. We stay in this hug for a long time. When we break, "Amy, you're a beautiful person with a beautiful spirit." He stops, "I can't ..." then he gently kisses me.

I want him next to me – touching me. This is the new me; I move the pillows, lie back, and motion him to lie next to me. He does. My legs wrap around him – hands caress him. Pulling him into me I kiss him. Soft – then not so soft. My skin is alive. I'm alive. "Just a second." I get up, look at him, and take off my shirt. I wonder if he can see my heart beating fast and furious. Next my sweats. He sits, eyes intent on what I'm doing. I chuckle to myself. Maybe there should be some stripper music. Not really – this feels so right. I unhook my bra and pull down my panties. "It's a tad cold." I go under the covers. He just sits on the side of the bed, not moving. "Come on – it's cold in here." He wrestles with the covers and joins me. Here I am waiting for him, wanting him, and he still has his clothes on. Guess I'm just going to have to help him. "Here." I tug at his shirt. He sits up and pulls his shirt off over his head. That's a start. Then off go his jeans. Just one bit remaining and I help with this. So, here we are. He's funny. I think he'd jumped at this chance – isn't this what men want.

Lying, skin on skin. My hands on his chest – strong. My legs open and wrap around him. Pressing against him. He responds to me – not guiding or directing me, only responding. My hand goes to his penis – he shudders – I pull away. I take his hand and put it on my breast. This is heaven.

He stops. "Amy."

Whispering, "Yes?"

He lets out a large breath. " I don't know how to say this. You're beautiful with a sacred and sweet soul. I feel like I'm in heaven. But ..." He looks away - my legs still wrapped around him.

"And?"

"I don't know how to say this, but can we just hold on to each other. Your skin is exciting – you are so beautiful, but ... maybe later I'll be able to explain. I want to sleep up against you, feel you in my sleep."

This is so strange. Don't know what to make of it. I was so ready just moments ago. I was the one starting this – wanting it. "You sure?"

"Yes. I know this is strange and maybe not even fair. To be honest I've been dreaming of this moment with you and now I'm unsure." Hesitating, "Do you want me to leave?"

"No. I do not. Come here, Ted – let's lie together." He scoots up against my back. We lie like this for the longest time. Our breathing in sync - in out, in out. Our skin merges. His hand is on my breasts – fingers around my nipple. No movement, just there. I revel in this more than is imaginable. I close my eyes. Don't know when, but we fall asleep. And so it goes for the whole night. No dreams, just the soft feeling of his skin against mine – breathing in unison.

I wake in the morning – he's still asleep. I lean up on my elbow - his face is beautiful in such sweet repose. And this is how I feel - never met a man like Ted - something very special about him. He opens his eyes – the sweetest softest eyes I've ever seen. We exchange small smiles - smiles of affection and care.

# TED

I have to leave Amy's. It's a workday and I need to let Stub out and feed him. Amy understands, offers me coffee, but I don't have time. "Got to rush if I'm going to get to work on time." After I'm dressed, "Amy, what a night. I need to thank you." Nervously, " I hope you're OK with it."

Amy pulls her shirt on. "It was good for me too." Adjusting her sweats, tying the drawstring. "Want to see me again?"

"Of course."

"When."

"Soon," looking at her clock. "Call me after work, OK? I've really got to boogy."

"OK. Hope you have a good day at work. Oh, and give Stub a pat for me."

"I will." Going up to Amy we kiss, then I draw her to me and we hug - heartfelt and strong. "Bye sweetheart."

"Bye."

Up the mountain, sun cascading its light through the tops of the trees - still too early to make it to the road – to my cabin. Amy's face is in my mind – in my heart. I flash on her in the pool, swimming – her long and graceful body. She is so beautiful – not just the outside, but her inner self that shines through her eyes. This is what I see and feel driving to my cabin. Up my small driveway – no need to back the car up. It's warm – it'll certainly start when I go back down. Stub is excited to see me ... and I'm equally as glad. His whole body squirms in delight. I'm sure he needs to go out. "OK, Stub, go on." He does, sniffing for just that right spot to do his stuff. Back and forth, nose to the ground - he finds that spot. More moving around – he pees on the old wheelbarrow. "Come." We go inside and I feed him. No time for coffee, got to get to work. Saying good-bye to Stub I begin my way to work.

Amy's been through so much. I truly hope she has turned a corner – is free from the past. Not necessarily free, but accentuating on the loveliness of her daughter. She glowed yesterday, especially telling about the party. I see her holding the potholder and smiling – joy filled. The taking of her daughter's life - inside twisting and turning, but she's brave – continuing in a positive direction despite her loss. This is not what I've done, but there's a huge difference. I'm the one who caused the pain and hurt. Forgiveness is much more than a meme posted on the Internet. I've not even searched for forgiveness – why should I. Seeing Stub just now, another wonderful expression of love. I'm able to show him my love. He doesn't have to forgive me – he just loves.

Then last night and recalling the very few times I've been with a woman – nothing special – just taking care of my physical needs. Needs? More like wants. At a party, meeting someone on a walk on the beach. Just casual on my part and I'm sure with them as well. This is so different. This is important - not just a casual encounter. The heat of her body next to mine – our skins merged in a dream world. The closeness is almost overwhelming.

With so much on my mind and in my heart I soon find myself at the gym. I'm actually a couple minutes early. The routine starts - wiping, mopping, emptying trash, polishing – just the regular routine. No broken glass as I survey the pool deck. The lifeguard stands in watch over three swimmers. In the shallow part of the pool a young mother is teaching her son to swim. He's tentative, yet she is patient. He puts his head under water and comes up beaming – his laughter is infectious. His mom glows. This is awesome. Without a prompt he does it again – so joyous.

Can't stay here forever, got to take out the trash. The sun is full on over the mountain throwing its light on the Welcome Gym when I dump the trash. Watching the sun, the thought - a brand new day. I have things to look forward to, not just doing the mundane. I stand in this thought. This is one thing I like about this job – I don't have to always hustle. Just need to get done what needs to get done, but no hurry. I'm almost invisible. That's me, The Invisible Man. I read that book. I'm a lot like that guy in the book. Not just at work, but my life in general.

Walking back inside. Amy says she's found a new path – not exactly her words, but it's what she's going through. She's open, friendly, and there's a light in her - she glows. Wonder what she thinks of me. Is there something here for me? Is it even possible for me to glow? Wait – I do glow around Stub – he's the light of my life. And I felt a peaceful contentment last night that I've never felt before. Just got to keep down the past, maybe throw it in the dumpster along with the other trash. The day rolls on and soon it's quitting time. Should I go swimming? Got my stuff from yesterday in my car. They'll be damp and cold. Not today – just go home.

Opening the door, Stub greets me. "Hi Stub." Our home routine – he goes out and I hang around the porch until he's done. My life is a matter of routine and that routine now includes Stub. My phone's ringing, pulling it out of my pocket.

"Hi," Amy with a cheerful voice.

"Hi Amy. How was your day?"

"Good. Alice called and we're going to swim together on Wednesdays, Saturdays, and Sundays." I'm jazzed about this. You go swimming today?"

"No. My stuff was still damp from yesterday. I mean I could have thrown my towel and trunks in the gym's dryer - can't go everyday and I've been good about going lately, so I skipped today. If I'd swum I would have missed your call. I have to say, maybe I should join the community pool - it's much nicer than the pool at the gym."

"That'd be cool. Do it, join the community pool."

I don't say it, but I can see her more often if I join the community pool. But it will cost. Stupid, me – I've certainly got the money now – no excuses. Come on. "OK. I'll join."

"Yippee. We can swim together – you me, and Alice."

"You sound so happy."

"I am happy. I've made two good friends – more good friends than I ever had in L.A. Isn't it amazing that so many changes can happen - even to this old woman. This has been the best decision I've ever made."

"It was a good decision for me too."

"What do you mean?"

Uh oh, what did I say. "Well, not exactly a decision, but I've met you."

"You're so sweet."

"I don't know."

"Ted, you're a good man."

Dark clouds cover me – bleak. Stop! Go away! Without thought, "No I'm not."

"Yes you are."

"You don't know me. We've just met."

"Ted, I know a good person when I meet them – you're a good and gentle person."

This is not going well. When will I learn to shut the fuck up. God-damn San Diego rising up again. Quickly throwing these thoughts away – at least for the moment. Things have been so positive – why can't I leave well enough alone. Don't want to put my disgust onto Amy - she's doing so well. I don't want to bring her down. And after all, I can be a good actor. "Thanks, Amy for the kind words." Pausing – what to say, "Sometimes I can get pretty down. Your words help. Thanks. And yesterday and last night ... just the best. Seriously, knowing you means a lot to me." Hope she believes me, at least the part that knowing her is important to me. Maybe, just maybe I can make a turn in my life, but to be realistic, forgiving myself is impossible, maybe not impossible, but I don't see it happening. They say miracles can happen, I'll see.

"You want to meet us Wednesday around 4:30 at the pool?"

"OK. That'll be nice. I get off at 4:30, but it'll only take a minute to get to the pool."

"Ted, knowing you is important to me too. Very."

"Thanks. See you Wednesday." I say good-bye and hang up.

"I've got a big problem, Stub. When everything comes out, Amy won't want to know me. She put me on the spot when she told me I'm a good person. What to do. Keep it all inside – seethe in my own hate. Amy deserves better than this. Tell and she'll hate me. Don't tell and my self-hate will destroy any chance of the relationship. Damn."

# AMY

Very interesting talk with Ted. I wish I knew what's going on with him. So loving and caring one minute - withdrawn the next. There's something he's hiding – something he doesn't want me to know. I know about hiding – I've been good at this – my forte. I'll just have to wait and see - be patient – after all, last night with him was beyond belief. I wanted him inside me – to be closer than close. I know he knew this, but it wasn't to be. But when he wrapped his arms around me all night – I was in heaven - so caring, holding me – strong in his arms.

The potholder on the bed draws me in. I want Alice to see it. I know she's at work. Gathering my things – once again deciding not to take my purse, I put my wallet in my pants. Good old men's pants with pockets big enough to put things in. Jamming the potholder in my back pocket I leave, but before leaving I smile at Emma. "Love you, my sweet girl." It's only a matter of a couple of minutes before I make the bell ring over the door of the Phoenix.

"Hey, Amy."

Holding up the potholder. "See what I made?" She beams.

"Want a coffee?"

"You bet."

She brings it to me. "Wish I could sit and chat, but I've got work chores to do. Jon tells us even if there aren't any customers there are always things that need to be done. He's right. This is a good place to work and Jon is a good man." Standing at my table. "Got a short story though. The other night a guy came in and asked to work for food. Jon says it's too much trouble giving chores to do – so he just gave the guy, a burger, fries, and a salad. He said this is what he does and to feel free to do it as well. Like I said he's a good guy. OK, got to get back to work."

When I go to pay, Amy tells me it's on the house. "No. I need to pay, don't want to get you in trouble."

"It won't be a problem."

"I know, but I want to pay." I leave a good tip. She's a working girl and needs all the money she can get. And after all I'm wealthy – not, but my retirement provides me with enough. Waving as I leave I have a date with East of Eden. The bell notes my departure. Just outside the café an young guy is walking and talking away. I once saw a guy talking very loudly to God in a phone booth. Didn't know you could call God from a phone in a phone booth, but anyway this guy has one of those phones in his ear. So, now it's hard to tell if a person is a bit crazy, or just talking on the phone walking down the street. This gets me going – why do people always have to be connected – feel lost if they're not. I often leave home without my phone. Music – that's what I need to find out about. I've seen a store on my way to the marsh that sells computers and things. Walking to it – another bell rings entering the store. I ask my question. I'm given a few choices - all very confusing. I gather this information. Maybe Ted can help with this. Thinking about the Marsh, but turn in the direction of my apartment.

Once there I get the book and drop it on the bed. Cake – there's cake left. Getting the cake I eat it at the table with Emma looking at me. "Good cake, Emma. That's what's so great about birthdays – cake and ice cream." I skip the ice cream and am ready to be taken away by Steinbeck.

# TED

I've been looking forward to this – thus the day drags on and on. Nothing unusual, just the same as everyday. Standing with my mop and bucket by the pool. Four people are swimming – the lifeguard watching them. Bet the lifeguards here have never even come close to making a rescue. 4:15. Good - almost time to go. I get everything completely ready so I can get out of here exactly at 4:30. Bam – I'm out of here.

Don't know what to expect – a little anxious. In the locker room, I take a deep breath, and walk out on the deck. Amy and Alice are by the side of the pool. Amy sees me and waves. I set my daypack down and walk over.

"Hi, Ted." Alice has a bright smile.

"Hi, Alice."

"Ready to go?" Amy asks, then licks her goggles and rinses them in the pool.

"Yup." I get me goggles ready.

Alice and Amy slide into the water and start their swim. I wait dangling my feet in the water. They return, do flip turns, and continue side by side. Both of them are so graceful, strong arm pulls, gliding through the water so effortlessly. It looks that way, but I know they're swimming hard – pushing themselves. That's what swimming's about for some of us – pushing ourselves. When they flip turn their butts come out of the water – I like this. I don't do flip turns – rather I rotate to my back just before the end of the pool and turn around. For me, flip turns take too much energy, but my turns are fairly fast and efficient. I'm still at the side of the pool. The girls - a beautiful sight. Time for me to get in the water. I do. I used to get in and right off the bat swim hard. These days I swim a few lengths fairly easy before I push myself. Swimming is solitary for me and I know it's been solitary for Amy as well. This is different. Instead of singing a song to myself – instead of random daydreaming – I've got Amy on my mind – easy to do with her only a couple of feet away - long graceful body. Guess to be honest, she's on my mind a lot. I'm taken out if this when I see Alice swimming butterfly. Gosh, she's strong – sweeping up and out of the water – powerful arms take her across the pool. When done right the butterfly is the most incredible stroke. I don't swim the butterfly. Continuing my swim and again this is a first for me – swimming with others. Stopping - Amy and Alice side by side are coming very fast to my end of the pool. They touch almost simultaneously – now standing - gasping for air.

"Wow, girls. Are you racing?"

Breathing hard, Alice answers, "Yes and no. Amy challenged me for these last two lengths. It was fun."

"I can't believe I kept up with you." Amy says, breathing hard.

Waiting for both of them to catch their breaths, "Want a sauna?"

"OK." They both say this at the same time and this brings a chuckle.

"I want to cool down a bit before getting in the sauna." And with this Amy puts her head underwater and blows bubbles. After a few minutes Amy leads the way out of the pool to the sauna.

It's dark as we enter – flash of intense heat. Someone's left a candle – it still has a small flame, but the whole candle has lost any shape and is a mound on one of the benches. I go to the upper bench and both Amy and Alice take seats on the lower bench.

"That was fun," Alice comments

"Yes it was," Amy answers.

"I really liked watching you two race towards the finish line. And,

Alice, the butterfly – you do it so well - very impressive. I think it's just too hard a stroke."

"It's what I swam in high school."

We sit in silence. I go down to their bench. Don't know what they're thinking. Looking at Alice and once again this strange feeling comes to me. In some way I feel I know her. I know I don't know her – have never met her until just recently, but there's something - just can't get a handle on what it is.

Amy wipes her brow and flicks the sweat away. Alice puts her feet up on the bench. I like the silence. So many times if there's silence I feel I have to fill the void by talking. Not now though. I'm almost in a meditative state.

I'm brought out of this when Amy suggests we go to her place and finish off the cake and ice cream. "Hey, I heard about the last time you girls had cake and ice cream – a lot of bedlam. Out of control I might add."

"I know. You missed out, Ted." A shrewd smile on Amy's face, she continues, "We'll be in control. I promise. Anyway the cake needs to be eaten. What do you say?"

"Love to," answers Alice.

"Ted?" Amy quizzically looks at me.

"I don't know." I do know – I'm just playing with them.

"You'd better." Amy, smiling ear to ear. I think she knows I'm only playing with them.

"Yeah, yeah. I'll join you. Just hope you behave." Then a thought comes to me, "You two like to race – lets race to Amy's." I know Amy has walked, maybe Alice has as well. Get a false competitive spirit going. Wonder if they'll fall for it.

"You're on big boy," Amy's smile is contagious. We're all smiles.

I get up. "Winner takes all. See you at the stairs." Leaving the sauna I hustle to the locker room. I don't look back, so I don't know about the girls. Quickly dressing, I leave, and don't see Amy or Alice. I decide to continue to play with them. I park my car a block past Amy's. I get out and hide behind a bush. They're casually walking. I see Amy looking about. They hesitate at the bottom of Amy's stairs. They're talking, but I can't hear what they're saying. I wait until they go inside. This is fun. I knock on her door. "Wow! You two are fast. Didn't think you'd get here before me. I'm impressed."

"Like heck you are." Amy slyly says. She goes to her cupboard and brings out the cake. She gets three plates – then the ice cream. The goodies on our plates. Amy looks at Alice - happy birthday, Mom."

Alice chimes in, "Happy birthday, Emma."

These two are quit a pair. Good times abound in Amy's small kitchen. I notice a look between them – then a nod – each of them grab what's left of the cake. Before I can do anything about it – cake is in my face – in my hair. The girls are uproariously laughing and I'm besides myself – these two are such brats. "That does it!" But there's no more cake to get even with. It's all over me.

"Having a good time, Ted?" A funny grin is on Amy's face. "We are, aren't we Alice."

"Yes we are." With a twinkle in her eyes, "Ted, do you have on one of those mud creams some of us use to look young and vibrant?" Emma laughs from her place on the door window. We all laugh.

Amy suggests I look at myself in the mirror in the bathroom. I do. Standing in front of the mirror, Alice juts in and takes a photo with her phone.

"Time for a beer." Amy gets us beer. "Let's sit in my massive living room, but Ted, you have to get the cake mess off – I don't want you spreading your mess on my bed." I pretend to sulk and go into the bathroom splashing water from her sink on my face. Drying off, it looks to be all gone. The chatter is light – easy going. I'm very relaxed and at ease. These two are a hoot and they feed off each other.

Alice gets her purse and brings out a small bag. "You guys want some?"

I know right away what this is. And yes, I do want some herb. Curious to how Amy will react. This is good because I won't have to broach it with her. She may be against smoking marijuana.

Amy responds, "Gosh, I haven't done this since high school. I don't know."

"I can put it away."

"No, if you want to, go ahead."

Alice packs a small pipe, takes a toke, and hands it to me. I take a hit, look at Amy, then pass it to Alice.

We do this once more when, "Hey, don't I get any?" Amy sticks out her bottom lip in a pout.

"Alice passes it to Amy. "Don't take too big of a hit – it's pretty strong - can make you cough." Amy's eyes bug out of her head, but she's able to hold it without coughing. We do this one more time. Without asking, Amy gets three more beers.

After she returns, Amy whispers in Alice's ear. Both of them point at me and laugh. Hearty gut laughs - knee slapping laughs. "What?"

"You've got ..." Amy can't continue.

Again, "What?"

"Tell him, Alice."

"You ..." Alice can't stop herself from laughing. Both of them are in hysterics. "OK. Let me catch my breath." She takes a couple of deep breaths, " You've got chocolate cake on your neck. You're such a pig. You can't even eat chocolate cake without getting it all over yourself. Don't you even know where your mouth is?" Once again, this drives them into hysterics.

"If you're going to treat me like this I'm going to go home."

"Oh poor baby boy." Alice with faux hurt feelings.

Amy adds, "Have we hurt your feelings?"

Mockingly, "Yes you have."

Things settle down. "This has been so much fun, but I need to get home. Stub's hungry and, for sure, needs to go outside."

"Alice, you've got to meet Stub. He's the greatest dog – so handsome, just like his human." Holy cow, this gets them laughing again. Tears are in Amy's eyes – tears of laughter. Laughing at my expense.

"You're laughing at me."

"Oh, Ted, of course we are," Amy answers. More hysterical laughing, this is all in good fun. I get up, so does Amy. She gives me a hug.

Alice, still on the bed, "You going to leave me out of the hugs?" She gets up and the three of us hug.

Just before I go. "Ted? Aren't you going to clean off the rest of the cake. I'd be embarrassed to go out like that." This sets them off again, howling in laughter.

"I'm not going anywhere but home." They laugh some more. Is there no end to this silliness?

"Bye girls. It's been fun." I leave them laughing. Out the door I go. What a day.

# TED

It's been a couple of days since hanging with Amy and Alice. The cake – the good fun. I think I should ... Phone rings.

"Hey, Ted. What's up?"

"Not a lot, just getting ready for work."

"Want to meet up after you're done work?"

"Yes." Trying to figure out what to say. Without thought, just blurt it out. "Want to come up for a beer?"

"Sure."

"Around 5?"

"OK. See you then. Want me to bring anything?"

"No, I've got it covered."

"Bye."

Hanging up, I check the beers. I'll have to get some more, maybe she'll stay for dinner. I'll get something for that too.

After work, shopping done, I go up Fickle Hill to see Stub, and get ready for Amy. Stub does his wonderful dog circle dance of joy when he sees me. I do a person circle dance in my heart. "We're going to have company tonight. Want to see Amy?" He doesn't answer. His mind is on taking care of his needs. I let him outside and stand in anticipation, wondering what tonight will be like. Standing on my porch when Amy drives up. Getting out, she smiles, and waves. Stub goes to her, she pats him - he wags his tail.

I'm still holding the grocery sack. "Hi, Amy. See Stub greeted you."

"Yes he did."

Entering the cabin, I put two beers in the freezer, the rest of the beer and the burger in the refrigerator. I pull out the two beers I had, open them, and bring one to Amy who's already made herself at home on the couch. "Thanks." I nod, then sit next to her. Stub comes over and plops on my feet.

"I still can't over how goofy you and Alice were. It was really fun."

"Yes it was. Alice is a hoot."

"You both are."

About to take a drink. "Wait. Let's make a toast." Looking up and a second later, "To having fun."

We click glasses. "Yes, to having fun."

We sit. My feelings are reflected on my face. I feel a small grin - sitting on the couch with Amy - Stub at my feet - in our cabin. She's grinning as well. This is very new to me and has taken me by surprise - going in a direction I know nothing about. Somehow I'm being pushed to where I've never been before - to a place I've never known existed. Maybe I should bring out my pipe, but no. Another time.

"I got some burger – want to stay for dinner?"

"Yup. That'd be nice. Do you have a cake?" She laughs.

"No, thank God." Laughing - we're both laughing.

"I'm having an awfully good time lately. I didn't really think a lot about what my life would be like in Humboldt. Just kind of got in my car and drove here. It was a super trip. I saw some fantastic things on the drive up."

"Like what?"

"Drove up Interstate 215 – it turned into a two lane highway, US 395. I saw Manzanar, Bodie, and swam in Trinity Lake - I wasn't in a hurry. At one point I was in Oregon - far from the coast – seeing the most beautiful sights. Oh, and I swam on the Smith River – what a pristine place." Looking up, she adds, "And I spent a night at Gold Bluff – wow what a place. In my whole life I'd never seen such beauty."

Taking a drink of my beer, "What's Manzanar?"

"It was an internment camp for Japanese Americans during World War II. Do you know about all of that?"

"Yes, but no details, just know we forced Japanese Americans into these camps all over the US. I've always thought it was so sad."

"Yes, it was sad. There was a museum. Racist articles about the 'Japs' not wanted. Photos of families – children in tow - getting on buses with their one allowed suitcase. They've replicated the dorms the people lived in and those damn guard towers. The people suffered in the bitterly cold winters – no insulation – away from everything that was familiar. What a shameful thing to do. And then it turns out the Army let some of the young Japanese American men join the service. Their unit, the 442 Infantry Regiment, was the most decorated unit of the war. Imagine those young men fighting so bravely for a country that hated them – that took their families from their homes, farms, and businesses – forced them to live in those damn camps. How sad. How could we have done that?" Waiting a moment, she continues, "Well, look at what we're doing now - separating kids from their parents at the border." Getting animated, "We haven't learned a goddamn thing."

"You're right. Just stay as ignorant as possible. Have you heard the controversy surrounding the statue of McKinley on the plaza? Another asshole."

"Yes, I've heard about it – they want to take it down … or something like that."

"Did you know the statue portrays McKinley reaching out to shake the hand of the assassin, just seconds before he was killed. Anyway, the city's going to put it to a vote and hopefully McKinley will soon be gone. Good riddance. Trump says to Make America Great Again. I don't think we've ever been great. On that note, you want another beer?"

"That'd be nice."

Returning with the beers, "I'm curious, what was life like for you in L.A.?"

"Well, you know about Emma - very hard for me. I didn't do much other than work – it took most of my time and energy."

"You were married, right?"

"I was." Looking up. She does this when she's thinking. "We had many good times together and when Tom asked me to marry him I immediately said yes. We were thrilled when we found out I was pregnant. My life – our lives were so wonderful. Our child was full of curiosity and, of course, her share of mischievousness. Tom was a good father. Then it happened, Emma was taken from us. Emma's death was so devastating – drove me into a deep, deep pit of despair. Our lives together rapidly went down hill. Tom wanted another child. I didn't. This caused all kinds of strife. I was terrified something would happen to this child too. I took birth control pills, but didn't tell Tom. One day he found them. He was furious and exploded at me. I know I was being untruthful in my life with Tom, but I just couldn't have another child. Tom wanted to know what else I was holding back, not being truthful about. After a couple silent days he asked if we could adopt a child. When I told him that I couldn't adopt a child he stormed out of the apartment - slamming the door. Our marriage continued to go downhill – argument after argument soon replaced by hours and days of silence. It's like his heart packed up and left. To this day I don't blame him – my love had gone into deep hiding – so deep I didn't think I could ever love again. He divorced me. Bitterness circulated around him when the decree came through. I've never seen or heard from him again. That's the short of it." She takes a deep breath and lets it out. "And you. You've mentioned San Diego. What did you do there?"

Damn. I shouldn't have asked her about L.A., now she wants to know about me. I've got to say something. "I was born at Mercy Hospital. Family legend has it that Dad got lost in the fog on the way to the hospital, but I guess I came out all right. Just did regular things, went to school, swam on the swim team, and played water polo. Had crushes on some girls – had a few friends – mostly guys on the water polo and swim teams. After high school I enrolled at San Diego State. I wasn't that interested in school though, but liked being a lifeguard until…" Fuck.

"What?"

"I don't know … nothing really." Amy sees through this and looks at me in a kind way

Fuck it. She's laid herself bare. Maybe I can tell her this, but I've got to be very careful – can't say too much, but here goes, "I was a lifeguard at the Silver Strand State Beach. Everything changed one summer evening. One of the chores before we shut down was to drive the jeep to the south boundary. There were no guard towers - just the beach and sand dunes. This was the first time I had done this. I was very pleased. I drove the jeep down the unguarded part of the beach. Heading south I was going fast – what a rush – faster and faster along the hard sand of the beach at the water's edge. Then abruptly the jeep went into a big hole in the beach that had been covered with water. I didn't see it - just thought it was the hard sand covered by a sheen of water. The jeep slowed, made it out of the hole, then stalled. I shouldn't have been driving so fast - what a fuck up." I radioed I was stalled. I waited – another jeep with the head lifeguard came. Looking at the engine - water had gotten into the distributor— that's why it stalled, he was furious because he knew I had to have been driving fast for water to get into the distributor. He was back at the beach because a man had drowned and where was I - driving too fast - getting stuck. My boss was disgusted with me - this was clear. I was also disgusted with myself—more than disgusted - I was devastated and shamed. How could I have fucked up so badly. I rode back with him up the beach to the main tower.

I'd never felt lower, the knowledge that I'd been responsible for a man's death - such a fucking shit. An irresponsible asshole and someone was dead. Hated myself. The next day I was called into the office by the head ranger and was told I no longer had a job, but if I agreed to quit there wouldn't be anything in my personnel file about the drowning. I really didn't care what the ranger told me, I knew I couldn't work there anymore, even if they would let me. A man had died. Later I was told the man had a heart attack and would have died anyway, but this didn't make me feel any better; I fucked up and that's all there was to it. I got into my VW and drove home. Not only was I responsible for a man's death, I had let the other lifeguards down - how could I face them? I stayed in my place for a week - not going out – not seeing anyone. This feeling of total failure has hung on me for years - still does."

"Oh, Ted." Sadness in her eyes. "So long ago. You feel guilty – I can understand." She moves about a bit – settling in. "You've been pretty hard on yourself. How old were you?"

"Nineteen."

"You were so young. Is there any chance you can let this go – I mean really let it go?" She waits for an answer I don't give. Slowly, she continues, "I also have a lot of guilt." She puts down her beer and closes her eyes. "All those years ago - the day Emma was taken from us. Why was she in the street without me. I should have been holding her hand when she crossed the street, but I wasn't. all those years ago and it seems like yesterday. We all fuck up; just some of us get away with it. I didn't. Not to be mean, but it was my daughter, not someone I never met. My daughter."

I move close to her and put my hand on her shoulder that's moving in a sad dance of sorrow. My God, what she's been through. Her face is so sad: a lone tear falls down my cheek. I hold her in my arms as Amy cries on my couch - in my cabin - under the ancient ones. What the hell happened to the joy we had only moments ago? Gone. She takes quick rapid breaths trying to stop the tears. Her breath slows down. Her head in her hands, very softly. "I love you, Emma." A little louder, "I love you Emma." Holding her head up, "You were and are the sweetest gift anyone could ever ask for. We shared our lives together – we had so much joy." Then in a strong and steady voice. "You are in my heart. You are strong. And

I'm going to be strong for you. Sad, yes, but I'm going to bathe in your presence, because you're always with me – always my sweet girl." No more tears. I see her strength. My sadness pales in comparison.

Turning to me. "Thanks for listening. You're a kind and sweet man." I don't argue this time. My emotions are out in the open. I told her about the death and she didn't tell me what a shit I am. I've never told anyone about it – been so ashamed. Then she shared her deepest pain with me. I want to help her be strong – want to hold her and be a comfort in her life. I will try my best, but the full truth about me is horrible and I don't think I can ever share it with her. I've carried this with me for 50 years. Impossible for me to change what I've held inside all of this time. But somehow there seems to be a shift. Thank you Amy.

There's still beer in our bottles. "Let's have another toast?" Amy says. Lifting our beers. "To good friends who listen and care." We repeat the toast and click our bottles. She snuggles up against me. After dinner I ask her if she wants to spend the night. She says yes. We crawl in bed and tonight we have the power of intimacy. In the morning she wakes me up, rolling on top of me. I'm in heaven.

# AMY

Back at my place I'm almost floating. Such a powerful night with Ted. I move the curtains on my window. I'm reminded about where I've been. It was like I put heavy blinds over my windows. I needed to keep out the light. I quit my job and just lived day to day – mostly crying my way through them. Eventually I got another job, but the only way I survived was to stuff and shove everything way down – hoping it'd stay there.

How odd, all of these years I felt like I'd led a fairly good life, but what is a good life. Certainly not defined by how much money a person makes – by how much power a person has. I told myself many times I was doing a good job – teaching my students about literature – helping them realize the importance of reading and writing. Knew I helped some with problems that seemed so dire to them - that were dire. The angst of youth: so many had no one to turn to and sometimes I was that person. Yes, I did help those high school kids and I knew they appreciated it: I could tell. Once in a while I'd meet an adult who had been one of my students. I could see the appreciation in their expressions when talking to me. One time comes to mind. I was in line at a grocery store when this young woman came up to me. She had the look of recognition in her eyes. She told me her name. Oh my, she was one of the sisters who, as girls, were living in that cheap motel – really run down. The girls' mother was heavily involved in methamphetamine. She dropped them off at the motel – no money for food. The older sister came to me after class one day and told me about her and her sister's situation. I called welfare, but they wouldn't do anything without involving the mother. I didn't know what to do. I decided to call the Salvation Army and bless their hearts they took food to the girls. After that we spent hours talking after school and became friends – a friendship between and adult and a teenager. This young woman wanted to thank me. She did and we hugged.

But still, a huge slice of my life was missing. I was so oblivious I didn't even know my pain was still deep in me – just so busy. Once in a while Emma would surface and I'd run and hide. No one was to know. But mostly my life became a matter of routine. Keep out the remembrance of that day. The remembrance of how the most precious person in my life was taken away. How it destroyed our marriage. No, it didn't destroy our marriage – I destroyed our marriage because I couldn't climb out of the misery that enveloped me. Maybe that's why I didn't have any close friends. Liked them all right, but that was as far as it went. I wonder if others saw my reticence - perceived the sadness that hung deep within me. If I were asked, which I wasn't, I'd say my heart was what my heart was. No one has a life without pain.

At Wildberries my pain went on a rampage – screamed its way into my life. I handled it with anger. Then yesterday it surfaced again, not in anger, but in a profound sadness. I've never told anyone about the guilt I have for Emma's death – no one. Even Tom didn't know and now I've told Ted. He didn't try to fix anything, just listened in care, put his arms around me, and held tight. Thankfully I didn't cover it with anger this time.

Ted suffers too, I can tell and when he told me about that man's death at the beach - how it was his fault; I saw his sadness and guilt. He's dragged this around all of his life. I have a strong feeling I'm the first person he's ever told. I don't know what it is, but I think he's holding even more inside - keeping everyone away. We're similar in this way, but I've truly broken free, and he hasn't. Maybe I can help him, but I do know one thing, he's helped me. Just being there for me is so different. Not just this, but the first night I spent with him – not wanting to make love, but he was so sweet to hold me all night. I think most men wouldn't have done this. I hope I can listen to Ted – be there for him.

Forgiveness seems to be a key. I've forgiven myself about Emma – for the ending of my marriage. I don't think Ted has forgiven himself about the man's death. Forgiveness seems to be a buzzword these days. "You have to forgive." It seems like a mandate and if you can't forgive you're a loser. Everything is black or white. People forget the nuances, the trickiness involved in life on this planet. I just know I feel blessed to have my love for Emma out in the open – no more hiding.

I certainly don't believe everything takes place for a reason - that God looks down directing us, or that some angel intervenes in our lives, but I have to think meeting Ted is almost a miracle – a miracle of the heart, because my heart is so open now. He isn't the reason for this, but somehow he is wrapped around me – a big part of these changes. I've never felt like this. Emma wasn't wrapped around me – she was me and I was her. But when she left, it all disappeared. Emma is out in the open now – her love and warmth surround me in the most caring way. I'm not stuffing her away anymore. I accept the love I have for her – the love she has for me.

I've opened up the curtains.

# AMY

Been swimming almost everyday. Still haven't gone to the schools to volunteer – there's still time for this. Holy cow, I feel there are still things to do, to accomplish in this life. I really didn't think what being retired would be like – just took off and here I am - changes abruptly cascading down on me. A large wave, not letting it crash against me, the chaos of the water – spinning - tumbling, not knowing which way to the surface; instead diving under the wave - tranquil below the chaos. Swimming under it, peaceful and calm. Popping up on the other side - seeing the massive wave pounding against the shore. That's my life now. I dove under my hurt – I'm on the other side.

Seeing Alice on a regular basis at the pool. She showed me interval workouts, swimming as hard as we can across the pool, once across we wait for one minute, then we swim as hard as we can back to the other side. We repeat this over twenty times. I'm completely exhausted at the end of each length we swim. Trying to catch my breath, but still in that exhausted state I do another - then another. The heart is our engine and I want my heart to be strong. Funny how I want my heart to be strong, both physically and emotionally. So great having a friend like Alice. I often visit Alice at her work in the early afternoon, the slow time at the café.

Ted and I spend a lot of time together. As kind and sweet and as he is, he's still a mystery – sometimes fading off into another world and when he comes out of this he's sad – I can see it in his eyes. When I ask, he says it's nothing, but that's not true – it is something. I'm feeling so good – so light that I don't let this get me too down. In time – gosh here I go again thinking of the future ... just have to be patient - he gives me so much. It's easy to see he deeply cares for me and I care for him in a grand way.

On this early evening I ask if we can smoke some pot. He agrees, gets his sack, puts some weed in his pipe, and we smoke. We listen to music, Stub cuddles up next to me. Drifting in the wave of the sounds – beautiful – deeper than I'd ever heard before. No talking, just holding hands on the couch. Ted gets a couple of beers. The taste - the carbonation cleans my mouth – tingles. Everything is highlighted. His cabin's so inviting. It's a comfort being here. Out the window - the trees like guardians. "Ted, lets go outside." We do and take a few steps away from his cabin under an almost full moon showing between the trees. Maybe two hundred years ago under an almost full moon maybe, just maybe, two people in deep repose stood at this very spot. Ted taps my shoulder and points to an owl sitting on a branch. In this still moment we watch until the bird silently flies off. "That's the second owl I've seen up here. This is a special place. You're lucky to live here." He nods and under these tall giants with who knows what other animals are watching us - we kiss. The depth of my feelings for Ted astounds me.

Back in the cabin we hold on to each other. Turning to Ted, "Sweetheart. I think I'm in heaven."

Leading me to his bed. "Where's Stub?" Stub had gone out when we did. Ted opens the door. Stub is standing, waiting, and quickly comes in. Taking off my clothes, I see Ted watching. I climb under the covers and watch as he takes off his clothes - a pretty handsome fellow. Getting comfortable, Stub settles on the couch. Dreams wait - our bodies free from clothing - free from anything but ourselves, we embrace, and hold on.

Yes, this is Heaven.

# TED

**A** shift is occurring – I can feel it. When I told Amy about the drowning I didn't know what to expect. Disgust – condemnation. Sure she'd lose all respect for me. But this is small compared to ... No, don't want to even think about it – damn it's never going to leave me. I've been wrapped in an inescapable realization at what I did, disgust, self-hate, and this has kept out anything to do with happiness, fulfillment – there is no room. Amy, and don't forget Stub, have opened my heart, but the battle continues. I want so badly to be free of my past. To do this is risky. Don't completely know why – maybe I'm so used to these feelings that I'd be lost without them – wouldn't recognize myself. But my times with Amy show me joy can be a part of my life. This is what's so different now. Though I haven't told Amy why I fled San Diego, maybe I don't have to. Maybe I can I live with these dual feelings – love and comfort crisscrossed with disgust and hate. Maybe the longer I have joy in my heart the smaller those other feelings will become – eventually fading away. To be sure, she was supportive about the drowning, but what my maddened hateful self did is beyond forgiving. I'm not up to the risk by telling Amy.

Stub and I take a walk. I take off my hoodie – tie it around my waist - it's really starting to warm up. The long, dark, wet-wet winter is starting to take its leave. I'm glad. Walking further a trillium splashes its whiteness. I stop; get down on my hands and knees to get a better look. The contrast is amazing. What do other people see? On the Interstates, cars, corporate signs and corporate businesses. Driving endless hours - only getting off to get gas or food - the need to get to their destination is of the upmost importance - the destination, not the journey. Then there's two lane highways going through rural America. Stop lights, stop signs, not going 80 mph. Old faded cafes, gas stations, and a handful of new businesses. Can see houses, farms, kids riding bikes, yard sales. The destination takes a back seat to the journey. Riding a bike – so much more can be seen – the pavement sometimes broken, rusty barbed wire fences, horses, cows, dogs barking. Watching out for the approaching dog. Sweating going up steep grades. The speed going down the grades - wind whipping the face. Birds calling out, or, "Johnny, you get home this instant!" Then there's walking like Stub and I are doing now. I'm able to stop, get down, and look at the miracle that is the Trillium. Just past the Trillium lies an old broken fence halfway hidden by blackberries - no longer separating anything.

Gosh, I remember seeing on the Internet that a man swims the Hudson River in his daily commute to work. I wonder if he swims home from work considering the flow of the river will be against him. Maybe he takes a bus or subway home. But what a super thing – his commute is a swim. Damn smart guy.

I'm glad I'm walking my way through life now - lucky to have the companionship of Stub. He loves me so much and I love him with all of my heart. Extremely fortunate to know and cherish Amy. I think she's fond of me. She is so sweet. Don't know if I can put the word love on it, just blessed. There I go again, afraid to admit or recognize what we have as love. The risk seems overwhelming. I'm such a coward. When have I really risked anything. When I was comfortable and proud of being a lifeguard I screwed up in the worst way a lifeguard can. A man drowned on my watch and when I leapt into love where did that get me?

Still on the ground, I've stopped looking at the Trillium. Wiping my pants of leaves and tree needles I get up. Stub's been waiting for this. We continue on our stroll – stopping – looking about - seeing the differences – some minute – so easy to overlook – too not pay attention to.

A deer! Stub starts off after it. "No, Stub. No!" he stops, looks at me, and returns to my side – not in shame, but with pride. Stub has a lot of pride. "That's a good boy, Stub. We don't chase deer." I pat him. He wags his tail. Our walk continues. Two ravens talk to each other in the branches high above. Wonder what they're saying - a remarkable animal – so intelligent. Many traditional stories about ravens. 'Till the dirges of his Hope that melancholy burden bore...Quothe the Raven, Nevermore.' This is all I remember of Edgar Allen Poe's poem, *The Raven*. Need to re-read it – it's been years.

All this on our walk. I've got a lot to ponder. Is it possible to make a get away from my self hate and disgust? Amy is helping me with this and she doesn't even know it. As Stub and I walk back to our cabin, "Yes, Stub – you're helping me too - love you, Stub." His eyes and nose intent on our travels. My guide.

# ALICE

So glad to know Amy. I really love having a swim partner. Swimming intervals is incredibly hard and Amy stays with it. Think I'll visit her. Leisurely walking past the plaza to her place – such a cool apartment – up above with a great view. Ted's car is parked close by. What a beater - an antique on wheels. Maybe I should let them be, but I haven't seen her in a few days. I'll just stop by; if I'm intruding I can just leave. Just hope they're not having an intimate moment – haha. No, seriously that would be embarrassing. Quietly I climb the stairs. They're talking. I knock. Opening the door, Amy grins. I say hi to Emma – then to Ted.

"What's up?"

"Nothing much – just hanging out. Ted brought this incredible photo." Amy shows me the photo.

"What is it?"

"Ted, why don't you tell."

I'm holding the photo. I don't know what to make of it. Some white robe or something. Ted tells the story of this photo and how it relates to Potato Boy. "Ted, this is very special. You were very fortunate."

"I know."

"Say, Amy, why don't you show me the carvings?"

"Good idea."

The three of us walk through town towards the Marsh. On South G Street Amy leads us to the trail to the Marsh. We leave the trail behind and walk through tall grass. A breeze blows across me - tilt my head back - smell - nostrils wide open. Ocean air fills my lungs - fills my heart. Then right there in front of me is the redwood log - blue/gray faces - expressive – can see their angst. I get on my knees and rub their faces. Closing my eyes I continue to feel the spirits in the faces on this log carved long ago. Amy and Ted watch. No one speaks and in the quiet of the moment we get up and continue our way to the ponds. This is very touching – the people put into this log – forever and ever.

Stopping, we sit on a bench overlooking the bay. The sun's directly overhead and its brightness accentuates our world. Momentarily the sun is covered by a cloud – instantly colder, but this passes and again we again sit in the sun's light. Ted turns, looks behind us, and points, "You see that rise over there?" We turn. "That's Mount Trashmore."

"Mount Trashmore?" Amy queries.

"When I first moved here the city dump was here – right on the shore of the bay – old refrigerators, stoves, cars, and general trash – oil seeping into the bay. When the City of Arcata decided to make the marsh, that mound is what's left of the old dump."

"For real?" I ask.

"Yes, for real. This marsh is more than it appears. Each pond further purifies the water from the city's sewer system. After the last pond it enters the bay. This has been a boom to salmon, oysters and the general health of the bay."

"Are you the town historian?" I ask.

"No, but living here for fifty years I've learned a few things. But in my fifty years I hadn't seen the woodcarving. It took Amy's eagle eyes and curiosity to find it. Now we all know."

An egret delicately lands in the shallows; slow and steadily walks until she finds a place to stand patiently and perfectly still waiting for that moment to catch her meal. Three pelicans fly over us out to the bay. It's high tide and the pelicans fly, looking down - then wings folded back – dive - streamlined they enter the water while thrusting their large beaks after a fish. How differently egrets and pelicans hunt for food. What a wonderful spot, what a wonderful day. So glad to be here with Amy and Ted.

Ted's a nice guy and I know Amy's smitten with him. Maybe someone is waiting around the corner for me. Jon? Never know - just know Amy's fortunate.

"Alice, this is where Ted got Stub. This place has so much to be thankful for."

Sitting on the bench with my two friends – looking out at the natural wonders that surround us - that fly overhead - that swim out of our sight. The Marsh is a place that takes the unclean and makes it clean and in doing so has become a sanctuary for birds, foxes, fish, and for people as well. Quiet, no talking - the sounds sometimes distant, sometimes near.

Then noisy gulls fly by. Probably the most talkative of the birds out here. Yak, yak, yak - they pass – their talking soon fades into the distance.

I get up, stretch, and look at Amy and Ted. "Want to go?" We move from this moment. "In the ten years I've lived here, I've only been to the Marsh three or four times. I've somehow missed how special it is. Thanks Amy for today."

"You're welcome." Then she adds, "There certainly isn't anything like this in L.A. The three of us are escapees from crowded out of control Southern California." She hesitates, then continues, "It doesn't seem that this is even California."

"You two know about the state of Jefferson?" Ted asks.

"I don't, do you Amy?"

"No."

"The northern counties of California contacted the southern counties of Oregon. People up here were serious about this. They felt the populace part of California was short shifting them, the rural northern counties. The southern counties of Oregon felt the same about the populace north of their state. They wanted to form the state of Jefferson. They even set up roadblocks on US 99 in Siskiyou County and were charging a toll. However, it was bad timing because a few days after they took action to form their own state, the Japanese attacked Pearl Harbor."

"Ted, the historian. I had no clue." I throw in.

"Even today we call it the Redwood Curtain. One more factoid. In 1970 Redding had around 16,000 people. There are now 92,000. Eureka's population in 1970 was 24,000 – it's now around 27,000. The reason why Redding grew so fast is that it's on Interstate 5 and Eureka is on old US 101. The flow of commerce is now heavily on the Interstates and communities not in this rush of commerce are slowly dying."

"Gosh, Ted – you know a lot of stuff," Amy asserts.

"It's just when you get to be as old as I am and pay attention to what's going on around you, some knowledge creeps in."

"Creeps in? Watch out Ted - creepy knowledge creeping in. Be careful, creepy knowledge – it's very scary." Amy laughs – I laugh. "Look out, Ted! There's some creepy knowledge to your right."

Ted turns and ducks his head. "Has it gone by?"

"I think so," Amy adds.

"Good that was close." Putting his hand through his hair, "Here you go again rousting me."

"It's so easy, Ted," Amy puts in.

"Yeah when it's two against one." And in the joviality of the moment we walk back to town.

# ALICE

**W**hat I thought about yesterday circulates in me. I need to see Amy. I've got a lot to talk about – to figure out. I call her and we agree to meet on the plaza. Once again fog is master – covering – masking me as I make my way to the plaza. Not there long when Amy comes over. "Hey, Alice. What's up?"

"I want to go over some things with you. I had quite a time yesterday. You want to go somewhere to talk?"

"Sure."

"How about the Marsh?" She agrees and we begin our walk. She's well prepared for this fog dressed day. As we walk along I want to talk, but hold back - we can talk at the Marsh. Gosh, I'm going to the Marsh a lot – guess I'm making up for all those years I rarely went. I'm leading the way to the carvings. "This was my first stop yesterday. I got down on my knees. I feel these spirits are in turmoil, and as with today, they seem to be floating in the fog. I kissed them."

I'm glad Amy's here – I need her. "One thing I like about the fog is it makes me almost invisible. Just go along my way unnoticed. This is how the fog affects me, but maybe things are changing. I'm glad to not be invisible to you. Yes, I like the fog, but I don't want to be invisible anymore. I want to be seen – maybe that's why I'm so sad for the figures carved in the log – invisible. Continuing on my way, a pelican flew over me - saw an egret patiently waiting to catch her food. Then noisy seagulls flew overhead yakking all the while - such talkative birds. I couldn't see where the pelican was flying. Then I realized I don't know where I'm going.

Fifty years old and still working in a café. Long ago, I somehow captured Mom's sadness, and I've carried it with me all these years. Never accomplishing anything – not making a mark or a difference. What happened to you and Emma makes my troubles seem so small, you persevered, and made a difference. I admire you for this. Anyway, this is what I thought about yesterday. I also did something out of the ordinary for me, I vowed to ask your help." I take a deep breath and release it. "I also remembered you telling me about your affirmations. I decided to look for an affirmation for myself. And in doing this I realized that two times on my walk I'd said negative things about myself. Negative affirmations. Negative self-talk. When I was able to see the pelican I felt he was free – soaring, gliding in air currents – few boundaries. That's when I came up with this – 'I am a free spirit.'" I take a deep breath.

"Wow. You had quite a day. I'm glad I've helped you. I think we've been helping each other. You bring out laughs I didn't know I had. I've laughed and giggled with you. You've helped me too. And swimming – the interval workouts – having a friend who wants to swim with me." Amy fiddles with her scarf. "I think you've come up with a positive plan. I know the affirmations are good for me. Every morning I acknowledge my worth. I, like you, have been hiding for many years. I just hid after Emma's death. Quit my teaching job and sat while my marriage dissolved. My hiding broke our marriage. It took a couple of years before I was able to go back to work. And when I did, I never fully opened up to anyone and that's how I was. Moving here I've had three blessings - you, the incredibly beautiful environment, and Ted. Let's make a deal that we'll be open, share our thoughts and dreams, and always care for each other." Smiling, she continues, "In fact, when we open up that's when magic can happen – the magic of love and care."

"Deal." Hesitating, "I didn't know I've helped you. This makes me feel good – like I've accomplished something. Thanks." Getting up I hold out my arms. Amy stands and we hug in a fog-covered anonymity. I can do this – break from my past – live in the moment – 'I am a free spirit.' I tell Amy I've got to go to work soon. We hug once more. I go to the Phoenix Café and Amy ambles up the street.

# TED

Spring has sprung - summer is on the brink. Picking up my seldom-used phone. "Amy, want to go to the Trinity River this weekend?"

"Yes. That'd be great.

"Can you invite Alice?"

"Sure. Let's hang up - I'll call her."

She does and a minute later the phone rings. Boy that was fast. "She'd love to go. You going to bring Stub?"

"I'd like to."

"I want Alice to meet him. This is going to be fun."

It's two days before Sunday and I pay close attention to the weather. I want it to be a good day – sunshine and warmth. The weather up here is so changeable – never know when the clouds will come. Generally speaking it doesn't rain in the summer, but it's early summer so it can be cold and cloudy. Things just rattle along. Work on Friday is ho hum. $10,000 – I haven't been thinking about this at all. I should start to make plans to either spend it or save it for a rainy day. This is so unlike me – get money – spend money – that's been my way. There's nothing I really want. Just keep it and see - kind of a safety net.

Sunday morning, the girls will be here in a couple of hours. What's it like out. A low fog has inched its way all the way up here. This is a good sign. To get to the Trinity River we'll drive up Lord-Ellis Summit 2,200 feet – then down to maybe 500 feet, then back up to Berry Summit 2,800 feet, then down again to the beautiful Hoopa Valley. These mountains keep the fog at bay. High clouds can make their way over the mountains, the fog can't. Almost all the weather here comes from the west – the ocean. A summer day on the coast in the 70's is universally rejoiced. In the summer just over Kneeland Mountain it's often in the 80s. That's what I'm hoping for.

Feed Stub, eat and wait for the girls to get here. The clock on the wall goes around very slowly – want this day to get moving. Finally, Amy's car pulls into the driveway. They get out – both smiling. "Ready?" Amy calls out.

"Yes, we are. I have to say I made a mistake. I should have driven to town, because to get to the Trinity River we have to over 299. That means driving back down to town. Duh."

"No worries. I'll drive. Not too sure your beater will make it." Amy laughs. "Have you checked your gas gauge?"

"You're funny Amy." Turning to Alice, "My old VW wasn't made with a gas gauge. Amy knows this – she's just giving me a hard time. Good thing I'm around to be a foil for Amy's humor ... and yours too, Alice." I gather my things and the three of us along with Stub tootle down to begin our little adventure on the Trinity River. Once past Blue Lake we rapidly rise up. Bright and dare I say hopeful - out of the blanket of fog – covering - hiding. The contrast is breath taking. I tell them about high clouds and how they affect the weather on the Trinity River - today we're fortunate.

Driving into Willow Creek I ask the girls if they want anything, because there won't be any more stores. They're good. "Amy, you check your gas gauge?" Giggles erupt. Steep hillsides - trees grace each side of the road. "We'll be on the Hoopa Reservation soon. This is their ancestral homeland. Tish Tang was a US forest campground. When gold was discovered here, the federal government took this small strip of land away from the Hoopa – greedy bastards wanted the gold. A few years ago the Hoopa got this land back. God bless America."

"Amy, turn here." We enter the Tish Tang campground. I ask Amy to stop at a turn on the small road. "Park here."

Getting out, we walk down a small trail that takes us to the Trinity River. This is the first spot the river is visible. We stop. Both Amy and Alice look out. Their eyes show their excitement. Quickly down to the water – then we walk up the river until we get to a place where part of the river breaks from the main flow. This section is only a few feet across and not deep like the main river. I cross this small section - the girls follow. After we cross there's a few big rocks. I go up and sit on one of the rocks. Behind this rock is a sweet sandy spot - somewhat hidden. We are the only ones here now, but still it's nice to be out of view. "Let's set up here." Alice throws down a blanket and Amy sets a small basket on it.

They bring out their swimsuits. Looking at me, I turn away while they change. Done with this, they tell me I can turn around. I do, then I start to pull my pants down. The girls don't know my trunks are under my pants. They turn. "Hey girls, no need to turn away – I'm sure you've seen this before – don't be so shy."

Amy turns – looking at her I slowly pull my pants down. She nudges Alice when she sees I've got my trunks under my pants. "Ted!" Oh boy, I got them this time. "Ted, you're playing with us?"

"I hope to tell you, but I'm not even close to getting even with you two. Ha" Amy's goggles fall out of her daypack. "Glad you brought your goggles."

"The water is so clear we won't need them." Amy says.

"I like to wear them because sometimes small bits of grit get in my eyes, but yes, isn't the clarity something. Ready to go?" We go down the river's edge. Stub sits. He's a good boy, and no matter how hard I try he doesn't want to go in. He finally steps in, very carefully, but not too far. "Guess Stub isn't going to go in. Stub, stay."

Pointing to the far side of the river, "We'll go there. The river is too strong to swim directly up it. I swim up the eddy. Even in the eddy it's not an easy swim." Swimming against the flow – steady arm pulls I make it to a rock and wait. It's only a matter of a minute before the girls reach me.

"My God, this is fantastic beyond belief. Never in my wildest dreams could I have ever believed such a place exists." Amy's enchanted – we all are. We continue until we come to a riffle and the water is too shallow to swim any further. We may have swum a quarter of a mile. Amy swims over to me and puts her hand on my waste and whispers, "Thanks, Ted." I'm so pleased.

Amy and Alice look so bright – looking around this wonderful place. "One time swimming here a turkey vulture followed me the whole way. Probably thinking this is unusual, maybe it's going to die, but I'm still here." Amy is holding on to a tree branch and Alice is eggbeater kicking in the water. Soaking in the beauty we stay at this spot. No one talks; the feeling of this place has taken over – no need of words. Finally, "OK, want to go back?"

"Ted can you show us how you spin in the water?"

"OK." Swimming with the flow of the river I turn over and over. The magic of the river is my friend. Stopping, Amy takes off, spinning – then Alice is spinning as well.

When they get to me – their whole demeanor is joyous. "Wow! That was something – something I could never have imagined." Alice's expression is soft, smooth, and joyous. "Ted, is this where you took the photo?"

"Just up ahead. We'll be there in a minute or so."

Amy continues swimming – Alice follows. I have to get going so I can show them the place. I surface dive and swim under them. Turning on my back I can see them - they look down at me. This is so precious. Can't swim on my back under water for very long - I surface next to them and stop. They stop. We're here. I don't have to say anything – they know. I swim over to the big rock on the left and put my hand to it and whisper a blessing of gratitude. "Thank you Potato Boy. Thank you river." The magic of this spot envelops us. We stay for a while bathing in this magic. No words, just soaking it in. Reentering the flow of the river we're soon back where we entered the water. Stub is waiting. Back at the blanket, still no words. Silently - thank you Amy, thank you Alice.

"This may be the best day I've had since..." Amy tears up.

Alice understands what Amy is trying to say. "Me too, Amy."

Amy wipes at her tears, then adds, "Special beyond special."

They brought cheese, crackers, wine for Alice, and a couple of beers for Amy and myself. We bask in the sun, Amy and Alice on the blanket, me on the sand. Stub looks at us. I get some cheese and a couple of crackers, get up, and walk a few feet away. I give Stub the food. When I get back, Alice asks, "Why'd you walk away to feed Stub?"

"I don't feed him from the table or from here for that matter. I don't want him to beg."

Stub is, of course, done eating – dogs eat so fast. Alice calls him over. He plops beside her. She pets him. He wags his tail. "See, I told you what a good dog Stub is," Amy says to Alice.

"Yes he is."

"Can he show off for you?" I don't wait for an answer. I walk a few yards away from the blanket. "Stub, come here." He does. "Stub, sit." I walk away, turn, "Stay." I continue until I'm out of his view. "OK." He comes running to me putting his paws on my stomach. "Good boy, Stub." Amy calls him – he goes to her wagging his tail.

The sun - fully overhead - I'm getting sleepy. I lie down on the sand next to the blanket, Amy saddles up against me. Alice lies next to Amy and Stub is next to Alice. Before sleep comes, Amy takes my hand in hers. Breathing slows down - I enter the sleep world. No idea how long I slept and when I wake up, Amy, Alice, and Stub are sound asleep. One soft white cloud floats over us. Amy slightly moves and whispers to me, "Ted, this is so wonderful." I lean over to her - a kiss on her soft lips reflecting her soft soul. Stub gets up and shakes - this wakes Alice. Drifting slowly out of our sleep, we lie still, looking up, and all around us in this special place, with special people.

It's getting late in the afternoon - time we go. We gather our things and head back to the car. Before going up the small trail to the car I go to the river, kneel, cup some water in my hands, drink, and say a silent blessing. Amy and Alice are there beside me, also giving thanks. Hardly a word is spoken on the drive back to Arcata. Amy drops Alice off at the plaza and takes Stub and me home. "I'd like to stay up here with you."

"I'd like that too."

# ALICE

Amy and Ted are having a great time together. How do relationships manifest – come to a positive and supportive place. Someone once said that a strong loving relationship is stronger than the two separate people. It went like this, two people in a solid relationship add up to more than two. Their energy feeds off each other and it adds up to three. Is that what's going on with them? In the little time I've known Amy, she's very open and there's a lightness in her step. I suppose my step is lighter as well, but not as light as hers. Having her as a friend is opening me as well. Amy listens and is there for me. Maybe it's in the telling. Never really had close friends – mostly acquaintances. I like Ted. He jokes around and is friendly, but there's a dissonance in him. Maybe it's just being a man, he doesn't show and reveal as much as a woman. I know this is stereotypical, but nonetheless it's there.

The phone rings.

"Hi Alice. What's up?"

"Nothing in particular."

"Say, wasn't it something at the Trinity River? What a place. Nothing like that in L.A."

"Yes, you can say that. Listen, can I come over?"

"Sure. I'll have coffee for you."

I bundle up – even though it was warm on the Trinity – it's still cold on the coast - especially this morning. Looking out my window the fog is present – has its hold on the earth. I walk briskly to Amy's. She has the door open for me when I reach the top of her stairs. I step inside, turn, look at Emma, and smile. "We're so lucky to live here, it's such a special place." Hesitating, I recall San Diego. "There's some pretty cool places in San Diego like the Sunset Cliffs, but nothing to compare with the Trinity River. Have you been to the Mad River? It's damn awesome as well."

"Yes. I went up there in the early fall – the water was cold, but I went in. So clear, like the Trinity. I love being in water. Makes me feel clean and dare I say – pure and alive. And then Ted took me to the Mad River at the Maple Creek Bridge this winter."

"I love it. It's one of my favorite places."

Amy continues, "Standing on the bridge in the midst of the river swollen bank to bank by the massive rain. The river was fast and furious. Can I tell you something off beat?"

"Sure,"

"While standing on the Maple Creek bridge, the river rushing helter-skelter – or so it seemed. Anyway, standing on the bridge with Ted I had this powerful feeling that when I looked down river from the bridge, the water rushing away from me - I felt it was like the sex act - the male exploding out. When I turned and looked up river, the water rushed powerfully at me – felt like a female accepting the explosive sperm of the man. It's funny because I felt I was both of these. I've never thought what it's like for a man having sex. Funny, standing next to Ted I had these feelings. I sure didn't say anything to him about my thoughts. We're close now; maybe I'll tell him what I was feeling."

"Very interesting. I've never thought about what sex is like for a man either. Of course I wouldn't have any knowledge about this – being with a man I mean." I try to keep a smile from my face.

"Yeah, right, Alice – no experience at all." We both laugh.

This is why I like Amy – she brings out the laughter and fun in me. I'm very curious to know more about their relationship, but I also don't want to intrude. Just let her tell me when she wants – not ask her.

"How are you doing with your affirmation?" Amy asks.

"I say it every morning. And sometimes during the day I'll say it to myself. I'm trying so hard to avoid thinking negative things about myself."

"Alice, maybe we only have so much room for thoughts and feelings. Negative thoughts can be so powerful and ever-present. By saying and thinking positive things maybe we can crowd out the negative. Anyway that's what I think." Amy continues, "Do you think people's inner feelings can somehow be perceived by others even if not on the conscious level?"

"Gosh, Amy – very interesting about how much room we have for our thoughts and feelings. Can people's feelings be conveyed, unspoken, to another person? Good question. I think so, but I don't really know."

"I've been thinking, maybe Ted picked up on my thoughts while we were standing on the bridge looking at the wild river. I've never met a man like Ted - kind, caring, and an awfully good listener, but there's something that's holding on to him – don't know what it is. Sometimes he drifts off and looks sad."

"Not to be glib, but we all have our sadness – can't always be happy."

"I know that, but I'm getting to know him pretty well. People, for sure, have sadness I'd just like it if he could tell me his. You and I have shared our deepest sorrows – cried – hugged – this felt so nurturing and whole. Sadness kept forever inside can fester and destroy. It could be he doesn't trust me enough. Or maybe I'm assuming more than there is. I tell myself to be patient – try to live in the moment as much as possible."

"I certainly don't know Ted as well as you, but I too feel something's in Ted he can't let out." Picking up my daypack. "Want to go for a swim?"

"You betcha." Amy gathers her things for the pool. We step out the door and Amy does a quick reversal. "Need more clothes – it's cold out." Pausing at Emma, "By sweetheart – off I go."

So sweet, Emma and Amy. I know I could never be as positive as Amy. No! 'I am a free spirit. I am a free spirit,' I say to myself walking down Amy's stairs. Got to catch all of these negative moments – throw them out. I think about Amy's affirmation, 'I am a swimmer powerful and strong'. I am too. Past Wildberries walking, "Say, Amy. Can I steal your, 'I am a swimmer, powerful and strong' affirmation? In fact can I steal, "I am a good person as well?"

"Of course. You are a powerful and strong swimmer ... and you are a good person."

Entering the water, "Lets not swim intervals. It's probably good to take a break from them once in a while." Amy is OK with this. When swimming I say my affirmations. They make sense – ' I am a free spirit. I am a swimmer powerful and strong. I am a good person.' These affirmations are helping. Yay!

Long, graceful, she swims along side of me. Amy is fifteen years older than me and she's such a good swimmer. I hope when I'm sixty-five I'll be in as good of shape as she is. Her body is svelte. I'm heavier than she is, but I like how I am. Comparing bodies – it's not really important. I just want to always be in shape – healthy – that's what matters to me.

We finish our swim and go out to the sauna through the thick fog. The sauna is so hot - love the contrast. Amy hums a tune. Her eyes closed – a look of contentment basks on her face. She stops. "That was nice, Amy."

"Thanks. It's the song Ted hummed in a whisper when he danced with me – so sweet.

"He what?"

"He whisper hummed this song and we danced – soft and slow."

"Wow. That must have been something."

"It was."

Amy is so lucky. Ted is a good man. But her happiness makes me feel kind of left out and sad – 'I am a free spirit. 'I am a swimmer powerful and strong. I am a good person'. Yes, I can feel alive and be in good spirits. Yes, I can do this.

# ALICE

This morning I bundle up in my bed covers, sit back, close my eyes, take a couple of deep breaths, and say, "I am a free spirit. I am a swimmer, powerful and strong. I am a good person." I'm breathing like Amy does – slow and steady. I don't know how long I say my affirmations, but when I finish, I open my eyes to this new day with a life that's changing. They're working – the affirmations. Want to listen to Stephen Marley. I get up and put iTunes on. Scroll down to Stephen Marley. His songs are so sensitive - of loneliness, love, and redemption. Just love his music.

*Inna Di Red,* "*My shoulders were as heavy as lead... So I took a walk inside. Doctor I I say – free our from this frame of mind.*" Taking a walk inside – guess that's what I'm doing. *Now I know,* "*...nothing's permanent in life – all except for change.*" I wonder if Amy knows Stephen Marley? If not, I'll share with her. I've fought against change most of my life and here it is jumping out at me. So afraid that I'd make the wrong decision – I sat on my ass – telling myself, at least I wasn't failing. Wrong! I was failing from the lack of trying – of taking risks. I'm ready now. The winds have changed – they're at my back pushing me forward. Of course it helps that I have a strong friend in Amy.

Maybe I should look for another job, I like working at the Phoenix, but maybe get a job that's more important. Amy has mentioned that she'd like to be a tutor. She wants to volunteer. I can't necessarily do that - I need money. Wonder if they'd hire a high school dropout to tutor. Probably not. I'll ask Amy what she thinks.

I know this guy who washes windows. He's brilliant and when I asked him why he washed windows for a living he told me since it was a mindless job he could think, plan, and dream while working. We are not measured by what we do for a living. I mean who does this measuring anyway. It has to be matters of the heart that are important. When people strive to be rich and powerful what portion of their hearts do they let go in order to attain their goals? I can get by with what I'm doing. And what I'm doing is working at the Phoenix Café. Jon comes to mind. He's such a good man. I know he's not married and I've never seen him with anyone – or heard him talk about a relationship. Hmmm. This opening of the heart is like an adventure - an adventure I want to share. This brings me to Amy; I've never felt this strongly about someone. We're like sisters – sisters of the heart - we share so much.

"Mom, I love you from the deepest part of my heart, but I'm going to toss out the sadness that wrapped itself around me – suffocated my soul – suffocated your soul. I'm sending you love, hope, and joy. Wherever you are I have faith that you have love, hope, and joy." Can't stop my tears. "I love you so much, Mom. I know you tried your best and that you loved me. I'm going to carry this love, not the sadness. Yes – the love we had and have for each other." Taking breaths, wiping my tears. "I just know you enjoyed the birthday party. I'm changing, Mom. Through a crack – small - these changes have entered me. I smile a lot now, Mom. I have friends and most importantly I have hope. I'm grateful. Got to get ready for work, Mom. Love you." After coffee and breakfast, I shower, and go out my door for another workday. Wonder if Jon will be there this morning.

After work - at the pool - Amy's in the water waiting for me. So much to tell her, but now it's time to swim. These interval workouts are exhausting. I feel the power they are giving me – or better said the power I'm giving myself.

Finally done with the torture, Amy turns to me after she catches her breath, "You know, I've never pushed myself this hard – ever."

"When I was in high school this is what we did, but I haven't done them since then – so, in a sense, these are new to me as well. We're two awesome old ladies."

"I wouldn't say that. You're 'older' I'm the one who's old." We chuckle.

# TED

Abrightness surrounds me these days. I grab it – want to bathe in it. In this lightness it seems my life is changing. It seems possible to feel valued. Amy definitely cares and I'm surprising myself how much I care for her. Can't teach an old dog new tricks isn't so. I am learning. I am changing - for the better. The $10,000 comes to mind. Maybe Amy and I can go somewhere – maybe Hawai'i. That would be so cool. Maybe this can happen, but looking out my window at my old beater – it's not going to last forever. I've got time to consider my options, besides I need to take into consideration my love for Stub – can't just leave him.

The battle inside me – and the winner is ... understanding and compassion – can't say the war is over, but compassion and care seem to be winning. Seriously it's not about winning – it's about having a meaningful life. Not the same old drag I've been doing all these years. A new energy in my steps – in my thoughts – in my heart. I can do this – having joy overcome the shamefulness of my past. Am I my past? In a way, yes, but I want how I am today to overcome the past – overcome my deep self-hate. The scales have not tipped one way or another, but I do feel the difference. Amy's face and her long graceful body circulates in my mind – in my heart. I'm keeping these new feelings, jump on, and go with the flow, like swimming down the river – at one. How odd so much has changed. I didn't even see the change until it became so large I couldn't ignore it. I've always been good at denying. Can't do that anymore – don't want to.

"Stub, you want to go outside?" He does and I let him out. Stub, you were the first opening of the door to my heart. How can I not love you.

Making coffee I turn on the radio. From the deep past *Mind Gardens* by the Byrds is on. I stop with the coffee and listen.

> *"Once upon a time*
> *there was a garden ...*
> *and there the sun came*
> *and the rain pouring down,*
> *the garden grew*
> *and flourished*
> *and splattered bits of*
> *of color on the ground.*
> *It took shape*
> *and symmetry*
> *and all of life abound*
>
> *But there came winds*
> *driven and a howling*
> *there came snow*
> *and I feared for the garden,*
> *so I built a wall,*
> *and I built another*
> *and roofed it over...*
> *And kept it from the strings*
> *of outrageous fortune.*
> *The killing wind could not get in,*
> *but when the sun came*
> *and the gentle rain of spring*
> *they could not reach the garden*
> *behind those walls.*
> *It would have died*
> *safely*
> *securely*

*died.*
*But as I walked*
*and as I learned*
*I tore the walls all down.*
*The garden*
*still lives.*

*-David Crosby – The Byrds-*

I'm stunned. I listened to the Byrds a lot in my twenties – just about my favorite group. Now it's back to me - the same melody - the same words that were a part of me, but forgotten until now. How serendipitous to hear this after so many years – so many years of hating myself. And 'the garden still lives'. Yes it does. At seventy years old it still lives. I've tried my best to protect myself from my own actions. I massively screwed up and have been paying the price for fifty years. It's about time I tore the walls down.

# AMY

**T**aking my phone out – want to call Alice. "Alice do you ever play games?"

"Of course. You talking life games? I've been doing that most of my life."

"Alice. Is this a negative thought?"

"Oh my goodness, it is. Damn. Thanks for calling me on it. I'm learning, but my old ways definitely creep in."

"I want to play Scrabble - haven't played it in years. Never that good at it, but I did enjoy. Anyway I picked up it up at the Salvation Army Store."

"Sure I'll play."

"I'm going to ask Ted. Let me get back to you." We confirm the days she's free and I call Ted. He's up to it, I call Alice back, and we set a date. The day arrives. I set my mattress on its side up against the wall, and arrange the pillows. Alice arrives with her bottle of wine. Soon, Ted knocks on the door. He's brought beer. I made chocolate pudding.

Sitting on the floor, Ted and I with our Cerveza Pacificos. Alice with her red wine. Alice brings out her stash. "I don't know, if I smoke, no way will I be able to concentrate enough to win." Beaming in the glow of friendship I mockingly continue. "I want to win and that is exactly what I'm planning to do – win."

"So, you're going to win. This high school dropout won't let that happen."

Ted watches us banter back and forth. "Amy, if you don't want to smoke that's OK."

Alice stuffs her small pipe and takes a hit. So does Ted and back to Alice.

"Hey, what about me?"

"I thought so," Alice throws in. With a couple of drinks and hits from Alice's pipe, we start to play. Not too far into the game - Ted makes a play – there's a dispute about the validity of his word. And guess what. I don't have a dictionary. How strange for an English teacher to not have a dictionary, but hey, I'm retired. We decide, that is Alice and I decide, that the other two players will determine if it's a real word or not. We make our decision against Ted. He pouts and says it isn't fair – that we are always going to discriminate against him.

"Oh, Ted – you're so funny. Isn't he Alice?" She agrees and we continue to play. We're down to only a couple of tiles and the scores are very close. Ted puts a word on the triple score. He's sure he's won, but Alice and I tell him 'zoology' isn't a word.

Ted loses it, "Not a word? You know it's a word. I protest!"

"Too bad, Ted – rules are rules," Alice says with a big grin.

Ted's a good sport and laughs along with us, but adds, "I'm going to have a dictionary the next time we play."

The evening is loose and free. We're chatting – mostly sharing about swimming. Alice tells us this story. "Our high school swim team had some really excellent swimmers and some who were just average. I didn't want to be an average swimmer. The decision was easy - I wanted to be one of the good swimmers - not just filling a space on the team. My senior year I went to a local swim club's pool in the evenings. And there I found myself five nights a week trying to keep up with the elite swimmers - took all I had – exhausted - keeping up - well almost. I was getting faster, but of course, so were the others. When I got home after these workouts, I would re-heat my dinner. I was so beat that I'd take a bite - then fall back on the couch. And this is what I did that whole year. The final swim meet of my senior year was going to determine who would be league champions. We were swimming against Hoover High - our rival. Not only was this meet going to decide the championship, it came down to the last race - a relay race. Amy, in relay races the fastest swimmer usually swims last - the anchor position. I was the third fastest swimmer on the relay team. Coach put me in the anchor position. I kept quiet - nerves on edge - wanting the league championship so bad. Our third swimmer came in a half a body length ahead of the Hoover swimmer. I knew I was going against Hoover's fastest swimmer. Off I went - pushing hard from the starting block – stretching - entering the water. Out the corner of my eye I saw the other swimmer. Pulling, trying to get the most air I could - heart pounding - just keep it up - keep swimming as fast as I can. On the last length of the race I was barely ahead of the Hoover swimmer. Then he pulled even with me. Reaching inside I pushed hard - harder than I ever had before – go – go - go - we have to win. Every inch of me pulled as hard as I could through the water. He pulled ahead of me. Harder – faster - heart breaking all boundaries – reaching – pulling – reaching – pulling - the fastest I had ever swum. I was even with him with only a few yards to go. Everything on the line - don't let him beat us - can't let him beat us. When I saw my hand touch the edge of the pool just a fraction of a second ahead of him I was delirious with joy – I'd done it. We won the league championship. After things calmed down I went up to Coach Lockwood. "Coach - why'd you put me in the anchor position - you know I'm not the fastest or even second fastest swimmer?" Coach answered, "I knew you wouldn't let them beat us."

"Wow, Alice – that's a great story."

"Yes a wonderful story," Ted asks, "So, your team was mixed?"

"Yes it was."

I really don't have swim stories – just in love with swimming - that's my story. The radio is playing, but no oldies to dance to and we sit on Amy's floor - sounds filling her small apartment.

# TED

**T**hings mellow out on the floor in Amy's wonderful little place.

"So, Ted, you're from San Diego."

"I am. That's where you're from, right?"

"Yes. When did you leave?"

"1969"

"That's the year I was born."

"Really. I was nineteen."

Amy gets up and brings me a beer. She asks Alice if she wants another wine. She does. "Alice, do you have a photo of your mom?"

"Actually I have an old one of us at the beach. Mom liked to hang at the beach and go swimming. Maybe I got my love of swimming from Mom."

There's a very loud screech and bang. "Wow, what's that?" We jump up – well jump as fast as we can and go to Amy's door. Out and down the stairs – there's been an accident on H Street. A large dual wheel Dodge truck has slammed into a small Honda – the Honda's pretty crushed on the passenger's side – glass and bits of its body are strewn about. Good thing there wasn't a passenger. The woman driver is pretty pissed off - the driver of the truck is very apologetic. Just glad no one was hurt – we go back upstairs.

Now we're on to car stories. I tell them this. "When I moved to Humboldt I'd been driving since the morning and was tired, but I had many more miles to go. Anyway, on the Golden Gate Bridge my car stalled and glided to a stop. Shit, a Highway Patrolman was right behind me. He got

out and asked what's the problem. I told him I thought I could get it running and asked him for a couple of minutes. When I said this I peered at
his vehicle. He didn't have a regular bumper – no, it was some kind a met-
al bar. I imagined if I couldn't get my car started that the railing on the
Golden Gate Bridge would swing out and he'd shove my old VW off the
bridge into the water below. Not really, just a funny thought. He looked
at his watch, 'OK. You've got two minutes.' I knew what was wrong. I
had a stuck float valve in my carburetor. I took out a large screwdriver
and banged away at the carburetor hoping this would work. This harsh
Highway Patrolman stood watching me. Nervously climbing back behind
the steering wheel, the car started up, and I was on my way."

"That's a funny story, Ted. Your car is definitely an antique."
Amy smiles.

"Oh, yes. The photo." Alice gets up to retrieve the photo. She returns
with her small purse and pulls it out.

Fuck – this cannot be! Fuck me! No! No! No! What to do? Standing
up – shock fills every pore of me. Words come out fast. "I've got to go."
Rushing out of Amy's apartment - down the stairs to my car. "Fuck me!"
Hands shaking, I put the key in the ignition, and start my way up the hill.
"This cannot be! Every good thing that's happened lately is all for nothing
– no damn good at all. I'm changing. Right. It's all over now. Amy thinks
she cares about me, but she doesn't know the real me. And Alice will hate
me for sure. I deserve their hate; I'm a fucking asshole. The real me has
blasted its way back into my life. Up the hill – I should just drive this off
the steep embankment – don't deserve any better.

Just like in San Diego when I thought I found love, then in an instant
it was ripped away, and was replaced with a violent madness. How fucking
sad, just when I'm feeling like I can have a life with care and affection it's,
once again, torn away. It's all my fault though – no one to blame other
than me - fucking asshole.

I don't drive off the edge and when I arrive home, Stub's waiting –

happy to see me. I'm so damn angry at myself I don't show any love to Stub – the always faithful loving dog. I quickly throw down beer after beer after beer. Got to cloud up – got to somehow get away. Looking around, I don't have a lot of stuff. I could pack up and leave. The room is spinning; no way can I drive anywhere tonight. Almost passing out, fortunately I make it to my bed. In this haze, I notice Stub. He's just looking at me. He's very confused. My anger at myself must be scaring him. With what's left of my goodness, I pet him, and invite him up to our bed. "Fuck me! Fuck me! Fuck me! You fucking piece of shit." So, it's all come back with a vengeance. I deserve this. I hurt so bad – need to hurt more. I slap my face hard, do it again. "I'm sorry. I'm so sorry." A flood of tears – feels like I'm drowning. Picturing Edith, "I'm so sorry, Edith. Your hate for me is real. It should be real – I'm a fucking piece of shit!" My tears turn to uncontrolled sobbing. I enter a dark deep place – no light – just a deep vast emptiness. A confused Stub, concern in his eyes – licks me. In between sobs, "Thanks, Stub." I hug him and keep him close.

# ALICE

Sitting in a state of confusion. "What was that all about?"

"Don't know, Alice. Gosh he just jumped up and left. It was like he saw a ghost."

"He saw a photo of Mom."

"You think that was it?"

"Don't know, just very strange. Maybe the photo reminded him of San Diego. I've had this vague feeling there's something he doesn't want anyone to know – that's hidden away from everyone."

"I have too. I'm worried, Ted didn't seem like himself, or at least what I perceive as himself. I hope he's all right. Our fun evening has twisted into something that's not understandable. I wish we could have ended on the good times we were having. Want another wine? I could use a beer."

"Yes, I could use a glass." She returns with my wine and a beer for herself. Not a lot to say and in this silence I drink my wine – slowly moving the glass around in my hands.

The phone rings. Amy jumps up to answer it.

"Ted?"

"No - wrong number. I'd like to call him, but maybe not. What would I say?"

"I think I'll be going. Got an early day tomorrow at the Phoenix." Amy walks me to her door. We hug. I look at Emma and tell her goodnight. On my way home I wonder what just happened. Ted moved from San Diego the year of my birth. He sees a photo of Mom and me and flips out. At least that's what appeared to happen - could be something else, but what. I'm really unsettled. Feelings circle around – not able to catch and understand any of them. The fog hides me on my walk home – this is good – I don't want anyone to see me. The balance I've been feeling is gone – replaced by not knowing – even afraid to know.

At my place it's lonely. I needed to get away and now I'm here. Who's here to comfort me? I need comforting – someone to tell me everything's going to be all right. There's no one. A dog. I should get a dog – a faithful and loving friend. Ted's dog Stub – he's a good pooch. Ted – don't even want to think about him. Something awful is going to happen and I don't want to be dragged into it. I'm going to put Ted away – at least for now. The feeling I had that Ted was somehow familiar – maybe it's true. He left San Diego in 1969– I was born in 1969. On my counter, a bottle of wine calls to me. Start to get a glass, but decide not to. I turn on Pandora. Undress and jump in bed. The music is comforting on this very uncomfortable night.

# TED

A realization I am alone – that I do not want to see Amy again and, for sure, Alice. And why would they ever want to see me. I wouldn't if I were them. Alice will hate me with all the power she has. I didn't say anything other than 'I've got to go.' Maybe they don't know. Who am I kidding. I'm sure if they don't know now – they'll figure it out. What then. How can I stay here – seeing Alice around town, her knowing what I did – hating me. I couldn't stand that. And Amy – she'll hate me too. I deserve this hate. I need to make plans to leave. Good I haven't spent that $10,000. I call work – say I'm sick and I am, both physically and in my heart. Fuck my heart. Stub stands staring at me. I feed him and let him out. He knows me better than anyone and sees my pain. I bring up a false smile and pet him. I'm sure he sees through this. I get back in bed, but before I do I turn off my phone – no need to talk with anyone. I'm gone, my soulless self lies in bed for hours. Don't even want to get up to pee and when I do I let Stub out. I usually go outside with him – not today. I feel bad for Stub – stuck here with this asshole.

I just stay in bed except to let Stub out. A hurricane of confusion slams me – just getting out of bed is difficult, let alone planning a life move. Phone still turned off - wonder if Amy has tried to call me. She shouldn't – she should throw me aside, I'm not worth her concern.

This continues through the weekend, on Monday I turn on my phone, and call in sick again. Quickly I turn it off without looking for messages. I can't eat. Stub's out of his food. I'm going to have to get him some. As fucked as I am I care for my loyal dog - got to feed him. Gosh, he doesn't care at all what I did those years ago. He just loves me now – no questions. I tried to live in the present – to be joyous and I thought I was succeeding – I was succeeding, but not now.

# TED

It's Tuesday. I'm going to work – still haven't turned my phone on. I drag at work, no curiosity about the swimmers – keep my mouth shut – got nothing to say. Kathy asks me if I'm all right. Guess I need to be a better actor. I tell her I've just got a lot on my mind. She seems to accept this. So, I just flop around all day doing what is needed for me to do. I wonder if I should even give them notice when I leave, because I am definitely getting away – have to.

Guilt wraps its ugly self around me. Can I really just leave and not say anything to Amy? And what can I possibly say to Alice – nothing. A huge part of me says, 'fuck it – just go.' But I also feel I should at least say good-bye to Amy. She's meant so much to me. I'm too goddamn ashamed to even want to see Alice.

So I trudge along with these disturbing thoughts. The only comforting thought I have is to leave and this isn't very comforting because when I leave – this all will come with me. Just when I was thinking I could do more than survive – that I could actually experience joy and way out on a limb – love. I had hopes for this – now it's dashed like large storm waves smashing against the rocks. I need to be like the rocks – blasted by super powerful waves – yet still there – ready for the next wave. Yeah, that's good for the rocks, but I'm not strong enough for these pounding feelings that are overwhelming me.

Maybe driving far away, or moving to Hawai'i isn't enough. Maybe I should get away from this fucking planet all together. No one would miss me – after Amy finds out the truth about me she won't care. The clock on the wall says 4:25 – good almost out of here. So, I've got a choice – flee or completely leave the whole fucking planet. Taken out of this, "Ted, you have a visitor," is announced over the intercom. "Fuck."

# ALICE

So nervous. When I stopped by Amy's I told her I wanted to see Ted - to find out why he was so shocked at seeing Mom. I asked her what I should do. She encouraged me. And now here I am waiting for him at the Welcome Gym. My heart's beating hard - hands are shaking. Memories of Mom envelop me. I need to turn - to run, but I stand my ground.

When he sees me – he's startled. He stops - looks at me - then down to the floor. We stay like this. It feels like the whole world is watching, but I notice in the periphery we're alone. How long will this stand off continue? I clear my throat, "Ted?" He looks up from the floor. He doesn't say anything. "Ted, can we talk?" Still no answer from him. "Please. Just step outside for a minute. Please." Well, if he won't talk – there's nothing I can do.

In a very soft voice, barely audible, "OK." I walk toward him, then past him, and wait outside. He comes out. "Let's go over to the soccer fields – we can be alone there." We walk across the road, past the Highway Patrol headquarters, and are soon standing on the green field.

"Ted, I need to ask you a few questions." No response from him. "What happened the other night after Scrabble?" Still no movement from him. "Was it the photo of my mom?" He isn't moving, just standing, hands down to his side. He's barely looking at me. "Please, I need to know. Was it the photo?"

In a whisper, "Yes."

"So, you knew my mom."

"Yes."

"I need to know. Mom's been dead for ten years. If you're a key to my past it's important for me to know."

He takes a deep breath, "Yes, I knew your mom. I was in love with her."

"What!"

"I was in love with her." Hesitating, he takes another deep breath, "I ..."

"Don't stop. Tell me."

In almost a whisper, "I raped her. I've carried this with me all of my life. Felt shame and regret."

"You raped her?"

His feet shuffle, "Yes."

"You fucking piece of shit! Goddamn you! I hate you! Oh you poor boy – you felt shame. You fucking destroyed Mom's life. She never got over it – carried it with her. She couldn't deal with it any more, so when she turned fifty-eight she no longer suffered - she killed herself. You poor thing – felt so bad. Fuck you. You destroyed her life. All those years of depression and deep, deep sadness. You're responsible you fucking prick! I'm glad you suffered, but you could never have suffered enough to erase what you did. I am the result of what you did! Do you see me?!" He's looking down. "Look at me asshole!" He's still not looking at me. I scream, "Look at me!"

He looks at me, "I'm so sorry."

I don't wait a second. "You're sorry? Oh, that makes it OK?"

"No, it doesn't."

"You bet it doesn't – then why in the hell did you say you're sorry – fucking scum!" He turns. "Wait! I'm not done. After what you did to Mom, you need to hear me out. So, you left San Diego after you raped Mom. Probably thought the police would be after you. Mom never told anyone. I didn't even know how I came to be. Mom never talked about my 'father'. When I'd ask, she'd just shrug it off - just said it was a mistake. So, that was my father – an unknown identity – a mistake. What was tragic, was Mom's extreme sadness. She could never keep a job – too many days in bed under the spell you cast. Hear me? The spell you cast over her made a life with love impossible. Then because of you, I carried around the same sadness Mom had. So, you didn't just fuck up Mom – you fucked me over as well." Anger building about to explode. "Want to rape me too asshole? Just fucking try! I'm glad you came over here so you can know up close how much I hate you! Will always hate you! Why don't you just fucking die - just die! No one wants you to live – you pathetic creature. Did it make you feel like a man raping my mom? Felt proud I bet. 'I showed her.'" Moving close, I take all the power I have, reach back, and slap this bastard as hard as I can. He staggers to one knee. "Go to hell, prick!" I turn, rapidly walking away ... I need to see Amy.

Up her stairs I knock on her door. I'm a mess, tears and I'm sure – a wild look to me. Her eyes large and concerned. "Alice? Come in."

"I saw Ted." Tears rush out of me – can't stop them. I'm crying so hard. "He .. he .. he raped Mom."

"Oh God." She leads me to her bed. We sit, our bodies snuggle up against each other. Amy gets up and brings a box of Kleenex, then sits by me again. Nothing feels good now, but Amy does give me some comfort. She doesn't say anything – we just sit, me crying and constantly wiping tears.

After some time of this, "Amy, Ted is my father." There's shock on Amy's face. "Mom never told me she was raped – and when I'd ask she just said her pregnancy was a mistake. But it wasn't a mistake – he raped her. I was born from a rape. After all these years I now know why she was so sad all of her life – how she was never able to get beyond it. And I've carried this hidden horror in me as well. And now I know – it's no longer hidden. I'm just spinning around – my feet aren't even on the ground."

Amy gets up on her knees - arms held out – drawing me to her. I fold into them; she holds me and I'm released - there are no more tears in me. Amy caresses my temples. Her softness and care are needed and I am in so much need.

"Alice – I want you to spend the night here," Amy says holding me in her strength. In all of my life I've never felt more loved – never needed it more.

"OK. I'd like to."

"I'm going to make dinner."

"I'm not hungry."

"You sure?"

"Yes, I'm sure."

"I've still got the chocolate pudding."

"You do?"

"Yes. I even have heavy whipping cream. Let's call that our dinner."

A weak smile sneaks up on my face. Thank God for Amy. "Yes a dinner of chocolate pudding."

After our dinner, Amy asks if I want to take a bath. I do. Her old claw foot bathtub welcomes me. I sit in this tub – feeling relieved – for this moment. Amy's put on the radio and some beautiful music flows in and around me. It's a relief to have some peace. Thought earlier that all peacefulness in me had run away – left me in a swirling ugly world of hate.

After my soak, I dry off, and get back into my clothes. When I emerge from the bathroom, Amy has a glass of wine for me and a beer for herself. We migrate to the bed, listen to music, and have our drinks. I'm sleepy. Amy pulls the mattress out a little from the wall, fluffs up the pillows, and we lie down – I want a peaceful sleep. "Thanks, Amy. I don't know what I would do without you." She smiles, we hug. A plain white muslin curtain frames her window – outside – stars. I close my eyes.

# AMY

Unfortunately Alice has an early shift at the café. Before she goes she says goodbye to Emma and me. Sadness accompanies her down the stairs. I feel so bad for her. What a miserable turn in her life. I fuss about, not knowing what I want to do. I'm trying my best to keep my new feelings intact – don't want to lose them. After hours of this I decide to see Alice – I'm worried about her. The bell rings over the door at the Phoenix Café as I walk in. Alice sees me and gives a small smile. "You get off at 4?"

"Yes."

"Can you come over after?"

"OK."

"See you then." Walking out the door I decide to go up to Redwood Park - a lot to think about. This has really shaken me and I can't imagine how much it's shaken Alice – probably beyond my knowing. I love Alice so much and I feel her hurt in me. Soon at the park, the grass field with the children's playground. Two mothers are with their three children - look to be between 4 and 7. Squealing in delight on the slide – the mothers tell them to be careful. They aren't – too much fun. I sit and watch. Joy is in the air, but not for me. Off to one side a couple is throwing a Frisbee. I go into the forest. I'm reminded of that day I fled Wildberries and came up here and how, on my walk up Fickle Hill, I came to Ted's cabin. It was a tumultuous day. And since then I've turned a corner. I'm grateful for all of the changes in my life. More whole than I've ever been.

My friend is suffering and I don't know what to do. Wondering her whole life who her father was. Now she knows and it's not comforting, in fact it's devastating. She's in a world of hurt. And Ted is ripped apart by his past. Not in a million years would I have guessed he could have done such an awful thing – beyond awful. Again, this was a long time ago. Is the Ted I know the same Ted who raped Alice's mom? Reaching down inside myself for answers. I see his face when I told him about Emma. I have to believe he's not the same person. I hope I haven't been fooled. I want to help, but don't know if I can. I want my friends to be whole. How is Alice going to deal with this – so much pain. On the trail – wrapped in these thoughts I come to a large redwood stump – maybe fifteen feet in diameter and ten feet high. Growing out of this redwood stump a new tree is growing and it's not a redwood. From the dead redwood, new life has taken hold. Out of the past we can have new lives. This has happened to me and I want it to happen for Alice and Ted - out of the past a new way of looking at things – a new way of being. With this thought, it's time to go home.

A knock on my door. I let Alice in. She says hi to Emma and we sit on the bed. "How are you doing?"

"Crazy – can't seem to wrap myself around the fact that Ted raped my mom – that I'm his daughter. People are supposed to feel joy when they connect with their long gone fathers, but how can I. Not only is there no joy – hate has taken over. I hate him so much. Just tootling along - all's copacetic. It's not! I think I was better off not knowing all of this. I was starting to enjoy myself – feel good – forgive myself for all the wasted years I spent in kind of a lock down. God damn it I don't want these feelings. This is so warped." She breaks down in tears.

Alice snuggles up to me - I try to comfort her. "You know, Alice, I too was, and hopefully still am, holding on to the lightness I feel. This is hard for me too, but I do know this is incredibly more difficult for you. I can't even imagine." Next to me, her body shakes with tears. Time is meaningless – don't know how long we are like this. I tell Alice, "I'd fallen for Ted, thought he was the best man I could ever know. And to find out what he did to your mom – so ugly – beyond ugly – don't even know how to describe it. But again, I know whatever I'm going through pales in comparison." I wish I could make this all go away - an extremely distraught Alice is beside me. "What are you going to do?" Alice is such a beautiful person – in so much pain.

"Don't know."

"I don't blame you for hating him."

"I do hate him, but Amy, I don't want hate to become who I am. I want to be, as you say, 'light'. I screamed and swore at him on the soccer field – called him names – told him how much I hated him – said I'd always hate him. I didn't hold back anything – I couldn't hold back – the dam burst. All those years of Mom's depression rose up – the sadness now warped into anger and hate. I felt myself as a young girl witnessing my mom's deep sadness – never knowing why. He stood there and I kept screaming. Finally he turned and left. That's when I came here. I'm so unsettled – everything is an incomprehensible swirl."

"How are you going to regain your balance?"

"Don't know."

"I can't tell you what you should do, but I can tell you what I've found out in this past little while. I've learned to share, to be open, and I did this by finally forgiving myself."

"Forgive yourself?"

"Yes, for Emma's death – she was in the street alone – I should have been with her. The break up of my marriage and for all of the years I spent alone within myself – not letting anyone in. I move here, meet Ted, let him in, and now this. It's almost as if a piece of my heart has been ripped out. Just when my heart is open the damn door slams shut. That's what I feel and I don't like it. But I'm holding on to the idea that the Ted in San Diego is not the Ted I've met. The first night he spent with me I wanted him to make love to me so badly. He didn't want to – seemed so withdrawn, but he held me strong in his arms all night. I hope this is the man I know. I want Ted to forgive himself, but don't know if this is possible. Forgiveness isn't an easy thing to do. I cannot possibly say what you should feel - I just believe Ted is a good person who's carried this guilt with him for fifty years. But I do know he hurt your mom and you in the deepest way and this hurt has affected you your whole life. I can't say you should or could forgive him."

"A while ago I decide to ask you for help. I sensed you could help me. Here I am. You care for me – you hold me in comfort. I am so blessed to know you. I don't know if I can forgive him. It's doubtful."

"He is your father." I hope she doesn't take this the wrong way, but it's true.

"I know, but I don't want him to be my father." Alice looks off to some distant place. "I am a free spirit. If hate takes over, I cannot be a 'free spirit.' I've got to look into my heart and make a decision of how I want to be."

"I love you Alice and I'll do anything I can to help. We're friends with a deep connection. Let's say our affirmations." Alice agrees. I sit back against the wall and so does Alice. Silently we say our affirmations.

I open my eyes; Alice is quietly crying – tears rise up in me as well. "I want to be that free spirit, Amy. I want love and joy in my heart. I want you and I to always be friends – offering support and love. I want to believe Ted's a good person now. I hope I can release the hate I have for him. Maybe I don't hate him, maybe I'm just very angry at the hurt he's caused. I'm going to try my very best to forgive him, if not forgive at least hope he isn't the same person who raped Mom. I just wish Mom had had the ability to get over her hurt. She tried and I know she loved me and I loved her and I love her today. I'm not angry she was so isolated, just saddened. I'm going to say my affirmations, 'I am a good person.' 'I am a swimmer powerful and strong.' 'I am a free spirit' that can soar in a golden glow. You know like how we see the bay - golden and beautiful. Oh, Amy

– thanks so much – I love you so."

"And I love you too. I want us to always be here for each other. And hey maybe eat cake - you never know."

Alice tries to smile, "Yes, cake."

"And the pool."

"And the pool."

"Tomorrow's Wednesday and after our swim we can take a sauna, then come over here for some cake."

A small smile appears on Alice's face. "Of course." We get up off the bed and wrap our arms around each other in the most caring way. Love abounds.

# TED

Edith has slammed into me and my heart isn't strong enough to resist the pain I feel. Wait – my pain? The torture I put Edith and Alice through is vastly worse than any pain I have. Such a shit – me – me – me. Fuck me.

Now I know – know the damage I've done. Two lives torn apart by me. Had a hard time with the immediacy of what I did – now this. Good – drive the nail in - worthless jagged soul ripped - not whole – only bits and pieces. I've plunged in a deep sunless world – should have died a long time ago – still here – breathing using life energy I don't deserve. That's me.

I have a daughter. Having children is supposed to be joyous – Not. I was never there to hold her – comfort her when she fell down and scraped her knee - tell her I loved her – watch her grow from a loving child into a woman full of dreams she'd share with me - No – None of this.

My legacy - hurt and deep pain. She hates me, as well she should – look at what I caused. Always felt shame, but I never thought about what it did to Edith in the long run. I wanted to hurt her and that I did. Just so fucking wrong. I'm an evil shit. A life never fully lived because of me. Killed herself because of me. How it hurt and damaged Alice, because of me. Life long hurt and pain because of me. Goddamn me – fucking hate myself.

I have to get away one way or another. Leave in my car – fly off to Hawai'i, or just end it all. If I flee the pain will still be there. I want my pain to end – selfish bastard. What I did is so powerfully evil – in me...

and in Alice. How can I even fucking shave in the morning looking at myself in the mirror. I can leave the $10,000 to Alice then take my leave – end my miserable time on this earth. The extreme hurt I've caused has battered my soul … and it should. End my life or flee. I roll around in these thoughts – in my bed – in my self-made misery. Misery I deserve. Oh, God, how can I make this all disappear. I can't.

Now it's out in the open - sure Amy knows. There'll be nowhere to hide. My whole life has been one of hiding – hiding from others and hiding from myself. No matter how deep I stuff what I did it always comes up, but not like this. This has blasted me – I'm down on my knees – not just from Alice's slap, but my whole being - worthless piece of shit. I've been able to go day to day for fifty years, not the greatest life, but now I can't even do that.

I've got to make up my mind. I'm all packed and ready to go – just need to tell the landlord and give notice at work. I really don't have to give notice – I can just skip out. Hard to concentrate on my next move - haven't told anyone I'm leaving – as if anyone would give a shit. So off to work I go – the silent janitor. I'm able to function at work. Function? More like walking around in a haze pretending to work. Good to be invisible among all of the yuppie gym rats.

I am grieving over the lost friendship with Amy – more than a friendship. I have great affection for her. Thought she had for me, but again, this will soon be gone, replaced by disgust and hate. Goddamn it, why did I let hate take control – be violent and ugly – why. Well, I did and there's no taking it back. What happened, happened and I'm to blame. Fuck me.

"Ted Lewis to the front desk." Now what. Slowly make my way to the front. Johnson is waiting for me. "What's up, Ted? You're slacking." To myself, 'you mean you even see me?' "The men's locker room is a mess. When was the last time you cleaned it?" I don't answer. "Well, it must have been a while ago. You need to do your job and if not you won't be working here any longer. Now, get back to work and I mean get back to it.

You understand?"

"Yes, I understand." Walking away from this I should just keep walking out of this lousy gym – this lousy job. But instead I go to the men's locker room. Expecting a total mess – it's not. It's somewhat dirtier than it should be, but not a disaster that Johnson made it out to be. Asshole. Doesn't take too long to get it all straightened out. Damn – they're watching me. I guess I've been slacking these past few days. Leave – stay - still haven't decided, but almost left just now. When I quit and leave – I'll be broke. God, I'm stupid – I've got that $10,000.

Glad it's 4:30. It'll be good to see Stub – have some beer and a smoke and just drift away from everyone. Oh no – Amy's waiting for me. What to do. Can't pretend I don't see her – she's only thirty feet away. Saying nothing, looking down, I go toward my car.

"Ted." I ignore this and keep walking. "Ted!" I make the mistake of looking at her. "Please. We need to talk."

I continue walking. Amy runs in front of me. I stop. "I've got to be getting home." I don't look at her.

"Alice told me."

"Great, now you know what a fucking piece of shit I am. Why in the hell would you want to talk to an asshole like me?"

"Because I need to."

"Well, I don't need to talk to you."

She reaches out to touch me. I jerk away. "Can't you see I'm not worth your time – more than that – I'm not worth anybody's time. I'm leaving, not just now - I'm leaving Humboldt. Good-bye." I walk around her and get in my car. It's up against the embankment. I put it in reverse, but Amy's blocking my way. "Goddamn you, move!"

She doesn't move. I'm stuck. Tears in her eyes. Why in the hell is she crying? I turn off the motor. What to do. Amy walks up to me sitting in turmoil – just wanting to leave. "Please, Ted, don't run away. You have friends here."

"No I don't, not anymore. I fooled myself for a while, but no longer."

"I'm your friend, Ted."

"No you're not."

"Can we please talk?" I don't respond. "Please."

Goddamn it, she's wearing me down. Can't leave – if I start to go, she'll just stand in back of my car, blocking my way. I get out and Amy leads me to the, now infamous, soccer fields. I follow. She stops in the middle of the field and I go up to her. Hard to look at her, but when I glance up there's great concern in her eyes. "OK, I'm here. What have you got to say?"

"Thanks for not leaving."

"I couldn't, you blocked my way." I feel so harsh – that's me harsh, ugly, and mean.

Amy responds, "Nonetheless I'm glad you're here with me. Will you stay and at least listen to me?" I don't answer – just look down at the ground. "I don't know exactly what to say." She hesitates, looks down, then up at me. "I'll cut to the quick. You are not the person you were in San Diego." I start to respond. "No, please let me finish. I've gotten to know you – I have great affection for you. I see you as kind and caring - a sensitive person. Someone I enjoy being around – someone who gives me a great deal of comfort. My life has opened up. You stayed by me even after I yelled – was ugly with you - called you evil. Remember? I do. Your acceptance gave me strength. When I felt weak you held me in your arms. That's who you are, Ted." I don't know how to respond. "This has caused me all kinds of angst. That person back in San Diego did beyond a terrible act. Hurt someone deeply. Affected her whole life. Affected her daughter's life. It was a horrible thing to do – meant to cause great harm. And it did. I know you've paid for it. Differently than Alice's mom or Alice, but it's influenced who you are. Hiding from everyone. Not getting close. It was and still is terrifying to you what you did. Do I think you'll repeat it? No you won't, not in a million years. It's not who you are. I know your heart.

I know you as a good man - struggling. We're all struggling, Ted. Me with Emma's death, Alice's mom, Alice, you. Everybody struggles with something - some just more severe than others. I'm old – I don't know if I'll ever meet anyone as good and kind as you. I don't want you to leave. Can you, at least, stay around for a little while. I'll be very sad if you go."

"You can't be saying this."

"But I am."

"I don't believe you. I fucking hate myself – how can you not hate me?"

"Because I know who you are. I'm not stupid you know – I can tell you're a good person. I've felt for a while there's something you were hiding – unable to let loose." She puts her hands on my cheeks – looking directly – very close. "You are not the person you were in 1969. No, you're not. You've been nothing but caring and considerate of me. I see you with Stub – I see your connection with the water – your reverence for... I just want you to know that what I believe is true – that I'm here for you – believe in your goodness – your goodness and worth. I'm grateful I know you. So, there you have it."

Fuck me. I want to flee, but this feels out of balance – not a good choice. Weakly, "OK."

"Let's go sit in the stands." I trudge along after her, not quite at her side – a little back. We sit. She scoots close to me – I back away some. Getting close can hurt. "I've forgiven myself about Emma's death – about my failure in my marriage – about being closed off to people since that day and you helped with this more than you realize. I've relied on your strength. The first night we spent together and how you didn't want to make love. I now know why. You held me all night. It was the most comfort I've ever felt. We've continued to grow. Gosh, sleeping with you, getting to know Stub, the rivers, your story about Potato Boy, our fun with the cake. But most of all you've helped me with Emma. I feel whole and in this wholeness you are a big part. I don't want to lose you." She wipes away a tear – looks so very sad.

So, if I leave I'll make her sad. Someone I care for – someone who is important to me. The war still rages in me – I want to believe I'm not the same person I was in San Diego. I want to believe, but fifty years of experience tell me differently, but a part of me - deep down – maybe she's right.

"Can I tell you about my affirmations?" She doesn't wait for my response, "Every morning I say these, 'I am a swimmer powerful and strong.' Then I say, 'I am a good person.' I am giving myself these thoughts. I want to crowd out bad thoughts I have about myself and it's working." She takes a deep breath, reaches out and takes my hand. I let her. "What's important is that you can forgive yourself. For me, it's easier to forgive someone else than to forgive myself. I've found this out the hard way." Looking me straight in my eyes, "I forgive you, Ted." She cries.

"Why are you crying?"

"Because I don't want to lose you."

# ALICE

Leaving work, I'm still trying to make sense of what I've found out. I'm just wandering around – no destination – just out. Too hard to stay inside my place – too confining. My heart needs the freedom, – not to be confined. I've been that way for too many years. The night ghouls are out in the plaza. I avoid them. The Humboldt Crabs are playing tonight –stadium lights are on - a roar from the crowd. A Crab has hit a home run. I walk past the crowd. Jon told me a wonderful story about Baseball Paul. He was very different. He walked around town wearing an Oakland A's batting helmet and carrying a baseball bat. He babbled as he walked. Someone went into the Phoenix Café and told Jon to not feed Paul any sweets – bad for him. Jon told me how impressed he was that the whole town looked out for Paul. At the first game of the season during warm ups, everyone stopped and Baseball Paul would go to home plate. A player standing close would toss him a ball. He would hit it a few feet in front of home plate and begin his slow awkward run around the bases. He was called safe at all the bases and crossed home plate after hitting his home run to the cheers of the crowd. That's the kind of place Arcata was then. Compassion – that's what was shown Baseball Paul – acceptance – caring. There's a message in this.

I keep walking past the bright lights of the stadium – past Safeway – to my place. I decide not to go in, but continue my walk. I make my way over US 101, then just before the Highway Patrol headquarters, I turn toward the soccer fields. I see Ted - see myself screaming at him - hate sucking out my goodness. Guess I was directed here to continue to try and figure out what to do. Amy has given me some good clues. Mom, I feel guilty for not understanding. Feel guilty because I wasn't able to help you. Guilty because my whole life has been spent in a shadow of sadness – a sadness wrapped tightly around me - unable to go past it and move into a fulfilled peaceful life. Things were starting to change. I admire Amy so much – she too was held down by guilt. Damn guilt – it can trap you. That's what guilt did – it trapped me – made me stuck – not going anywhere – no changes possible. Guilt is so goddamn strong and its strength held me down for so long. Amy has strength – she's broken away from that guilt. I want to be free of my guilt as well, but mostly I want to be free from hate.

My new direction has been altered with anger and hate. At least I recognize this. Something only a little while ago I wouldn't have seen. I want to be rid of the guilt I have, what good has it done me. "Go!" I want to be free from hate. "Go!" I startle myself by yelling this. Looking around I'm all alone – good. "Go! Go! Go away!" An idea hits me. Thinking about my sadness and guilt I take my hand, put it on my heart, then I make a quick motion as if I'm throwing the hate and sadness away from me. I do this three times. I have to take care of myself and maybe this will help – this and the affirmations. When I have an ugly self-thought I'm going to do this.

Now for my hate for Ted, and I do hate him. Or do I? I'm going to see him around and how will I react. I now know stuffing things inside doesn't work. What to do. Going to the stands I sit and say my affirmations. Opening my eyes just in time to see an owl fly overhead. I'm pretty sure owls hold no hate – their spirits are free to fly. 'I am a free sprit.' I have to rid myself of hate or it'll destroy the goodness that's inside me - that is me. This in itself is new for me – knowing that I'm a good person. I want to remain this way. Ted, yes you were a fucking asshole. Then it hits me. Amy changed – I'm trying to change – I was having some success at it. So, maybe Ted has changed. Do I judge Amy and myself on how we were or how we are now? This is a revelation about Amy and me. Maybe it can be with Ted. I hope so.

My feet are on the ground walking home. The swirl of confusion has left me for now. Hope I can hold on to this. 'I am a free spirit. I am a good person' walk with me this night.

In bed, the thought of Amy as a teacher enters me. Amy is teaching me. Wham, this hits me. It's said that you can learn from adversity. Is this true? Mom flashes in my eyes. I let myself get dragged down by Mom's sadness – really dragged down. It was wrapped around me so tight that I couldn't see any light – only darkness. Hiding in her room day after day I heard her crying and didn't know what to do. So, I became sad as well and I've worn this as my protection. It's affected me my whole life – this sadness. Will I be able to learn – to be free from this? Fifty years is a long time. And do I see Ted as a cruel and ugly person? No I do not.

Maybe this is a beginning. I drift off with this thought circulating in me - 'I am a free spirit'.

# TED

Days continue as if in a dust storm - so much debris clouding my way. Sure I was out of here – then Amy burst in – wouldn't let me leave without talking to her. Standing in back of my car – not letting me go. She's something. The balanced side of me appreciates this very much. This is countered with – Fuck it – I'm gone. Like the blindfolded woman holding the scales of justice and in this case what is the right action or feeling to have. I have to make a choice, but how. So damn indecisive all my life. Not now though. A decision has to be made one way or the other. I see Amy's face. She tells me I'm a good person - that I'm not the same person who lived in San Diego. I am and I'm not, but the scales the blindfolded woman holds are tilting to Amy. Picturing her tears when she told me, "Because I don't want to lose you." This touches me deeply.

Have to take care of Stub and he's almost out of food, so I go to the store. Getting out of my car at Wildberries. "Ted." It's Amy. I feel ashamed, but I don't turn and flee. She comes up to me. "Are you doing OK?"

"Don't think so." Who is this woman – not giving up on me when I was so ready to run – to be the victim, but I don't want to be a victim. Besides, Alice and her mom are the victims – victims of my hate and ugly violence. Somehow I've turned this into all about me. Damn selfish. Miraculously, Amy stands in front of me.

"Can I ask you a favor?" Not waiting for me to answer, she continues. "Can we go to Maple Creek?"

"Oh."

"No, seriously."

What to do now? Not that hard – either I say yes, or no and in this silence.

"Come on, it'll be good. I know it. I have my swimming stuff and a couple of towels in my car. What D'ya say?"

Her sweet smile is so engaging. I let out in almost a whisper, "OK"

"Sweet. Let's meet up at your place."

This came from out of the blue. Behind the wheel of my car, up I go. Nervous – not knowing what's going to happen. At my cabin I get my trunks, swim goggles, and towel. Amy drives up. "Can I bring Stub?"

"Yes, but would you mind if Stub stays home this time? I love him to pieces, but I want today to be just for us. If this isn't OK, Stub can come."

"No, it's all right."

In the shadow of the trees we drive up Fickle Hill. Silent – no words - passing under the trees – in and out of shadows. Finally at the bridge. Every time I see the river I'm comforted - wish I was this time – too damn unsettled. We park and walk down to the river - clear inviting – the essence of life. We put our towels down.

I watch Amy her take off her jeans and white blouse – she's wearing her swimsuit under them. Turning away I put on my trunks.

"Shy, are you?"

"Yes."

Amy stands at the edge of the river. She points across it, "Let's swim to the tree." We swim across the river to the tree. Amy cups her hands and puts water on the tree. "When we came in the winter the river was way up, the roots got plenty of water. See how the roots over the rock don't reach the water?"

I cup my hands and also give the tree water. Swimming up river, we rest, and swim back down. Amy's spinning as she goes – such a strong and beautiful swimmer. We get to a pool of water just before some riffles and sit – the magical world surrounds us – a couple of very white puffy clouds slowly drift above us. Trees, so green mix with the blue sky and white clouds. We start our swim up river again. After doing this a few times we get out of the water. The sun is warm - there's only a slight breeze blowing up river from the ocean.

"I love this place - thanks for showing it to me."

I lie down, shut my eyes. Amy lies down and puts her hand in mine. Oh my. The sun is warming me up. Amy's eyes are shut - I look at her. She is so sweet, kind ... and to me, very beautiful. She stirs some, opens her eyes – she sees me looking at her.

In this moment – light on her face – soft – she glows. "I've got an idea. Let's go up past that riffle."

We swim up to the riffle, get out, and walk carefully over the river rocks – rounded from water flowing down this river for centuries. We find a sweet sandy spot and sit.

An osprey flies over us using the wind currents – she soars. "I am a free spirit," Amy says. I ask her about this. "It's an affirmation I have. Actually I borrowed it, the osprey brought it to mind."

"I am a free spirit. Gosh, it feels good saying this."

"Ted, we are free spirits." She turns to me - puts her hands on my shoulders. I shut my eyes, her lips press gently against mine, and softly she kisses me. She pulls down her swimsuit straps – a sweet smile shows on her face. She stands - takes off her swimsuit. A shy glint in her eyes. I take off my swim trunks. She leads us to the water. We're immersed in this life giving water. Amy is so beautiful. I'm enveloped in her charm and grace. The water touches every inch of us. Overhead blue, the river flowing all around us – every inch of my being seems cleansed. A gentle breeze sweeps over us. We share this. Amy takes my hand and leads us out of the water.

Putting her hands on my face, she draws me to her, and kisses me. She lies down on the sand and looks up to me. Her body smooth – her soul beautiful. I lie beside her under the sky – next to the river – the giver of life. She draws me to her, and kisses me. This kiss - strong – from this strong and wonderful woman. Amy looks up and softly says, "Yes."

Warm - moist - strong - hard - inviting - this place - no thoughts – just this moment. And then the miraculous moment when two become one. I could be here forever. We lie in this sweet repose for a long time.

I softly ask Amy if she wants to go.

"No I don't. I never want to leave this."

"Me neither." Skin on skin we continue to lie under the sun in our magical moment. Don't know how long we are like this.

After some time, Amy asks, "Should we go?"

We both get up. Back in my trunks – Amy in her swimsuit - we walk back to the riffle we got out of – get in, and go with the flow of the river. Seeing our towels I start to go to them. "Wait, Ted." Amy swims over to her tree. I follow. It's over our heads. Amy treads water, cups her hands, and puts water on the tree. I do the same. The sweetest expression I've ever seen, "This isn't my tree – it's our tree."

"Amy …" colors intense – water the essence wrapped around me - in the river, "I love you."

"I love you too, Ted. With all of my heart."

# THE END

## ABOUT THE AUTHOR

Ron Ramsay Hagg was raised in Burbank, California.
He spent many years in Humboldt and Mendocino counties, California.
He has also lived on the Big Island of Hawai'i.
He currently lives in Arroyo Hondo, New Mexico.

He may be contacted at:
Ron Hagg
po box 434
Arroyo Hondo, New Mexico 87513
ronhagg@hotmail.com

Made in the USA
Lexington, KY
10 December 2019